The Gold Mohur Tree

Joyce Mackenzie

ISBN: 978-1-909609-74-7

This edition first published in 2013 by:

Thistle Publishing
36 Great Smith Street
London
SW1P 3BU

Cover image © Rahul Singh http://www.flickr.com/photos/raahulsingh

one | home

1949

The jungle was never far from our door in Bihar and its continual presence gave me a strange perspective. The sterile, ordered daily routine for nine months of the year, cocooned in a boarding school at the foot of the Himalayas, contrasted dramatically with holidays at home. But was it home? Did I belong in this rural environment? The village children who had been my companions had long grown up and gone. Some married and moved away, others dead of the cholera epidemics that struck the area periodically down the years. I was eighteen and alone emotionally and often physically, estranged from a mother who did not love me and from the sister who she did, often smacking me for little or no reason when my father was not present. It was 1949, India was now an independent country and so much had happened in the years before, including the Second World War. But for me, I suppose it all began with my encounter with the Garial.

I had been talking to Ramesh, a fit and pleasant young man my father employed to look after the gardens. I often helped him in the vegetable plot behind the gardens. He didn't speak any English but Bengali was practically my first language and we got along well enough. He had been chopping down an old palm tree, past its best and unproductive. I had put out my hand to touch the bark that grew like scales upon its rough surface.

'Just like the crocodile, Miss, the one that swims down there in the river.' He pointed over to where the river ran at the bottom

of the valley and I had shaded my eyes. It was the first time I had heard of crocodiles down there. 'They'll rip off your arm if you get too close,' he confided, 'or maybe even your head.'

I giggled nervously at this, but spoke to my father later that night. 'Nonsense, Jo,' my father had reassured me. 'That young man is telling you fibs. Why, if there were crocodiles in that water, don't you think the whole village would be filled with women without arms? '

He laughed uproariously at his own joke and I could smell the whisky deep-stained on his breath, a fact that saddened me. But he was my father and I loved and trusted him. He certainly had a point about the women who scrubbed and washed and rinsed their families' clothes in the river every day.

So, the following morning when Ramesh began his stories again, I told him what my father had said. He merely smiled, shook his head and wagged his finger at me, saying, 'Just don't go down into the river, Miss. Garial or not.' As I left he shouted an additional warning: '*Mut karo*' (don't do it).

I, of course, didn't like to be told by anyone what to do, and certainly not by this young man who was laughing at me as I ran away from him. I went straight down to the river bank, past two women washing their clothes as usual, past the big rock on which you could see the high-tide marks of the monsoon-swollen waters and jumped and splashed straight into the shallows. I'd show that Ramesh, I thought. My father knew far more than he did, and if he said there were no crocodiles, then that was good enough for me. Besides, it was so very hot and my clothes clung to me with perspiration so I didn't hesitate. Hoisting my skirt and wading out of the shallows I ventured deeper. I was now almost waist-high in the river with the waters swirling around me. I saw the women I had passed, leaving their washing, standing up and pointing, then they began to wave and shout and I saw Ramesh running down the hill towards me, and just at that moment a great current caught at my legs and pulled me off my feet and I was swept down the river, the water coursing around boulders, throwing my head under and then back out again and against the slimy bank. The younger of the two women was running like a tigress after her prey, trying to keep up with my course, throwing out the end of the sari she had been washing, and flicking it towards me in the hope I could grab a hold of it as I neared the bank. My screams now became loud and frantic as my grasp at protruding roots and reeds became weaker as the swirling current was carrying me ever deeper down river.

It was Ramesh who saved me. He had taken the saris the women had been washing, tied them together and knotted them round a tree and lowered himself down the slippery bank, ten or twenty yards ahead of me, grabbing me and scooping me up in his arms as I was being sent sweeping past with the swirl of the current.

He hauled me up the bank and sat me on the grass, while I vomited the river water I had swallowed. As I sat wheezing and coughing and shivering with fright he spoke gently saying, 'Garial, maybe; but dangerous currents, definitely. You should have known that, Miss Jo. You have lived here long enough. The river is more dangerous than the creatures it houses.'

If I thought that being nearly drowned was bad, worse was to follow when I got home. Someone had run to tell my parents what had happened and they waited in the courtyard for me, sitting grimly at a table, my mother pouring tea, and father a large whisky. The factory doctor had also been summoned and he dealt per- emptorily with my wounds, cleaning my cuts with iodine, stitching a deep gash on my leg. Once he had been dismissed the tight line that was my mother finally lashed into action.

'What on earth did you think you were doing, you stupid incon- siderate girl!' Her grip on the tea cup was so tight she almost broke off the handle and had to put it down with an alarming clat- ter to stop herself doing just that. 'How many times have you

been told not to go in that river? How many times?' Her stare was unnerving, and I couldn't hold it. I lowered my eyes to the ground, shivering even more within the blanket that now covered me. 'Well, my girl,' she continued, 'this is the last of your silly little exploits, the last time I will put up with your nonsense. Tomorrow I shall start making arrangements for us to leave for Calcutta.'

'No!' I wailed looking desperately at my father who was usually my stalwart defender, but on this occasion he merely poured himself another whisky and looked away.

'Don't you answer me back, Josephine!' It was rare for my mother to use my Christian name and when she did, it meant one of two things, each as bad as the other: a taste of the strap or a spell of solitary confinement in my room with no book or pen and paper to keep me company. 'And there's another thing, in the time you have left here you are absolutely forbidden to consort with that disgusting, unwashed and painted half-naked young man who calls himself a sadhu. Heaven knows what you're up to with him halfway up that hill. Is that understood?'

My mouth fell open, indignant at what she was suggesting, though it took a while for the words to come out, for the defiance and anger to build enough to spur them on. 'But he's a holy man,' I finally whispered, and so he was, one of the multitude of such spiritual men who had inhabited India for centuries and spent their lives denying themselves physical pleasures in order to pursue wisdom and vision and to try and pass on their spiritualism to others. He had been my greatest friend and confidant since I was small and I had come across him one morning on the hill, sitting meditating in the lotus position with his back against a large tree. My ayah Mini was with me at the time. She feared him but his silver-painted arms and ash- covered body, his coiled matted hair, piled high on his head, and the strange-smelling herbs he burnt in a small brass urn, which was always beside him, had not deterred me, and over the years he had taught me many good things. Yet, he had never been able to explain to me my repetitive dream of a young woman in a blue dress who danced with me.

'Josephine!' my mother's voice came to me like a slap. I raised my face towards her own and saw nothing of myself in her features. 'This peculiar friendship between a young *white* woman and a half-naked young man, wearing nothing but a red loincloth and sitting doing nothing on a hill, is utterly unacceptable. It must stop this minute. I can't imagine why your father has turned a blind eye to it all these years.'

Rose, my sister, had arrived and stood behind me giggling at my discomfort, blocking my escape.

'Daddy?' I asked, but no help came from that quarter. 'Dad,' I pleaded, yet again, 'I've known the sadhu since I was a child. Why can't I speak with him? He's always taught me good and decent things. You know there are people who treat sadhus like gods in their religion. He comforts me and has never said or done anything harmful.'

'Your mother is right, Jo,' was all he said.

And so it was, that just over a week later, I found myself on a train with my mother and Rose heading for Calcutta and though I didn't know it, the great journey of my life was about to begin.

two | calcutta

1949

My father had booked a first class compartment for us on the overnight train to Calcutta. We had our evening meal, almost in silence, and the car had been loaded with our clothes crammed into cases, and the inevitable cold box. It was a short but sad journey for me to the station. Dad helped us on to the waiting train and saw we were comfortable. Fresh bedding laid out on bunks with well-laundered sheets awaited us. He hugged Rose in farewell and I clung to him weeping and whispered, 'I love you, Dad.' I noticed there was no embrace for my mother. Instead he simply handed her our tickets and some money, saying, 'Look after the girls, I'll phone you at the weekend.' It all happened so quickly.

The guard blew his whistle and Dad jumped down from the train urging us to keep the windows closed and on no account to get off at any of the stations on the way to Calcutta. I looked out at him as we drew away from the station, the train slowly chugging, a solitary man with his back to us, his brown wavy hair thinning at the top, looking as if it could do with a cut, his shoulders slightly hunched and his step slow. I wanted to scream and shout, 'run after us, don't let us go.' This was the man who had walked with me in the forest as a child, teaching me what not to touch, what not to put in my mouth, and tutoring me on the health-giving and healing effects of the non-poisonous plants and berries that grew so freely. Not a backward glance. Had he forgotten

I was the fruit of his loins? Had my mother's constant carping and mean and quarrelsome nature turned him against me?

But instead, my mother closed the shutters over the windows and I was left facing her with a feeling that someone had stolen my stomach and replaced it with a hard mass of indeterminate proportions and for good measure was tightening a ligature round my neck.

Now, in the swaying carriage as I moved our cases in the restricted space, I stood facing her; two boxers swaying together, waiting for the first punch, with good and tried pugilistic skills. A deep hurt swirled around me and as I looked at her, her pointed features, straggly brown hair and piercing blue eyes didn't strike fear into me any more. We were both now without a champion. I was eighteen, taller than her, stronger than her, and I told myself I would never let her hit me again, punish me or abuse me.

I dozed fitfully. My dreams were strange and confused.

Vali Finlayson, my close friend through my schooldays, was laughing and screaming in the back seat of a car as I was being taught to drive by her father Edward, and took a corner too sharply.

I had spent so many happy times with them during school holidays as he was the manager of a steelworks not far from my father's factory. My dream took on nightmare proportions, and. I was in the cool water of the river with the garial circling me with a swishing sound and Vali shouting and saying, 'Don't worry, Jo, garials don't eat redheads, it gives them indigestion.' I woke with a start and smiled to myself. It was just the kind of silly thing that Vali would have said. I would miss her fun and laughter and the kindness of her mother Ruth. Vali had been the self-styled clown of the class.

I realised why I'd been dreaming of rushing breezes and cool river water. I was hot, clammy and thirsty. I rose quickly and helped myself to a drink from the cool box and wiped myself down and

dressed quickly. Rose and mother were fussing with their hair and lipstick, as if anyone would notice.

The train was slowing down and mother had opened the shutters. As I looked out no paddy-fields met my gaze or cows and bullocks ambling idly by, nor was there any sign of the lush green banks of the river. We were approaching Howrah station and would soon be mingling among throngs of people in an ever-growing and over-populated city of millions. Screeching and groaning the train shuddered slowly to a halt. We waited in silence for mother's friend to find us while coolies banged on the glass and mouthed offers of cheap help with our luggage.

The platform was crowded with sleeping bodies waiting for trains that perhaps they had already missed. Beggars crowded round passengers who had disembarked, their leprous stumps stretched out to almost touching point, asking for a few paisa, some accompanied by small naked children, their bellies swollen, their thin arms telling of malnutrition. Two mangy dogs, with scarcely a hair on their emaciated bodies, were pulling at a discarded stale chapatti in a corner, and vendors shouted loudly, offering tea and snacks from large brass plates balanced precariously on their heads. And, as for Rose, her face was etched in blank horror, her eyes watering.

Fortunately my mother's old friend Mrs Hunt and her son Jeb were not long in finding us and after hurried introductions it was Jeb, who with the help of a coolie, swept up our cases quickly and expertly onto the luggage rack atop a waiting Hindustan car and ushered us out of the fetid atmosphere of a crowded station.

Five of us and our baggage were a tight squeeze. Jeb edged his vehicle into the early morning rush and we sat in a traffic jam on Howrah Bridge for over twenty minutes. I let the wave of noise overrun me, ignoring my mother's chattering with Mrs Hunt. I noticed Rose looking shyly, almost flirtatiously, at Jeb. Good heavens, Rose, I thought, he is so much older than you.

Rickshaw-pullers and cyclists ringing their bells incessantly, and shouts from car drivers hooting their horns, desperate to move, formed a deafening background to my thoughts. I wondered why we had come here and why my mother had, selfishly, seen fit to leave my father alone at this crucial time, coping with a business which we all now knew had become far from lucrative.

Jeb stopped his car near a small block of flats in a quieter area of the city. I noticed a taxi rank, a few small shops and a youth hostel nearby. The apartment my mother had rented was on the first floor. A large plant, crying out for water, languished in a pot at the front door; withered and drooping, a symbol of what our lives might be now. Like the plant we too had been green and fresh of spirit and surrounded by the waters of the good things in life. I would feed and water the plant and it would surely flourish again and survive. Would we?

Mrs Hunt handed my mother the keys. She had done her best with the cleaning of the shabby furnishings and bed linen. The accommodation consisted of three bedrooms and a bathroom, a dining room, kitchen and sitting room together with a small area off the dining room which had been used as a study at some time. One bedroom had its own access to the stairs. Mrs Hunt had stocked the refrigerator and hired a cook/bearer to help us. He was preparing lunch when we arrived. Jeb helped with our luggage and promised to call back later in the week.

It was going to be some time before we ate. Mother asked the cook for tea and toast. Lukewarm tea and unbuttered toast with a pot of marmalade were served on a tray, on which there was a decidedly grubby tray cloth.

We sat in silence, Rose trying hard to hide her tears. I got up and opened the windows. The air was stifling.

My mother spoke hesitatingly, 'Well, Josephine and Rose, do you have anything to say?'

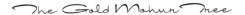

Rose shook her head. 'What a bloody dump this is. Could you not find something better,' I replied.

Rose started to weep.

'Riches to rags, Rose. You had better get used to it, gal. No ayah to clean and run around and pander to you now. You will have to be just like me. Just like me,' I repeated, as I picked up my luggage and headed for the room with access to the stairs.

I heard her shout after me with a tearful catch in her voice, 'Nobody wants to be like you, Josephine Willis.'

At this point the cook/bearer came through to the sitting room to tell us lunch was ready.

'What have you cooked?' asked my mother politely.

'Stew, Memsahib, Good for the babas' he replied, almost apologetically.

The only good thing that could possibly have been said for the stew was its accompaniment of mashed potatoes. Bits of tough, unrecognisable meat floated in a grey substance which passed for gravy. Fortunately Mrs Hunt had provided a large bowl of fruit for us. I rose from the table and decided to clean my room. Disinfectant in hot water and a half-hour scrub soon freshened up the stale atmosphere.

Rose was sitting and snivelling. I still had the bowl of soapy water in my hands when she asked me to clean her room for her, feigning a headache. I did it for her reluctantly. She was two years younger than me. At sixteen she was cosseted and spoilt and had never lifted a finger to do anything for herself.

It didn't take my mother long to dismiss the cook. She told him he was not suitable, paid him a week's wages and let him go. Mother was an excellent cook so there wouldn't be a problem for a few days.

'What are you going to do about someone to cook for us on a permanent basis?' I asked.

'Don't fuss, Josephine. I'll manage to get a young lad and teach him my ways,' she said confidently.

I started to laugh. 'That'll be entertaining, Mother, considering you hardly speak any Hindi. Your vocabulary seems to extend to a few futile commands. Telling people to shut up, hurry up or buzz off in Hindi won't do the trick, I'm afraid. Perhaps you can phone dad each time you want to instruct the cook.' She pursed her lips but didn't reply.

Transport was a problem. My mother had never driven a car. Taxis were expensive and not safe for young girls. Before we left Ranchi my father had spoken to us seriously about our safety in Calcutta. He knew there was social unrest after the assassination of Mahatma Gandhi in January 1948 and he impressed on us we should be very careful not to put ourselves in danger. Uncle Edward had taught me to drive and now I needed additional lessons before attempting to launch yet another car onto the already chaotic Calcutta roads. I would have to sit a driving test.

Mother had been constantly on the phone to Mrs Hunt, and Jeb visited us a week later at teatime to offer us some help. Mother had baked a cake and Rose served him with tea and a slice of cake, shyly simpering and smiling at him. He was not unaware of her attention. Jeb Hunt was almost twice her age. Would he be interested in her? She was just a child.

He turned his attention to me and before he could ask me any questions I said, 'I have quite a few things I would like you to help me with please, Mr Hunt.'

He interrupted, saying, 'My name's Jeb. I'd like you both to call me Jeb.'

'Well then, Jeb,' I continued. 'First, can you recommend a driving school? I can drive on country roads. I need to know the streets in Calcutta and I'll need a licence. Can you advise me where to buy a reliable second-hand car? Also, do you know of a decent secretarial college? I must do a course before I apply for a job.' He seemed taken aback at my idea of obtaining work, but didn't comment.

He laughed a trifle nervously, saying, 'I'll try and fix some stuff up for you later in the week. I can't manage the weekend. You see I'm a Bookie and that is my busiest time.'

True to his word, he came to the flat on Wednesday afternoon accompanied by his mother, who was helpful in suggesting a good secretarial college. Jeb had arranged a driving instructor and said he had seen a small second-hand Morris 8 which he thought might suit me. However, he suggested he take me to the college, the driving school and to view the car.

Disapproval was already etched on the face of my mother and jealousy hung like a dark cloud over Rose, as she sat pouting and sulking, the attention having been taken away from her.

'Indeed not,' my mother said curtly. 'Josephine will need a chaperone.' Jeb's mother, May, started to laugh. 'You've been out of touch quite a while, Babs,' she said. 'Young people date freely these days. Besides I should really take exception to your remarks. Jeb is trustworthy.'

'Very well,' Mother said, reluctantly giving way.

Rose was enrolled into dressmaking classes, and Jeb, over time, became an integral part of our newly established household, making himself indispensable to my mother, and to Rose, doing all the little jobs they no longer had any servants to do for them. It suited Jeb well enough and we liked his company, ultimately being allowed to attend a few of his luncheons and swim in the pool attached to his rather elegant house, a short distance out of Calcutta.

Jeb Hunt was in his early thirties and seemed to pay far too much attention to Rose, in my opinion, but Mother didn't seem to object and I had no intention of whipping up waves in the already murky river of our lives.

three | dean

January 1951

And so for almost two years the mundane pattern of our life went on, and by the time I was twenty we had settled into an uneasy peace.

The driving instructor of poor habits, spitting out beetle juice constantly, and displaying a difficult temperament, had put me through my driving test easily, and I was the proud owner of a second-hand Morris 8 which Jeb had chosen for me. I had obtained a junior post in a mercantile house, the salary being adequate enough to keep the car on the road and help with some of the household expenses, food in particular, as I was able to visit the New Market to obtain fresh meat and vegetables. Mother still cooked without assistance but she had employed an English-speaking ayah to help her. Despite the fact Rose had acquitted herself with distinction at her sewing class; she repeatedly refused to do dressmaking on a commercial scale, saying to me high-handedly and rudely, 'Young ladies of the Raj don't work.'

Mother and Rose were not interested in the real Calcutta and I spent many days on my own feeling the throbbing pulse of this great and vibrant city. I explored museums, old cathedrals and stood in awe when I visited the tomb of Job Charnock, said to be the founder of the Raj. The Zoo and Eden Gardens and the Victoria Memorial were a relief from the crowded parts of the city and well away from the slums and many garbage strewn areas.

Rose and Mother spent more time than ever together, doing their dressmaking, going out to tea with friends they considered fashionable and important, and Rose occasionally off to goodness knows where, with Jeb. They seemed to be living in some sort of genteel past of which I was not a part, unwilling to realise and accept the full implications that the Raj was over and that things had moved on and this was now an independent country. Every European mercantile assistant that left his post to return home was replaced by a young educated Indian. What of me?

One dull day of daily routine followed another, often interspersed with quarrels with my mother and ill-tempered conversations with Rose, fuelled by the fact that I constantly suggested she obtain some sort of lucrative work. My father too, now seemed to reject me. I had phoned him asking if we could spend a week or so with him as I had leave due to me, but he had said 'It's not possible just now, things are difficult and money is tight.' I realised that soon, I might be the only wage earner in this family.

My life was now like an empty coracle, floating down a slow and polluted river, ever slowly onwards, unwanted and heading for whirlpools and rocks, but kismet was not about to forget me entirely and picked me up and put me on a fresh path of life which would, for a short time, hold much joy.

So then, in the heat of the summer, in May 1955, I met Dean Mitchell, an American Marine working at the Consulate, and for a few short months, a spark of joy held me in its grasp.

I had joined the Swimming Club and went for a quick swim after work each evening to cool off. I had also entered for a few of the events at a forthcoming Gala, an ambitious act on my part as I would have to swim against many strong and stylish swimmers. I had decided to get as much practice as possible so swam a good few lengths each evening.

It was quite late and most of the swimmers had gone home. The flat tiles surrounding the pool were very wet and as I walked to the shallow end, I slipped and fell into the pool, landing heavily on another swimmer. Strong arms were holding me. I stood facing a well-built young man.

'Are you OK?' he laughed after helping me to my feet.

I nodded and lifted myself on to the edge of the pool. I was embarrassed. He got out of the pool and sat beside me.

'It's not often I have young women throwing themselves at me,' he teased. 'By the way, my name's Dean Mitchell. And yours?'

'I'm Josephine Willis'

'Well, Jose, let's swim, I presume that's what you're here for,' he said with a cheeky grin.

We spent the rest of the evening swimming and getting to know each other and had a cold drink together at the bar. He was entertaining and attractive. It was quite dark by the time I had changed to go home and he was waiting for me at the exit. He offered me a lift and I thanked him saying I had a car. He walked me to the car park but before I got into the car he smiled at me, his blue eyes dancing with fun and laughter and said, 'Jose, what about a date. I think I need some compensation for being assaulted by a redhead. Would you like to go dancing on Saturday night?'

At first I hesitated and then agreed, and asked him to collect me at seven, knowing full well my mother would not approve as she had said we were not to speak to men in uniform, constantly repeating, 'They are merely soldiers from God knows where.'

I was dressed by half past six and lied to my mother that I had been invited to a dance, never daring to tell her he was an American Marine.

'You have no right to accept dates without my permission, Josephine. Who is he anyway? How did you meet him and where are you going?'

'I was introduced to him by a friend at the Swimming Club,' I lied again. She didn't have time for any further questions as Dean

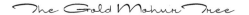

arrived to collect me. He came into the sitting room and smiled and nodded his approval when he saw I was well groomed and dressed for the occasion. I introduced him to Rose and my mother. Before any embarrassing questions were shot at him he said, 'I'll take good care of her Mrs Willis. She'll be home by midnight.'

I knew it wouldn't be the end of the matter but Mother never mentioned him or my friendship with Dean for the next couple of weeks.

Jeb had taken Rose to what Mother insisted was the cinema. We were together in the sitting room having coffee after our evening meal when she raised the question of Dean Mitchell.

'Josephine,' she said, and I knew by her tone our conversation would be confrontational. 'Why do you constantly lie to me? You lied as to how you met Dean Mitchell. I have it on good authority he is merely a Marine who often picks up girls. Calcutta society expects certain standards of behaviour from young women of your background.'

I started to laugh at her pomposity. 'Calcutta society,' I mocked. 'What is that supposed to mean? There's no such thing. Mother, stop living in the past.' I thought she would let go, but she continued.

'I've written to your father about you.' This time I knew she lied. She had done no such thing. 'Your behaviour in my view is decadent and no decent young man would like to court you in the present circumstances. In the meantime you are to stop seeing that American fellow.'

'His name is Dean Mitchell, Mother. Why is he unacceptable to you? How is it that Rose is allowed to date Jeb Hunt, a man years older than her? What do you really know about him? Are you being fair to me? Dean is good company and a considerate escort and an amusing companion.'

Her irritation with me was now at a peak and she spoke angrily. 'An escort and a companion? If that is all, why do you kiss him goodnight outside the Swimming Club? You've been seen on several occasions. Similarly, your behaviour when you dance with him is immodest to say the least. All that jitterbugging as you call it. What sort of dance is that supposed to be? Vulgarity, nothing else. I believe he plays the piano with the band sometimes as a guest artist. His arms are around you wherever you go. I am not putting up with it any longer. Educated young ladies don't behave in this distasteful manner. Josephine, this isn't America and if you get pregnant your father will disown you.'

'So, so, so,' I said rudely. 'Who's been telling tales? Yes, we kiss. It's normal for boys and girls to kiss goodnight, or didn't you know. What a farce this is.'

Having finished my coffee I left the room and turned in for an early night. Once again I lay in bed in dingy surroundings asking myself how could a mother dislike her first-born child so much. Why? What had I done to make this possible, and the hurt and anger I felt made me lash back verbally time and again.

I continued to date Dean for several months. I had a special love for him but not a grand passion. I just loved him for his happiness, good nature and returned his love for me. I knew his time in India was coming to an end, but kept putting it to the back of my mind, fooling myself it would never happen.

He phoned me on the last Friday before he left. 'I'll collect you at eight Jose. Don't dress up, we aren't going dancing,' he said.

He was punctual but far from happy. I jumped up into the jeep and he drove in silence to a block of flats. It was most unusual for him not to chatter to me. The lift stopped at the third floor. He explained the flat belonged to a friend and he had the key. 'He's on leave for a month.' Jose, don't look so anxious. Look at me, I'm your Dean, I'm not a rapist or an axe murderer.' We laughed together. 'I just need a quiet time with you tonight,' he said.

He went through to the kitchen while I looked around the small flat. It was clean and simply furnished. Dean brought a tray

of sandwiches and cold drinks through to the sitting room and placed them on the coffee table. For the first time since I had known him he was serious and spoke slowly while we ate.

'Jose, I will be leaving Calcutta mid-week. I've been given my marching orders and I'm sorry I can't tell you where I'm to be posted.' There's only a vague possibility I'll be back in India. I won't lose touch with you, Jose. You're very special to me. I'll write to you as soon as my feet touch the ground. Be sure and reply to me.' He paused and spoke emotionally and softly. 'Our time together has been too short, just five short months. It's difficult. You must meet my folks and you must definitely keep in touch with me. I'll make arrangements for you to come to the States. You'll like our house. It's not a bad little patch.'

I was upset and he comforted me, holding me close and kissing me tenderly. He was enthusiastic about my visit to America, but he didn't realise how difficult it would be for me, with so little money. It was an exciting prospect as I had never left India, but in my heart I felt what he was suggesting was almost impossible. He had been my first love and I would never forget him.

He took me home and held me close on the landing of our rather run-down flat. 'I'll always hold you like this in my dreams, Jose, and I know that Jose will always kiss her Dean.' We embraced for the last time and as he left me and ran down the steps, a part of me wanted to run down after him, a part of me perhaps always would. And as I stood on those steps watching him go, watching him wave, I wondered how my life would go without him, how things would change.

four | a new role for jo

April 1952

I missed Dean. I missed everything about him. I missed his tenderness and his smile.

Each day on returning from work I asked Rose if there was mail for me. 'There are plenty of bills, Jo dear,' she would smirk, or sometimes giggle.

After a few weeks I stopped asking. I felt a sense of rejection and my self-esteem was at a low. Why had Dean been so insistent about keeping in touch? Where was he? Had he met with an accident? Had his posting been to a war zone? I wept each time I thought about him.

If I had found him attractive then, even with his funny GI haircut, his regular features in a face that lit up when he smiled, girls from his home town might also have found him appealing. He was fit and vibrant. He would have been welcomed home with great love and relief at his safe return, although it would have been for only a short time before his next posting.

In a time of war, would he ever return home again as a well-rounded young man or would the ravages of war send him back into the arms of those who loved him and whom he loved, broken and twisted in mind and body, if at all? Would Josephine Willis with her pale green eyes and unruly red hair be a distant echo? Surely a spark of love would remain in his heart? But then, I knew that sparks of love were not fanned into eternal flames by long separations.

As the days passed into weeks I began to believe Dean had forgotten me, a fact that amused Rose greatly. The post I held, which at first seemed acceptable to me, now became drudgery.

Diwali, the festival of lights had come and gone as had Christmas, without much good cheer in our small household. Mother had roasted a chicken, which was a real luxury at the time and I bought dress materials for mother and Rose. It was, however, a truly dismal affair.

And as the New Year dawned for me in1952, I thought bitterly, what was I doing with my life, sitting and typing endlessly for a small wage? The British and many Anglo-Indians had left Calcutta for Britain. Some of the vacancies had been filled by young male typists or Indian girls. A young man, by the name of Anil Basu, who now occupied the desk next to mine, always seemed in a hurry to go home. I asked him if he lived far and whether transport was difficult for him.

'No, Josephine, this job is merely feeding me and paying a few bills in the meantime. I'm doing an accounts course for a year at college. I hope to get a better job if I qualify well. The course is from five to eight each evening. The new term starts in April.'

'Are there any places still available?' I asked.

'Possibly, phone and ask,' he replied.

I phoned and made an appointment for an interview. The course was at the Suffee College, the same place where I had learned to type. The Principal was pleased to see me and offered me a place. He warned me I would have to work hard.

'Accounting is not typing. It's not a fun thing, merely to keep a car on the road,' he said smiling at me. Anil also said the course was difficult. I enrolled; the work indeed proved difficult but I persevered. I gave Anil a lift home each evening and he often helped me with small problems in accounting which I didn't understand easily the first time round.

And so at twenty-one, in the searing heat of April 1952, in an ever deteriorating situation in Calcutta, where Mother Teresa opened her home for the dying and where beggars were on the increase and several demonstrations of one kind or another took place, I took a new direction, a new road, and a new role.

I now had different companions – poor but clever students, who were mostly of my own age, working during the day and trying to take a step at a time up the ladder of success.

On several evenings a week I joined my colleagues at a very small Indian restaurant close to the college. The clientele were mostly young students. Though sparsely furnished with long wooden tables, and folding metal chairs designed to seat a dozen people, it was kept spotlessly clean. The mouth-watering aroma of freshly made chapattis, parathas and vegetable curry made from seasonal vegetables, blotted out the stench of the garbage floating in the drains outside, but not the sight of hungry young children begging for a few paisas to feed themselves. Their swollen stomachs and wide eyes told of malnutrition and guiltily we gave them money for food, the restaurant also supplying them with leftovers at closing time.

I wasn't immediately accepted, though. What was an English girl doing in a place such as this? Only gradually did I become one of them and we sat and ate our evening meal together, arguing and exchanging views in a friendly way.

My mother and Rose dined early leaving me to fend for myself. My mother still cooked, helped by the ayah, who also pandered to Rose.

Still, three months into the course and I was much happier, enjoying my work and Dad usually phoned on Saturday evening after closing time in the factory. I looked forward to his weekly call.

On a particular Friday evening the phone was ringing constantly. I ran to answer. It was my father's voice speaking through a poor line with a good deal of crackling. He had to shout to make himself heard.

'Jo, your Uncle Edward died of a heart attack last evening after dinner. Poor Vali, she's in a terrible state. Can you hear me, can you hear me?' he kept shouting. 'Send her a cable and write immediately. I will represent the family at the funeral on Monday. I know you can't come. I'll explain to Vali.'

'Yes, I hear you, Dad,' I replied but the line had already gone dead.

five | london for jo

1953

After the funeral, Vali and her mother sold up and left for England, never to return again. Mrs Finlayson, always known to me as Aunt Ruth, was an excellent organiser and they soon settled well in England. Vali had been a good correspondent and after many depressing letters from her and comforting ones written back by me, she started to enjoy London even though the aftermath of the war was still in the hearts and minds of many people.

She spoke of shortages in her letters. She missed the lush tropical fruit. 'Oh, Jo,' she wrote. 'What would I not give for a nice basket of mangoes, the ones your father grows in his garden?'

But soon enough it became obvious she was beginning to enjoy life in London, and her correspondence was full of amusing incidents. The letters always ended with a few lines written by her mother invariably urging me to visit them. But I had a course to complete and it took a year of hard work every day, and every evening, to finally complete it, working through the searing heat of May and June and splashing my way to evening classes during the monsoon, whilst Rose and my mother socialised idly, ignoring our unfortunate circumstances. My hard work was, however, rewarded and I passed my final examination in the following April of 1953, with merit.

No parties or congratulations were offered by either Rose or my mother. My father did, however, send me fifty Rupees with a letter saying how proud he was of my achievements. I was grateful

to him as I knew the financial situation was difficult for him. I thought wryly that in the halcyon years of his life, his gift to me would have been in the hundreds and his enthusiasm would have been as a cloak of joy surrounding us. Today his praise was, of necessity, muted. Jeb Hunt very kindly bought me a box of chocolates from Firpos, a shop selling luxury confectionery.

April, as usual, was a blistering hot month, and when a letter arrived from Aunt Ruth, once again asking me to visit them in London, I felt the words were like a breath of fresh cool air ready to revive me in mind and spirit. She even said she would send me a ticket through BOAC if I gave her the proposed date of my travel. After that there were no problems as my father had arranged passports for the whole family in case we had to leave India at short notice. I planned to spend a month with Vali and Aunt Ruth and I was excited at the prospect of seeing the country of my ancestors.

It was May. The year was 1953 and I was twenty-two and buzzing to see Vali again. I arrived at Heathrow at six in the morning and knew a long wait was inevitable, as the Finlaysons were not early risers.

I collected my luggage and some hot tea and found a seat in the arrivals lounge. I looked around me at the throngs of people going about their business: passengers, airport staff and those waiting for friends and relations to come off flights. The airport was busy but clean. No vendors, no small barefoot children in rags, sneakily relieving themselves against a wall and no adults coughing and spitting carelessly as they went about their business.

I thought of our friendship over the years. Vali was a pretty child, popular with her peers but at school, routine had not sat easily on her shoulders, and her pranks often bordered on the dangerous or bizarre, her behaviour often hiding real fear. She had a fear of the sound of conch shells being blown late at night in the valley, not far from the school. The Nepalese ayahs at the school had explained the meaning of prayer flags, the wheels of intercession used by the lamas and, of course, the blowing of the conch shells. She knew they were blown to ward off evil spirits as part of a burial service, the corpse having been swathed in strips of unbleached cloth, in the sitting position, and buried with difficulty deep in the hard frozen earth for all time, but each time we heard them at night, she slid deep into her bed, sometimes weeping and bizarrely whispering, 'Don't let me be buried alone.'

The warmth of the waiting room, together with the hot tea and anti-sickness pills I had taken, all conspired to make me doze and hallucinate. I dreamed of Vali. I could see us both in school Vali sitting on a swing, her bare feet touching lush green grass that was dotted with small yellow and purple flowers. I looked at her and smiled but she slowly disappeared, ghost-like, into the Himalayan fog. A shadowy figure, with a hazy light where her face should have been, appeared in her place. Blood was at her feet instead of flowers. I woke with a start to see Vali running towards me, vibrant and smiling.

I stood up as she threw herself into my arms, and we clung to each other laughing and crying at the same time. Aunt Ruth was not far behind, and she hugged me too saying, 'Oh, Josephine, forgive us for keeping you waiting. It's lazy Vali who's to blame, as usual.'

It seemed strange we had no male family member to help us carry my bags out of the airport. Vali must have had a similar thought as she put her arm round my shoulders saying, with a catch in her voice, 'No daddy to help us now. Mum and I miss him so.'

Aunt Ruth drove to their home and on the way I constantly commented, 'So different, so clean.' She parked the car at an attractive block of flats.

'This is where we live. It's called Kensington,' she said.

The bumpy flight in an Argonaut had taken its toll. After a substantial breakfast, I asked if I could rest for a while. It was past

midday when I awoke. Vali was keen to show me as much of London as possible. She wanted to take me shopping, have lunch and show me the sights all in a day.

'Come on, Jo, shake a leg. Get up and wash and dress. Everything will be closed by the time we get there.'

'Vali, I can't spend a lot of money shopping in London. Dad's business is in a bad way. It's not like the old days. I have had to penny-pinch almost all the time I've been in Calcutta.'

Aunt Ruth heard us speaking and came into the bedroom. 'I'm so sorry,' she said. 'I had heard rumours before I left India that your father's business was not doing well but didn't realise it was so bad.' She sympathetically put her arms around me for a moment or two.

I smiled ruefully. 'I've been working as a typist and this last year I've done an accounts course. I'm grateful to you for this holiday. I really need it. I hope to get a better job when I go back. Dad is really unable now to support us all. As for Rose and my mother, they don't realise how serious the situation has become.'

'Well, Josephine dear, let's enjoy this short break together before you face difficult times. There's nothing to stop us sightseeing,' she smiled.

And so we spent the next week sightseeing. We visited the Tower of London and Vali said to me in a deep mock serious voice, 'You'll get your head chopped off here if you continue to be a naughty girl.'

She was bright and full of fun, just like she had been as a young girl. She insisted I accompany her to parties. After the first one, I wasn't prepared to go to a second.

I had absolutely nothing in common with the wealth of the guests there, nor with their extreme style of dress, behaviour and language. It was pure affectation. One young man with lank blond hair flopping over his forehead like a miniature sheaf of wheat and a slight lisp made a vulgar pass at me. At the end of the evening Vali was so drunk we had to take a taxi home.

We lunched out together the next day and I tried to speak to her about her drinking.

'Vali, what on earth are you doing? Do you really enjoy parties like the one we were at last night? Everyone seemed to be drunk. Did you see what that stupid chap with the lank hair did to me?'

'Yes,' she giggled, 'I saw him pinch your bum. He was only teasing you, Jo. Lighten up. This is London, and it was just a bit of fun. People are still depressed after the war and the Blitz. They try to forget the terrible things that happened, destroying their families, their livelihood and their way of life. I call it false fun. It'll pass. That chap, James, you are so indignant about lost his father and an older brother in the war. Jo, we were so protected in India, we didn't realise what war really meant. You have got to try and understand the devastation that took place here.'

I knew she had a point and tried to understand. After all, Dean had told me something of the war and what it had been like fighting in it. Oh, Dean, I thought, where are you now? And perhaps it was that sudden stab of sadness that made me say what I said next.

'And the drinking? Is that fun too?' I asked.

I knew I sounded like a Victorian nanny but I felt she needed to be told. 'You could barely stand by the time I got you home. Having fun is one thing but getting that drunk is just plain silly. Don't you have any other friends? What about hobbies? You used to ride and swim so well in India. How can you spend all your time with such people?'

Vali smiled oddly, and it was only then that I noticed a slight tremble in her fingers as she poured another cup of tea, how a vein was throbbing on the left side of her forehead and how very young and vulnerable she looked. I could have forgiven her anything at that moment.

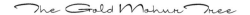

'Oh, Jo darling' she said, her voice pitched far higher than was her norm. 'Of course I have hobbies. They're called Men. Isn't that enough? Stop being such a pain in the nether region.'

I was quiet then, and worried by her attitudes, behaviour and a strange nervousness, more so when the next evening a rather nice young man by the name of Jonathan came in to ask her for a date and she brushed him aside quite cruelly. Noticing my surprise she said, 'He's got no money, darling. He's only a junior lawyer who handles our affairs.' There was such a sneer in the way she said these words that I had no reply for her.

I couldn't understand her obsession with wealth. Her father had left enough money for her to have a generous monthly allowance though she wasn't able to touch the actual Estate, not yet at least. Not that she needed it, for her mother also subsidised her. And I couldn't understand her moods, warm-hearted at one moment, bad-tempered at another; she seemed to swing between two extremes. At school she had always entertained us with her pranks, and I wondered now whether this apparently new exuberance was a part of her evolving personality, or whether there was something seriously wrong.

I didn't go the next party Vali was invited to, though she went all the same. I decided instead to spend the evening with Aunt Ruth. As Vali was about to leave I realised the young girl I knew had become a beautiful woman. The blonde hair arranged high on her head shone, and her skin glowed. He long pink chiffon dress swirled around her as she came out of her bedroom, showing her small pretty feet in silver high-heeled sandals. She had a white wrap in her hands. She looked so like a fragile flower. No wonder Uncle Edward had always asked me to look after her when we were alone together on days he had taken me shooting for wildfowl and snipe in the forest.

'What do you think, Jo?' she said, waiting, just as she always had, for my approval.

'You look beautiful, Vali. What more can I say?' and I meant it. 'Have a nice time,' I added as she left, closing the door and leaving a drift of exotic perfume behind her. I could hear her heels clicking as she went down the steps to the waiting taxi.

That evening Aunt Ruth cooked steak, as a special treat, for our evening meal, and I enjoyed both the meal and her company and felt at ease with her.

'Josephine,' she said at one point, leaning over the table and taking my hand. 'I would like us to go to the bank tomorrow morning. I can't bear to think of you living like a pauper in India while we are so well off here. You must have some money as a cushion and we have the means to provide it. I really am upset to know that you're struggling financially. How on earth did your father manage to allow his business to get into such difficulties? He had a very good income at one time. As for your mother and Rose, well I know what you mean about them living in the past, and more than that I'd rather not comment.'

It should have been an awkward moment, but it wasn't. Aunt Ruth was Aunt Ruth and had known both myself and my family for years. I told her what little I knew about Dad's business going down the tube and accepted her offer with gratitude. And then, we moved on and spoke about Vali.

'She's so beautiful,' I said, 'and seems so fragile. Do you know about her drinking, Aunt Ruth? Don't you think she's mixing with the wrong crowd? I would hate to see her get hurt.'

"Well, that's another matter, my dear.' Aunt Ruth sighed as she spoke. 'She's a young woman now, not a child any longer. All I can do is to warn her. I would ask just one small favour of you, Josephine. You and Vali have grown up together. Look after her if you can. We are...' she stopped, corrected herself and said, 'We have been almost like family.'

I put my hand on her arm. 'It's all right, Aunt Ruth. Don't worry. I'll look after Vali, in any way I can. Maybe it's just a phase she's

going through. I can't see Vali acting the sophisticate for long. She's always been too full of fun.'

The next morning Vali didn't accompany us as she said she was unwell. Her face was red and blotchy and she looked as if she had been crying.

Aunt Ruth and I lunched together in a small restaurant and she took me to her bank where she opened an account and deposited ten thousand pounds in my name. It was a large amount of money, far more than I had expected, and at first I had objected saying it was too much.

'It's for emergencies, Josephine,' she explained. 'I know you're careful with money, but sometimes circumstances take the upper hand.'

She also arranged for me to have five hundred rupees in cash so that when I arrived back in Calcutta, I would be in funds. I thanked her for her generosity saying I would pay the money back to her once I was able to stand on my own two feet financially.

We walked through a park on the way home. I noticed sadness in Aunt Ruth's demeanour. It was mid-May and the daffodils and crocus were now well gone. In their place was a lush green carpet of grass and newly planted summer annuals, yet to bloom. May in India was dry and hot and the earth was barren.

This should have been a happy time for me, but there seemed to be a sense of finality in our slow walk in the park, almost of foreboding. Aunt Ruth had to sit down for a while on a nearby bench and was quite out of breath, though we had only taken fifteen minutes of our promenade.

'Oh, Jo,' she said, once she had got her breath back. 'I'm so glad you came to see us. I'm not too well. The hospital is running some tests, though I'm sure you'll have noticed my breathing is laboured. I fear the worst, darling. And I must ask of you a favour.'

She clutched my hand as she said this, and then I realised the true import of the gift of the air tickets, the trip to the bank, and knew what she was going to say, almost before she said it. 'I need you to look after Vali. She has nobody to care for her, and her spirit is not strong. The loss of her father was a heavy blow. Please don't lose touch with her. She needs a guiding hand. She so often doesn't seem to be in control of her actions.' Aunt Ruth had to stop at this point to gather breath, and the almost rasping sound of her breathing was alarming, but I stayed quiet until she spoke again.

'Now, apart from the money I have just given you, I have made provision in my will to see that you and Vali are secure and at the very least have a roof over your heads. I know you'll eventually come home to Britain. There isn't anything more for girls like you in India.' She stopped and shook her head sadly.

'Your poor father, he will end his days in the India he loves. For him there's nothing here. He was such a handsome young man. No wonder your......' she stopped and took a deep breath. What was she about to say to me? 'Yes, Aunt Ruth?' I said. 'Is there something you need to tell me?' She shook her head. 'It's nothing dear, old stories of India often bore the young.'

I was saddened by what she had told me but not as surprised as I might have been, what with the air tickets and the trip to the bank, and having already seen Vali's style of living for myself. And despite the sense of duty I now felt, the rest of my visit with Vali and Aunt Ruth was pleasant and restful for all of us, with no bitterness and no arguments.

The last day of my visit was tearful for us. My flight was an evening one and Vali packed my case for me while I dressed. Eventually we were ready to go for one last lunch before I left for Calcutta.

As we came out of the restaurant the spring sunshine caught Vali's hair and seemed to wrap her in a golden glow. This was the picture of the girl who was like a sister to me and the same picture I wanted to hold in my heart and mind forever. She held my

hand in the car and hugged me several times in the airport. I now knew the loss of her father had affected her deeply.

The short time I spent in London seemed to have restored my health. I felt fit and well. Aunt Ruth handed me an elegant shopping bag. 'You need this, Jo, darling; it's just something cool to change into before you leave the aircraft in Calcutta.'

Aunt Ruth hugged me then and whispered in my ear, 'Thank you, Jo, for all you've done. I know I can rely on you when I'm not here. If I don't see you again, my dear, then may God bless you and may life be kind to you and may my Vali always have a friend like you to rely on.'

six | destiny's meeting for jo

June 1953

A month of pleasant living with Vali and Aunt Ruth had been too short, and as the aircraft took off I promised I would do my utmost to lift myself out of the difficulties I now faced, but I knew I had to do it alone.

The BOAC flight from London to Calcutta had a long stop-over in Kuwait and almost continual turbulence during the remaining leg of the journey made sleep impossible. The flight had been delayed and we landed late on a very hot summer night and were met by a team of disinfectors, spraying the inside of the aircraft, which dispelled any idea I might have had of walking off an international flight dressed elegantly in a summer dress with the aroma of expensive perfume around me.

I waited for my case to be unloaded and carried my luggage to the Customs desk. The counter assistant who searched my case upset the neatly folded clothes Vali had packed for me in London, generously including several attractive summer dresses of her own, together with bottles of perfume, some of which were confiscated as they were in excess of the amount I was allowed to bring into the country for my personal use. A cynical thought came to mind. Whose dressing table would they grace by tomorrow morning?

I asked at the enquiries desk for the timings of the bus to the city centre. I was informed the evening and night service had been discontinued as the bus had been stopped on the lonely

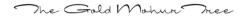

Dum Dum to Calcutta road on a previous occasion and passengers robbed of their money and valuables. I was facing a long stay at the airport.

As I walked towards the small restaurant for a cold drink a voice behind me said, 'Would you like a taxi, there isn't a bus until morning?'

I turned and looked into soft grey eyes set in a tanned face and saw with a shock that he was Anglo-Indian. What was he doing driving a taxi? I had no idea. What I did know was how extremely attractive I found him at first sight, and felt embarrassed, blaming the long flight for playing tricks with me. He was speaking again.

'I'm registered with the Police and the Airport Authorities. You'll be safe with me.' He produced a small card from his pocket with his name and photograph. Adrian Greene the card shouted out in bold letters giving his age as twenty-seven.

'How much is the fare to Calcutta,' I asked.

'Whatever the meter says, Missy,' he replied cheekily.

'I'm Miss Josephine Willis, not Missy, but that's fine, I'll hire your cab.'

He merely smiled, picked up my case for me and we walked together to the car park. His taxi was parked at the edge of a row of cars beneath a Gold Mohur tree. Even in the dim light I noticed it was in full bloom, its flamboyant red and fleshy umbrella-shaped flowers covering the tree, pausing and waiting to be dashed to the earth by the ferocity of the monsoon yet to come.

'I love that tree,' I said. 'So spectacular and beautiful.'

With barely an upward glance he said, almost to himself, 'Love and spectacular beauty; two things that never last.'

He opened the door for me and made sure I was comfortably settled before getting into the driver's seat and leaving the car park. I gave him my address.

A deep voice with a lilt woke me. 'You are home now, Missy.'

I had slept all the way in the back of Adrian Greene's taxi, fearlessly, trusting him. I paid him his fare and gave him a tip. He carried my case up the stairs to the flat. I had carelessly left my front door key in my dressing table drawer when I had left Calcutta for London, so now I rang the doorbell repeatedly.

We stood together on the landing. I could feel the heat from his body in the sultry night air while we waited. He took a step to one side and looked at me. I was embarrassed and stared into space in front of me, hoping that Rose would hurry up and open the door.

'You can look at me,' he said. 'There's no charge.'

Before I could reply Rose came to the door. He put the case inside the hallway, said goodnight and left.

Instead of a welcome home Rose snapped, 'Why are you so late? Mother and I have been waiting up for you for ages. We thought something had happened to you.'

I had thanked the taxi driver for carrying my case up the stairs but Rose, annoyed at having been woken, spoke irritably, without a hint of a welcome in her voice or demeanour.

'You took a taxi from the airport at this time of night on those deserted roads, with nothing but a few mud huts on either side? You're mad. You could have been raped or murdered or anything.'

Mother came out of her room having heard voices. 'Oh, you're home, Josephine,' she said. 'There's a salad in the fridge if you're hungry. I've made up a divan bed for you in the small study. I've had to let your room as it has a separate entrance, as you well know. We'll speak in the morning.'

And that was it. Such was my welcome home.

The divan bed was as uncomfortable as ever and the overhead fan squeaked at every turn. I opened the window to give myself some air in the room. My sleep was fitful and full of strange dreams.

I woke early. The *roti walla* was coming up the back steps. As I opened the door to him he started shouting, asking who I was and demanding payment of fifteen rupees, swearing at me in Hindi as he spoke, not realising I understood every word he said. He didn't have his bread basket with him so I assumed he was owed money and was not going to supply us with bread. I closed the door, went to the bedroom and got fifteen Rupees from my purse and paid him. He had used extremely foul language. I lost my temper, caught him by the collar and said, 'If you shout and swear at my back door once again I will have you arrested by the police.' I spoke in Hindi using similar invectives, much to his surprise. He left mumbling to himself.

My mother had come into the dining room having heard raised voices. Though she didn't speak Hindi she knew full well what had taken place.

'Don't try and emulate your father. You can't behave like that here. I'm so ashamed. People in the other flats must have heard you swearing, Josephine.'

'You're ashamed, Mother? No. I'm more than ashamed. Fancy owing the bread man money. Why are you buying bread from street vendors anyway? You know his bread could be contaminated. I'm going to Flurys to get bread, the same as I always did.' For once she didn't argue with me. Rose made breakfast.

'It's only a month I've been away. Why are you in such debt that you are unable to pay the bread man?' I asked after breakfast.

Mother went into her bedroom and brought out a slim folder with several papers in it and handed it to me.

'You had better see these papers, Josephine. Your father has not been sending me enough money to keep us going comfortably and without your help this last month, it became impossible. I can't argue with him any more. You had better speak to him.'

'I've just come off a flight and am faced with this. I'll see what I can do. Why can't you and Rose think of some sort of work?' I said irritably.

It was a futile comment. Neither of them had any intention of working. It was below their dignity. My mother was trying to act like a memsahib of the British Raj while we were on the brink of poverty. I gave her two hundred rupees from the money Aunt Ruth had let me have.

'Please use this carefully until I manage to get myself some sort of work. It is money Aunt Ruth gave me and there are no sinister implications.' So, nothing had changed and Rose and my mother once again looked to me for financial help.

I noticed she was tearful as she took the money from me, thanking me almost reluctantly. I had never had much kindness from her. Still, she was my mother.

I unpacked my case to get myself some fresh clothes. Rose's curiosity got the better of her. She came to see what I had brought from London. As I unpacked she looked with real longing at the perfume. She had so little real luxuries that I felt sorry for her and let her help herself.

The morning papers had been delivered. I poured myself a cup of tea and took it to the room I was now to use as my bedroom. I looked at the 'positions vacant' column very thoroughly. One advertisement caught my eye. It was for a junior accountant with some secretarial skills. I phoned and was given an interview for Friday at ten. The girl who spoke to me stressed that if I didn't have original certificates I needn't bother attending.

I asked Rose if she could alter one or two of the dresses that Vali had given me as they were a little fussy for my taste.

'I'll help as a thank you for the perfume, provided you don't interfere and shout at me. I'll do the alterations my way,' she pouted.

My car wouldn't start and I would need transport if I was to job hunt. I walked to a nearby garage and explained I needed transport urgently. They agreed to tow my car away, promising to let me have it in working order in three weeks time.

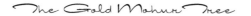

I was up early on the Friday morning and showered and dressed well before the time of the interview. The dress that Rose had altered now had a simple neat round collar and I thanked her, promising to let her have some money. Like my father, she was clever with her hands.

I decided to take a taxi to my interview as I didn't know where the offices were and got into the first one in the rank, not far from the front gates of the flats we lived in.

'Do you know how I can get to Joint India Enterprises?' I asked the taxi driver.

I had spoken in Hindi as most of the taxi drivers didn't know any English.

'*Ha,* (Yes) Missy,' was the reply.

I looked at the driver and laughed saying, 'I'm so sorry, I didn't look into the cab properly. I beg your pardon.'

It was Adrian Greene.

'I'll drive you round but it's really walking distance from here,' he said smiling.

When we arrived at the offices of Joint India Enterprises, I had a better look at him in daylight. He was very athletically built and his smile revealed even, well looked-after teeth. His grey eyes still attracted me. The dress I was wearing had a slim skirt and I had difficulty getting out of the taxi. He put his hand in mine to help me out of the back seat and then seemed embarrassed.

I paid him and as I turned to go into the building where the office was located, a crazy notion came into my head. I looked back and asked, 'are you married?' He laughed and replied, 'no, Missy, are you?'

I just shook my head and smiled at him, a little embarrassed at my stupid question and at all the thoughts that were rushing through my head, and that Adrian Greene was in every single one of them.

seven | a job, a date and the beggar boy

June 1953

I was early for my interview. A pretty Chinese receptionist ushered me into an air-conditioned room and invited me to wait. After about half an hour the door opened and a middle-aged man, balding and slimly built came into the room. I stood up as he came towards me. We shook hands. In a very clipped English accent he introduced himself.

'I'm Lance Rooter, head of this branch of the company. I presume you're Miss Willis?'

'Yes, I'm Josephine Willis.' I replied.

'Will you come this way please, Miss Willis' he said smiling politely at me.

I followed him down a short corridor into a bright sunny room. A large desk was set at an angle in the centre. A door opened into a small adjacent room. It contained a desk, a typewriter and numerous filing cabinets. As I handed him my folder containing my certificates he indicated I should sit opposite him.

He was reading the papers I had handed to him when a bearer opened the door and brought in tea and biscuits.

'You're certainly an industrious young lady and have not wasted much time since you left school,' he said kindly. He asked about my schooling in Darjeeling while we drank tea together. He then spoke about the post he had vacant.

'You'll need to work two days a week for a chartered accountant Mr Mackie. He is connected with several companies. He
has the use of an office here. He's been to Darjeeling and
says parts of it remind him of Scotland. If your application
is successful, my company will pay you for four days a week.
Mr Mackie will make arrangements for the other two. Can you
work on a Saturday? Some of the candidates were unable to
work at weekends.'

'It won't be a problem,' I replied. He handed me two letters
and asked me to copy-type them. 'There's no rush. Accuracy is
important,' he said.

I read over the two short letters and typed the first one
rather quickly. I noticed a typing error in the first. The second
letter had a spelling mistake. I took the letters through to him
and commented that I had corrected the errors in both letters.

'Thank you, Miss Willis,' he smiled. 'The mistakes were deliber-
ate to see if you were efficient enough to correct them.'

'My name is Josephine, Mr Rooter.'

'Your test is satisfactory, Josephine. I can offer you the post
if Mr Mackie finds you suitable.' He sighed. 'He's being so difficult.
We seem to have come to an impasse. The last girl who worked
here emigrated to Australia with her parents. She got on so well
with Mr Mackie. I'll take you through now.'

In a nearby room, with the door open, a broad-shouldered man
was looking out of the window. He had a cup in his hand. He was
tall and blond. Mr Rooter knocked gently on the open door to gain
his attention, and coughed once or twice, almost as if he didn't
want to upset him.

'Craig,' he said rather loudly.

The man swung round.

Good heavens, I thought. A small helmet with horns and he
would have been a Viking. I closed my eyes and gritted my teeth
for a moment or two to control my laughter. He ignored Mr Rooter,

nodding his head as if to dismiss him. He looked directly at me, taking in my appearance.

'Hem, a redhead' he mumbled, and then cleared his throat and said distinctly, 'I'm Craig Mackie, and who are you?'

'Josephine Willis, that's who I am,' I said slightly cheekily. I realised I would have to hold my ground with this man.

He didn't shake hands with me. Instead he indicated that I should take a seat at a small desk at one side of the room, pointing to it arrogantly. A large amount of paperwork littered the desk. This strange introduction was clearly meant to be intimidating. Even a year ago I would have said to him, 'You're bloody rude' and walked out. Today I had to eat humble pie. I needed money.

He grunted a bit and then said. 'What name are you known by? Josephine is a mouthful?'

'I'm sorry, Mr Mackie. Josephine is the only name I have.'

'A pet name maybe?'

'Sorry, I'm not a dog.' Was he deliberately trying to rattle me?

He cleared his throat a couple of times and then pointed to the papers on the desk saying, 'See what you can do with these. They will possibly take you over an hour. I'll leave you to it.'

He left the room. I looked through the papers. Copy invoices, receipts, delivery notes and several small folders with miscellaneous papers were all jumbled together in large brown envelopes. I could find no ledgers. This was a simple but tedious sorting-out process. I opened the desk drawers to find some folders. Whoever had worked here before had been methodical and tidy.

I was starting to feel thirsty and hungry. It was one o'clock when the door opened and Mr Mackie came in carrying a double-handled basket.

'You can stop now. I think we should have lunch,' he smiled. Did he want an accountant or did he want a playmate? The work he had given me was nothing to do with accounts. I had sorted out

somebody's chaotic business housekeeping. He put down paper plates and glasses and opened the package he was carrying. The sandwiches and cold drinks he had brought in were very welcome. As we ate he now spoke to me in a friendly way.

'I believe you've just returned from London.'

'Yes, I've spent a month with friends after completing a one-year accounts course here in Calcutta. London was quite an eye-opener for me. You see, I was born here and it was the first time I had left India.'

'Your papers say you were in school in Darjeeling. Now there's a place. Absolutely beautiful. You were very lucky to be at school in such glorious surroundings. I had a holiday there. It's something like Scotland in parts. I'm a Scot, Josephine.'

'Yes, I know. Mr Rooter told me,' I said.

We finished eating and he looked at what I had done. He was taking quite a long time to make up his mind.

'You'll suit me,' he said smiling. 'Come in on Monday and sign the necessary papers. I'll advise Mr Rooter the long search is over.'

I thanked him and got up to leave. His parting question amused me. 'Josephine, do you always wear high heeled sandals and paint your toenails?'

'No, only for interviews with chartered accountants.'

As I closed the door behind me I heard him laughing.

I walked home slowly thinking if I had been wise to commit myself to working six days a week. When I entered the flat Rose was sewing. My mother was out playing bridge.

'Well, Jo, did you get the job?' she asked. 'You have been away for such an age.'

'Yes, Rose, I did get the job. Perhaps you could help me by altering a few more of the dresses that Vali gave me.'

'Of course,' she said, nodding her head in approval. 'I'll see to it tomorrow, Jeb and I are going out shortly.'

'Rose, just listen to me for a moment. Jeb Hunt, though quite a nice fellow, is far too old for you. I think he is manipulative. What's the attraction? He isn't even good-looking. He's almost twice your age for heavens sake.'

She didn't let me continue and snapped at me saying, 'Mind your own business, Jo. In any case, looks aren't everything.'

The lack of enough private space and the fact there were no green areas of our own to use had made us irritable with each other.

I went to my room and lay on my bed. The interview had been exhausting for me. I saw Jeb for a few minutes when he came to collect Rose. They seemed happy together despite their age difference. Before they left Jeb said he would be having a Sunday barbeque soon after some necessary work on his pool was completed.

'You'll, of course, be invited, Jo,' he said before they left.

On Monday I walked to work among the throngs of people going the same way. I wished I had my car. Mr Rooter was at his desk when I arrived and he gave me some hand written letters to type. The offices were pleasant and at lunchtime I realised there was no canteen on the premises. I went downstairs and saw a vendor a short distance away from the office. I bought a couple of oranges, a banana and a bag of peanuts from him. It would have to do until I got home.

A small ragged beggar boy was sitting on the first step of the office building. He smiled at me even in his poverty. I gave him some money. His eyes were large in his thin little face and he scampered barefoot over the hot pavement towards the vendor to buy something to eat.

And now at the end of the day I walked slowly down the stairs. I hadn't found the staff particularly friendly. Maybe I

should try somewhere else for employment. Once again I joined the throngs on the pavement. Above the chattering crowds and the shouts of the vendors I heard a voice behind me say, 'Good evening, Missy.'

I turned to see Adrian Greene, dressed smartly in white trousers and a blue shirt, smiling at me. He caught up with me, held my arm and pulled me towards him so that we would not get parted in the crowd.

'Got a date with someone who hasn't turned up?' I teased.

'Someone fabulously rich and very beautiful was due to meet me here, but you'll do,' he replied.

We could barely hear ourselves speak.

'Let's cross the road here,' he said. He held me by the hand and we ran across the road together like children, walking across the tram lines avoiding the thundering trams carrying their human cargo back home.

The few benches on the grass in the *maidan* were occupied with mostly office workers having a short rest before they returned home for their evening meal. We walked until we found a dry spot beneath a tree and sat down.

A vendor with a large kettle and small earthenware cups stopped near us. Adrian bought tea cynically commenting, 'I wonder what the memsahibs of the Raj would think if they saw us now. An English girl, sitting and drinking tea from a *chatty* bought from a vendor, and horror of horrors, accompanied by an Anglo-Indian taxi driver?'

'I'm not concerned with what people think. Josephine Willis does what she likes. That's the first thing you need to know about me.'

'Well, did you get the job, or do I have to run my taxi back and forth to that office forever? Goodness knows how many candidates they've interviewed. Ridiculous.'

'Yes, I'm on probation, though. I'll see how it goes. How did you know there was a vacant post there anyway?'

'I've been running candidates back and forth for a good few weeks. It was becoming a joke among the taxi drivers. You're very lucky. Jobs are difficult to obtain nowadays, especially for Anglo-Indians.'

'I'm not an Anglo-Indian,' I said.

'I know, Missy, but I am. My grandmother was French. She knew no English and I was brought up to speak French. My father was Anglo-Indian. He was in the Indian army.'

'Are you a taxi driver full-time?'

'No, I'm a medical student in my final year. I'm short of money so drive a taxi in what spare time I have. I need to keep myself solvent. The taxi is owned by a friend of mine, Ranjit, who owns several taxis. I drive for him as often as possible but I only get a percentage of the takings,' he replied.

I wondered if it was true.

We finished our tea and then walked towards the flat, not saying very much as it was impossible to hear each other speak among the noisy throngs of people.

We arrived at the entrance to the flats where I lived and he turned and faced me and took my hand in his.

'Would it be possible for me to date you?' he asked.

'Yes, why not,' I replied.

'It won't be every day as I still have a lot of study to get through and quite a lot of work on the wards.'

'That's fine,' I said nodding in agreement, 'but could I have my hand back, please?'

He was embarrassed as he seemed unaware he was still holding my hand. We said goodbye and I walked up the driveway to the flats.

Rose had arrived home a few minutes earlier and had stood in the porch listening to every word. As I walked towards the steps I thought what on earth was I doing? Well, it would be entertaining. I was so bored with my surroundings. It was only a bit of sheer

bravado and what Vali would have called a cool stunt with a good-looking man. Was it a stunt too far? I barely knew him, but was attracted by this unusual and charismatic man. My thoughts were interrupted by Rose who was standing in the middle of the sitting room as I opened the door.

'I knew your small window of sanity wouldn't last, Jo,' she said acidly. 'Wait till Mother hears of this latest ploy of yours. I saw you holding hands and strolling with that Anglo-Indian taxi driver. Are you completely mad? Your carry on with that damn stupid marine before you went to London was bad enough but this is completely unacceptable. You don't even know who he is.'

'He's a medical student, Rose,' I said calmly, not knowing if this was really true, which only seemed to enrage her.

'Don't lie, Jo, you know he's nothing of the kind. He's Anglo-Indian and drives taxis, for heaven's sake. When Mother questioned you about what you did when you were out with Dean Mitchell you used to say you were jiving. What excuse are you going to come up with this time? She'll give you a good thumping, you just wait and see.'

By this time I was standing facing her.

'You jealous cat,' I said quietly and started laughing. 'What a nice cabaret you're giving the other tenants of this building, what with all the windows open, and you shouting your head off at your older sister. A fine way to behave, Rose.'

Rose went the colour of the more pink varieties of her namesake, before stamping her way across to her bedroom and slamming the door behind her.

eight | dating adrian

July 1953

Adrian often met me after work and walked me home. Sometimes we walked to the *maidan*. We watched hockey and other games being played, and at other times we found an empty bench and sat and talked, although this was made difficult by beggars asking for money. On days when he had the taxi with him we were able to sit and speak to each other in comparative peace.

My mother wouldn't allow Adrian to visit me in the house. After an ill-tempered refusal she put up a wall of silence. She was afraid of banning me from seeing him altogether as I'd become her main means of financial support, my father now able to send her only enough money for the basics of life. It was an uneasy situation, laced with a great deal of bad temper.

Work too was a strain on me with Saturdays being particularly tedious and difficult, as Craig Mackie took time on a Saturday to teach me, increasing my knowledge of accounting day after day. Unfortunately tempers often flared as he sometimes lost patience with me, running his fingers through his mop of curly blond hair, his blue eyes looking at me in such a way as if to say, 'don't you dare give up on me.'

The one good spot of news was that I finally got my car back from the garage. It was a Thursday and I sat in the car park in the evening after work and saw Adrian standing waiting for me. The little beggar boy was sitting on the steps of the office near him. I tooted my horn and shouted out of the window.

'Adrian, give the child some change for food.'

He got up and walked towards me. 'Let's have a go in this car of yours, Jo,' he said smiling.

I got out, handed him the car keys and sat beside him. Before he started the car he said, 'Incidentally, I gave the boy his meal at the vendors while I was waiting for you. If I'd given him change he might have had it stolen from him. I paid the vendor and he chose what he wanted. It's such a shame. Who does he belong to? He's such a skinny little fellow.'

He drove to the Strand by the banks of the Hooghly. It was a pleasure sitting together undisturbed and he managed to park near a walkway. Children were running ahead of their parents in their brightly coloured clothes. Two seemed to have escaped from the supervision of their parents and were playing at the edge of the river covered in mud.

Although I had been the instigator of our relationship, expecting just a bit of fun, I had an uneasy feeling I was losing control of the situation. We seemed to be on the brink of something far more serious. Did I really want this? He had so little laughter within him, but then poverty and light-heartedness were uneasy bedfellows.

'Why so quiet today, Jo?'

'I'm tired.'

The skies had darkened and people were returning home by any means they could find. Some had cars, others took rickshaws. The street lights had come on and we watched the boatmen lighting their lanterns, one at a time and attaching them to their crafts where they bobbed about like giant fireflies with the movement of the dows, and the other small boats in the water.

He kissed me in the gloom of the evening, and pointed to the Gold Mohur trees in full bloom on the other side of the road, their blossoms glowing like fireflies in the light of the streetlamps.

'Just like you, Jo. Bright and unashamedly flamboyant and the glow is my love for you,' he said sentimentally.

'I think I love you, can't you feel it? I love you, Jo.'

He cupped my face between the palms of his hands and kissed me again, this time sensually, deeply and insistently and then a pause grew between us like a chasm. I didn't know how to respond to him so I said nothing and drew away.

'I can wait,' he said, and though there was disappointment in his tone, I felt there was also a touch of anger within him that I had not responded positively.

We drove home then, and Adrian parked the car under the porch.

'I can't see you tomorrow,' he said. 'I am working all day at the hospital.'

I just stood there on the steps and watched him go, more confused than I had ever been in my life.

It was early in our friendship and I felt he had tried to dominate me.

The weeks passed and our strange dating pattern continued into July. We had nowhere to go and the early rains now made it difficult for us to sit comfortably for long periods in the small Morris 8, without the windows steaming up, or to take a walk along the river bank. I was home later than usual and my mother could hold her silence no longer.

'What time do you call this?'

I wasn't in the mood for this interrogation, and answered rather rudely, 'It's the same time as the clock on the wall shows.'

'Don't be impertinent. 'I've already, just today, posted a letter to your father telling him about your disgraceful behaviour, so I'll say no more. You'll be taught a lesson by me in my own good time. Wait and see. The whole of Calcutta is talking about you.'

'The whole of Calcutta,' I repeated after her in mock horror. 'What fame! Who are these tittle-tattlers? Shall I send them letters of thanks? What's wrong with going out with a good-looking educated young man who will be qualified as a doctor very shortly?'

'Don't lie, Josephine,' she hissed. 'Everybody knows he's only a taxi driver. Stop making up fancy stories about him. Some of my friends have been driven by him on several occasions. What do you want? To marry him? Live in a hovel on a taxi driver's earnings? An expensive boarding school education for what? Where will all your grandiose ideas go then?'

I didn't think I'd ever seen my mother so angry. But this time I didn't even bother to reply. I was too tired and too confused, and had no idea what I wanted then, nor what I felt for Adrian.

I turned from her ready to go to my room but she came after me and swung me round by the shoulders. I was face to face with her and was sure she was about to hit me as she had done so often in the past when I was a child. I took a step back and put my hands up to ward off the impending blow and shouted at her, 'Don't you dare touch me, Mother. Don't you dare.'

With sorrow, I knew in my heart that this time if she had struck me I would have hit her back. – God forgive me. My own Mother.

She returned to her room with a slow step.

This was the night when fear and comfort - strange companions - visited me in my dreams. The young woman in the blue dress who laughed and played with me so often in the dreams of my childhood now wept, as I stood dangerously close to the edge of a precipice, while the sadhu, with his eyes shut and his face gaunt, chanted and prayed for me, pleading with his gods to keep me safe and not allow me to fall. I could almost hear his repetitive chant of prayer and comfort as I woke to a new day.

nine | a message from the grave

It was Saturday and I assumed we would finish work at noon as I had gone in earlier than usual but Craig Mackie had been tetchy, and when I said to him, 'Mr Mackie, would you like me to make you coffee before I go,' he had humphed a bit saying 'I'm Craig. Call me Craig, I'm fed up with this Mr Mackie business and I'm sick and tired of this infernal heat and rain and the sight of poverty outside the window each day.'

I was amazed at his strange outburst and really had no answer for him and he then continued looking at me hard with his piercing blue eyes, as if he was examining my very soul. I shook my head at him and started to pack up and close my desk as it was way past noon.

'You're getting into deep waters in your personal life,' he said. He obviously meant my friendship with Adrian as he had seen us together many a time.

'Thank you for your concern, but you don't need to worry about me. I'm a jammy swimmer,' I replied as I was about to leave the room.

Downstairs, Adrian was waiting for me. He was sitting on the step talking to the little beggar boy. He had once again given the little fellow his lunch.

He was a bit subdued and as we walked towards my car he spoke so softly I could barely hear him above the noises on the street.

'I've a sad task to perform today, Jo. Will you accompany me?'

'Yes, of course, I will,' I said, although I had been hoping to go somewhere pleasant for the afternoon but didn't show my disappointment as he seemed particularly distressed.

I gave him the keys to my car and he turned the car round and drove in a direction that was unfamiliar to me, until we came to a small cemetery and then turned off into an open entrance.

The wrought-iron gates had been removed, possibly stolen. Heavy chains in loops, some badly rusted, surrounded some of the graves.

We got out of the car and I felt very uneasy at our surroundings. Adrian held my hand and led me down a pathway. Weeds had sprouted and multiplied through the cracks in the cement. Some of the graves had been vandalised; statues and ornaments had been removed. Bits of wings off stone angels, decorative flower pots and parts of marble cherubs lay strewn near graves, forming a macabre scene.

We walked through uncut grass and a tangle of weeds and rubbish. The graves that had been left intact had been eroded by the weather over the years. Where the writing was still legible I noticed it was in French. Large pillars, domes and urns and a few pyramid shaped monuments covered in moss, cast their shadows over small gravestones of children, as if they were mourning their untimely deaths in perpetuity.

Beggars and vagrants had been using the shelter of the domes as housing. Cooking had taken place between the gravestones. What were we doing in this sacred place that had been so badly desecrated?

We came to a small section of moderately well tended graves which were much newer. We stopped at one of them. Adrian spoke quietly.

'This is my mother's grave, Jo' Today is the anniversary of her death.' His voice broke as he said the last few words.

I touched his arm gently in an act of sympathy saying, 'Oh, Adrian, I'm so sorry, so very sorry, and I'm moved that you've chosen to share this moment with me,' I said in a whisper.

The gravestone told its own tragic story. She had been in her forties when she died. I stood motionless, not knowing what to say to comfort him. After a long silence I heard him say, 'Kneel with me Missy and say a prayer for her soul.'

I knelt and we said the Lord's Prayer together. He continued to pray silently. I clasped my hands and shut my eyes waiting for him to finish. I felt afraid in this deserted place, almost of another land, forgotten and timeless. I started to shiver.

Adrian rose from the graveside. He had noticed I had shivered and put his arms around me. The warmth of his body against mine comforted me.

'Why are you shivering? It's a balmy evening,' he commented.

I had no reply for him as I didn't want to speak of my strange fear in the cemetery. I looked at the name on the grave. It read Frances. It stood out bold and clear like a message for me. I knelt again and touched it, passing my hands over the name several times. Adrian didn't stop me. Instead he said, 'That's to be the name of my first child. Do you like the name, Jo?'

Afraid and confused I replied, 'We're here to remember your mother whom you loved dearly. Why are you speaking of children, yet unborn?'

'Jo, don't start an argument with me, please.' He spoke almost angrily.

We were standing over his mother's grave and I knew it was an emotional time for him. All I could do was to put my arms around him. He was getting very agitated. We stood motionless in each other's arms.

He then led me to a bench a little distance from the graves. The grass here was quite long and the squawks of the crows seemed to reach a crescendo, resounding in my head. I could smell the coal fires and the acrid smell of the cow pats being burnt as fuel

to cook the meagre scraps that the beggars were preparing as a meal. A sense of nausea was starting to take hold of me. It was getting dark. The large spiral monuments were casting peculiar and sinister shadows around us. I felt I was in some strange and damned place. Everything was fetid. It was disgusting. The fight for survival goes on, I thought, no matter what the odds.

We sat for a short while on the bench and Adrian put his arm around me and started to speak.

'Many years ago a French ship carrying a large number of people coming to work in India had cholera aboard before it docked. Several perished, children and babies amongst them. They are all buried here and that's why it is called the French cemetery.'

'Who put up all these huge gravestones?' I asked.

'That's a mystery, Jo. Very few people ask to be buried here now. I don't know why my mother wanted to be interred here. It's not the best of places but it was her wish. It's a dreadful place, but I loved my mother and visit her grave each year. I also question myself. When I think of my mother, my French blood speaks. In the hospital I am Indian.' He paused.

'I don't know how to say this to you. I often feel like two people. Both of me, if I could coin a phrase, have a burning desire to succeed in life. You see all these graves. If these people had stayed in their own country, then perhaps they might have lived longer and. not lost their lives so young and I wouldn't have been of mixed race. Where do I belong, Jo? I often feel I have no identity. Anglo-Indians and others of mixed race were often ignored in the heyday of the Raj.'

I sat silently beside him, not knowing how to comfort him. He put his hand in mine and said, 'Forgive me, I'm very troubled. My feeling and conscience are in turmoil when I visit my mother's grave, and especially today. She sometimes expressed the wish that I should join the priesthood. Standing at her graveside I become aware of this fact, but I cannot reconcile myself to live in poverty and celibacy and constantly tend to the poor. I try to practise my religion and worship God each day, but I have to achieve something in my life. I hanker for success. Is it wrong, I wonder?' I didn't reply and almost in a whisper he added, 'And now there's you, Missy.'

He drove me home. His circumstances, together with the fact that he was unacceptable to my family, was beginning to put a strain on our relationship. The easy flirtation I thought I had started was turning into something much more serious, one which, maybe, I was not strong enough to handle. I knew the sensible thing to do would be to end it, but where was the fun in being sensible?

ten | dean mitchell returns

September 1953

I hadn't seen Adrian for a fortnight since the visit to the cemetery and the odd conversation at his mother's graveside still disturbed me. I was hurt that he didn't come to the office after work and there had been no phone call. I, on the other hand had no idea how to contact him. I didn't know where he lived as he had refused to let me know, saying 'You don't need to visit hovels, Jo.' Why then had he abandoned me after his outpouring of love? Did he feel he had said too much in an emotionally charged moment? And each day I felt lonely and deserted, and the posturing of Rose was certainly no comfort.

Jeb Hunt had eventually had his pool refurbished and phoned to invite us to a barbeque and a swim on the following Sunday. Since his invitation Rose had developed a strange smug attitude with me saying, 'So, where's your boyfriend, Jo? Lost?'

On Saturday evening she was frantically putting the finishing touches to a floral dress.

'Surely you're not going to wear that to a barbeque' I said to her. 'That dress is far too pretty, it'll spoil with the mess of a barbeque and people splashing in and out of the pool. You know, you could make a fortune designing clothes. I wish I had a talent like yours.'

'Jeb has asked me to be the hostess,' she replied curtly. 'I won't be swimming.' She was obviously in no mood for general chitchat with me.

On Sunday morning I was up earlier than Rose and put on a swimming costume under a pair of shorts and an open-necked blouse. That way it would be easy to change. Rose was still fussing when the door bell rang. I opened the door to a stony-faced Adrian. 'Jeb sent me to collect both of you,' he said.

'Hello, Adrian,' I said as lightly as I could though he was obviously as embarrassed about the situation as I was. 'Have you been very busy at the hospital?' I enquired, but he didn't answer my question, merely saying, 'The taxi is waiting.' He turned away from me and went down the steps.

I got into the front seat and Rose settled herself in the back. He drove out of Calcutta, and as we left the city behind us she suddenly decided to speak to me and her words seemed to be something she had rehearsed several times; something she had been told to say.

'You shouldn't have sat in the front seat of the taxi. It isn't the done thing for young women to sit beside a taxi driver. You should be here in the back with me.'

I looked at Adrian and saw his jaw tighten with anger. He had clenched his teeth, refusing to exchange insults with her. He couldn't afford to jeopardise his livelihood.

I turned in my seat and looked at her. 'Shut up, Rose, just shut up,' I said.

The rest of the journey was in total silence.

The large wrought-iron gates were opened for us by a *durwan* as we arrived at Jeb Hunt's house, and Adrian drove to the large gravel area, the well used taxi grinding and crunching to a halt on the newly laid drive. He opened the door for Rose who got out, fished around in her pure and produced a brown envelope and handed it to Adrian saying, 'Jeb said to give this to you. It's the fare,' and without so much as a thank you she walked towards the house where bearers had started to set up tables. I sat quietly in the taxi until Adrian collected his thoughts and emotions.

As we sat together I waited for him to speak. He tried to hide his distress and hurt. His speech was curt and his accent clipped.

'I can't put up with these engineered insults, Jo, nor am I your lap dog or poodle and I will not be a part of a group of men begging for your favours. Oh, yes, I know Jeb Hunt quite well. I drove him to the race course just the other day, and he spoke about your strange habits. I may be poor, and just an Anglo-Indian taxi driver in the meantime, but I have morals and.......'

I wasn't prepared for his lecturing and false notions fed to him by Jeb and now realised why he had stayed away from me. I got out of the taxi, banged the door as hard as I could go and said, 'Believe what you like.'

He turned the taxi around to face the exit and drove off without another word, crashing the gears in anger.

'I'm not finished with you, Adrian Green,' I muttered as I walked towards Jeb standing and speaking to a small group of people. As he saw me he left them and walked towards me saying, 'Glad you could come.' He then took me by the arm saying, 'Come with me for a minute, Jo.'

We walked together to an area of open ground some way from the pool and he explained to me why the land had been cleared of trees and shrubs.

'I'm having a bungalow built for my mother in this area. It's a lovely spot, don't you think?'

I was too upset to discuss property development with him. He changed the subject when he realised I was not in the mood to enthuse about his plans.

'Jo, I want you and Rose to stop quarrelling. I also think you should end your silly flirtation with Adrian Greene before matters take a serious turn. I know Adrian well. Leave him alone. He's studious and rumour has it that when he completes his medical course he wishes to enter a seminary. That's what his mother wanted for him. He was very attached to her. There are surely more suitable men in our own circle of friends for you to date. Please behave yourself, Jo, and don't add to the already difficult situation your mother and Rose find themselves in. Remember you're British and part of a family.'

Jeb had always been considerate towards me and now his attitude surprised me.

Upset, I shook my head and with real sadness said, 'You knew all along Adrian is a medical student in his final year. Why didn't you convince my mother and Rose that this was the truth and, far worse, why turn Adrian against me, hinting that I see other men. You know I don't. For heaven's sake, you know it's not true. You have hurt both of us deeply.'

He didn't reply and instantly I thought the rebuke should be mine. 'You are years older than Rose. She is just an untutored young girl of nineteen and I feel you are manipulating her for your own ends and nothing more. I don't think my father will be pleased once he finds out about this relationship and I can assure you, my father is a force to be reckoned with. Guns and fists are no problem for him. I think my mother has put you up to this. Has she?'

His attitude changed and with a hint of fear he said, 'Don't take this in the wrong way, Jo. I only meant it as kindly advice. Come, let's enjoy the rest of the day.'

I walked away from him and with a final backward glance I said politely 'Please don't interfere in my affairs.' I felt I had lost a friend and was convinced that it was my mother and Rose who were the instigators of this sly and vindictive plot. And then I remembered my mother's warning. Was this the result?

A small group of Americans were standing together speaking to each other and as I passed them one of the men with his back to me seemed remarkably similar in build to Dean Mitchell, but then I had been upset and was probably being fanciful.

I went indoors, changed and got ready for a swim. I swam a few lengths, enjoying the cool water, and then got out and sat at the edge of the pool.

The man with his back to me turned round and I could have been struck by a thunderbolt, for there was Dean Mitchell in the flesh. He walked towards me. I was, by this time, sitting on the grass beside the pool and he came over and sat down.

'Well, Jose, have you learnt to read and write yet?' he said.

'I don't know what that's supposed to mean, considering I never heard from you after you left Calcutta over eighteen months ago,' I retorted.

'Jose, I wrote to you once a week for at least three months and I never got a reply. Did our friendship mean so little to you? Since I returned to Calcutta a few weeks ago I've phoned your flat twice, about ten or eleven on Saturday morning, only to be told by Rose that you didn't want to speak to me.'

'Dean, walk with me,' I said at last. He held my hand and pulled me up. We walked towards the wooded area where Jeb was to build his bungalow. He was still holding my hand as we walked and his very touch brought a lump to my throat. He had been such a special person for me at a difficult time. We found an open grassy area and sat down together.

'Dean, I've never received a single letter from you, nor have I been told of any telephone calls. I work on Saturday mornings and I was not at home. I was hurt when you didn't write because you promised faithfully you would keep in touch. Each evening when I returned from work Rose told me there wasn't any mail for me, even without my asking her.'

I stopped speaking and then said almost in a whisper. 'Yes, that's it. Why didn't I think of it – it was Rose. How could she, how could she,' I repeated. Dean was looking at me with disbelief on his face. I shook my head and continued to speak, 'Forgive me, I was convinced you'd found a girlfriend in America and I was history. I thought so badly of you for so long. Damn Rose,' I said angrily. 'She must have destroyed the letters. She must have, she always collected the mail from the box as I left for work early in the morning before the postman arrived. How could she have been so mean?

'I went to the Swimming Club on Saturday and you weren't there,' he said. 'You seemed to have vanished.' He laughed before saying, 'I began to think you didn't exist and I had dreamt it all.'

He then said, 'Jeb says you have a new boyfriend. Is it true? Is there someone new and important in your life?' He paused before saying 'Is it possible for you to come out with me?' I didn't answer his questions but hedged. I needed a few moments to think a little.

'As I've just said I work on Saturday mornings, I seem to do nothing else but work these days. We need the money. As far as a boyfriend is concerned, the answer is yes and no. I'm seeing someone but we're having a bit of a blip in our relationship just now. Forgive me, Dean.'

'I'm so sorry, Jose. I've thought of you so often while I've been away and couldn't understand your silence.'

We walked together towards the barbeque area. Rose served us. She was embarrassed when she saw Dean with me. I smiled at her politely in front of the other guests saying, 'Thank you Rose,' and then went across to her and whispered in her ear. 'Just you wait until I get you home, you little bitch.'

Dean and I sat on the grass and ate together. We talked of the times we had gone dancing together and I told him about Adrian Greene. He was upset at what I said. I got up, changed and thanked Jeb. Dean took me home. Before going up to the flat he said quite seriously, 'Relationships that blow hot and cold should be avoided. It only makes for unhappiness. I'll phone you. Please come out with me,' he asked for the second time.

'Yes. I will. Just give me a week or so to sort myself out,' I said.

It was so strange. He made no attempt to kiss me. It was as if we had met for the first time.

I made myself some tea, thinking I would have a quiet evening and an early night. There was nobody at home. I dozed on the

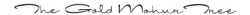

couch and it was the sound of the key in the lock that woke me. Rose and Jeb came in together.

Jeb looked at me as if he was surprised to see me. 'Rose was tired, Jo. She wanted to come home early. I'll go back in a little while. My friends will stay until they've finished all the beer.'

'Why, Jeb, you shouldn't have bothered bringing Rose home, she could easily have flown home on her broomstick,' I said bitterly.

'What nonsense is this, Jo?' he said irritably.

'Nonsense,' I repeated after him. 'Sit down, the two of you and listen to what I've got to say.'

'Rose, you are conniving, sly and evil. You destroyed every letter I got from Dean while he was away, and you never even told me he'd phoned once he'd got back. Why did you do it? I've never harmed you. What gave you the right to say I didn't want to speak to him and that I had a new boyfriend? You're not my spokeswoman. Now I want you to tell me in front of Jeb why and how you destroyed my mail.'

'No, I didn't burn the letters' she said guiltily, starting to weep.

'Burn the letters!' I exclaimed. 'I never said burn. I said destroy. So you burnt the letters. Such a lot of letters couldn't just disappear.' I then addressed Jeb.

'When Rose was a child, she cried when she didn't want to admit anything or when she didn't want to do anything. That's why she's only half educated. Watch her now; she's pulling the same stunt. Rose can barely read or write properly, but she would get a triple 'A' for sly, vicious behaviour.' I looked at my sister straight in the eye and said, 'You're a liar and a thief. How could you do such a thing?'

Rose left the room crying, her sly and hurtful behaviour having been revealed. Jeb was quiet for a few moments and then spoke trying to excuse her.

'Your mother didn't approve of Dean Mitchell and now she's faced with a worse scenario. She totally abhors your association with Adrian. Her standards are not the same as yours. You're not as strong as you think you are, Jo, and he's not for you. It's a dangerous game you're playing.'

Quite why it was so dangerous he never told me, as by then he'd stood up and gone to comfort Rose, an act which I found as despicable as anything Rose herself had done.

eleven | violence in the name of love.

October 1953

October heralded in the cooler weather.

The past few weeks had been difficult and confusing. I refused to speak to Rose and she to me, and though my mother must have known what was going on, none of us was keen to air the subject further.

I tried to get in touch with Adrian at the hospital, without success, but he was keeping his distance and I realised I must have hurt him more than I had meant. Dean phoned often, and eventually I relented and agreed to go to the cinema with him and for coffee afterwards.

It was a good evening, and one we repeated often, though the times had changed since we were last together, and we no longer were dancing, the music having changed so much, as had the bands. We seemed to have moved into a much more adult relationship somehow, and though I thought of Adrian often, it was with Dean that I now spent my little free time.

It sometimes felt as if he was guarding me rather than dating me. We visited the swimming club and swam together but our laughter was muted and I held back from him – Adrian Greene was in my heart and mind, even though Dean's company was light-hearted and refreshing. Once again and unfortunately for me, he was due to leave India. He had only been sent out to replace a sick colleague until a permanent replacement was found. I would miss him.

He cooked a meal for us on one of our last dates. He seemed keen to tell me of his plans for the future and spoke seriously as we were having our coffee after the very substantial steak he had cooked.

'Jose, my time abroad is over, especially India. Mom wants to see the family united again. My father's business is expanding. He's making a lot of money and wants us to share in his good fortune. The building trade is very buoyant at the moment and my brother Luke has joined him and I hope to follow suit. You would like our home, it's a nice patch.'

'Dean, bless you. I am pleased you have a caring and happy family. You know you are very special to me,' I said, holding his hand.

'Apparently not special enough, eh, Jose?' he replied. 'What are you going to do? Forgive me if I've appeared to be distant from you at times but I didn't want to press you into making decisions you might regret. I know you still have Adrian Greene in you heart. Why?'

He got up and paced the floor. He seemed upset. 'Jose, come with me to America. This is second time around for us and we still barely know each other. I have some money put aside. We could tour a bit and perhaps you could get Adrian Greene out of your system. I'll arrange a visa for you if you let me have you passport. There shouldn't be a problem. I'll take full financial responsibility for you. Why do you keep hankering after Adrian? He hasn't bothered about you for the past few weeks.' He paused and looked affectionately at me. 'Oh! Jose, for heaven's sake, don't do something foolish that will ruin your life.'

I looked at Dean and thought a lot of girls would find him irresistible. He was uncomplicated, yet full of charisma; no strange hang-ups, full of fun most of the time, and very importantly he was gentle and considerate towards me.

'Thank you for asking me,' I said. 'My family life is almost impossible at present, but I'll give you my passport and think seriously about your offer.'

He put his arms gently around me. 'Jose, I've told you, the financial responsibility will be mine.'

He took me home and kissed me goodnight. He smiled at me and said 'Jose will always kiss her Dean and Dean will never do anything to hurt his Jose.'

Annoyingly for me, once again the little Morris 8 was out of order. I often wished I could have afforded something more reliable. On Saturday morning I had to walk to work. I should have asked Craig to collect me. As I approached the taxi rank I noticed Adrian was sitting in the third taxi. The window was open and he was reading a book. I intended to pass by without speaking to him. He had made it quite plain he didn't want anything more to do with me. He was in full control of himself. What was it that attracted me to Adrian Greene? Instead of ignoring him my emotions got the better of me. I looked into the taxi and said cheekily, 'Good morning, taxi *walla*.'

The book in his hand was a small prayer book with a gold cross embossed upon it.

'Sorry, but I can't compete with God,' I remarked.

He turned and looked at me.

'No, Miss Josephine,' he mocked, 'but you're making a damn good stab at competing with the Devil. In fact I think you're winning.'

I couldn't answer him and continued walking, the tears welling up in my eyes making me stumble on the pavement. There was a screech of brakes behind me, and I felt the whoosh of a rickshaw pass me by far too close. Then a taxi pulled up and the door was flung open, and Adrian was there, gritting his teeth.

'Get in Jo, we have to speak sensibly.'

I tried to push past him without answering. And without warning he picked me up bodily and dumped me in the front seat and banged the door shut. The pavement was crowded but not a single person remonstrated with him and I felt a pulse beating in my throat as we drove along at breakneck speed, and I remembered Jeb's words of warning – he's not for you, and wondered what Adrian was about to do.

We got to my office and he stopped the taxi, and I shakily put a few coins on the dashboard for the fare. He picked up the money and flung it on to the pavement much to the delight of the *chokra* boys who were scrounging nearby.

'You are to stop this rude behaviour,' he hissed, 'I will see to you later.'

I ran up the office stairs and while I was running started laughing with nervous relief, trying to explain the episode away as a childish quarrel, unwilling to see in Adrian's behaviour any actual violent intent.

Craig was already at his desk.

'What's so funny, Josephine?' he asked.

When I told him what had happened he was far from amused.

'Do you think it's a laughing matter for you to be manhandled in public? I don't see anything amusing about this incident. We have agreed not to speak about your association with this taxi driver. As far as I can see you have pressed the self- destruct button.'

He changed the subject.

'I would prefer to discuss our trip to Ranchi. Mr Rooter and I have business there and I'll be very pleased to have you with us. We can drop you off at your father's factory.'

'Thank you, Craig. I'm very grateful,' I replied. 'We should leave sooner than later and definitely early in the morning. May I suggest we don't try short cuts and stick to the Grand Trunk Road as we're approaching the winter months and it gets dark pretty early. The side roads are dangerously pot-holed after the monsoon and get pretty dodgy and sometimes nearly impassable.'

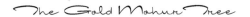

Craig merely humphed in assent and then said. 'Point taken.'

We continued working until early afternoon.

After work that afternoon, Adrian was waiting for me at the foot of the stairs. He had calmed down after his outburst in the morning. He followed me as I walked down the road and asked in a civil tone. 'Could you please get into the taxi now, I need to speak to you reasonably.' I didn't reply and he said firmly, 'Get in, Jo.' I didn't want a repetition of the morning's behaviour so got into the taxi and he drove silently towards a very poor area of the city.

Was this where he lived? I felt so sorry for him. I held back my tears. His behaviour was my fault for trying to use him and the fault of my family for rejecting him. How dare we look down on him for his background and his poverty.

He parked outside a large ill-kept block of flats and spoke softly to me, 'Take a good look. 'This is how I am forced to live, worlds away from your comforts. Look at this garbage-strewn courtyard. Why do people live like this? I'm not taking you into my room. Ranjit, who owns this taxi, has been kind enough to let me have a word with you in his flat next door. It's clean and attractively furnished.'

We sat silently together in the cab for a while without speaking. Did I really want this relationship?

'There's nothing I have to say to you, Adrian, but why insult me without good reason?' He didn't answer, and after a moment or two childishly I said, 'I hate you.'

'Love and hate are very close companions, Missy,' he replied.

Ranjit had opened the door of his ground-floor flat when he had heard the taxi draw up. He had been good enough to let us use his home to try and sort out our differences. He let us into his flat and smiled and wished us well before he left.

We stood in an attractively furnished sitting room, facing each other, almost in an attitude of combat. Adrian took hold of

my wrists and pulled me to him kissing me so roughly that my lip started to bleed. His hold tightened on my wrists and he said, 'Tell me Jo, tell me now and speak truthfully. Are you playing the field behind my back with other men. Jeb says you are. I need commitment from you. I may be poor but I am far from stupid.'

He didn't wait for a reply. 'Tell me now,' he said harshly.

His hold was tightening on my wrists; his temper rising uncontrollably and I felt as if my hands were bloodless. I had on a thin metal cuff bracelet whose sharp edges cut into my left wrist as the metal bent in his vice-like grasp, and as I tried to break free from him, twisting my hands, the metal slicing my flesh like a newly sharpened knife, and puncturing a vein on my wrist. I shouted out, the searing pain. too much to bear. His grip relaxed and I was able to break free from his hold, the blood spurting from the cut.

'God, what have I done to you?' he said, panic in his voice as he saw blood staining my clothes. He let go and I wrapped my skirt round my wrist as tightly as possible to staunch the flow.

I woke in a hospital bed. The cut was deep and long and I had needed sutures in my wrist.

He was by my bed when I awoke and I turned to him and said, 'Look what you've done to me with you silly jealousy.

His face was drawn and his manner anxious but he left my bedside without apology.

Later I heard from a nurse that he had advised my mother I had met with an accident. The nurses at the hospital were concerned and refused to believe my story that I had fallen and cut myself on a piece of glass on the pavement. I was allowed to go home with my wrist and hand heavily bandaged. A senior nurse came to see me before I left the hospital.

'Now, Miss Willis, once again relate to me what happened to you. How did you get such a deep cut on your wrist? You obviously were not trying to commit suicide. The bruising is severe on both wrists. They look like heavy pressure marks. Did someone tie you

up or hold you down by your wrists. I have worked in hospitals for a very long time, my dear. This is an assault case. Who are you protecting?'

I thanked her but couldn't bring myself to tell her the truth. She sighed as she spoke again.

'Bear this in mind. You shouldn't protect anyone who has done this to you. Shield him and you will suffer worse assaults in the future.'

No one came for me. I took a taxi home.

Whatever else, I wouldn't let Adrian be involved. I told myself repeatedly, he didn't mean to hurt me. It was a one-off accident, borne of sheer frustration with me, and it was partly my fault. I felt I couldn't jeopardise his career at this stage. I believed him when he said he loved me but by the same token he shouldn't have been so rough. I thought that for the sake of sanity I should leave this man but a strange passion for him within me would not let go. It was a stubbornness of heart. I felt a great pity for the circumstances of his life. He needed to be encouraged to succeed. I told myself he needed to be supported and most of all he needed to be loved by me, and I had to show it, just a bit more.

Once home, mother was out, but Rose gasped at my bandages, and persistently questioned me.

'Lady Nagalot,' I said eventually. 'Just get out what you've been bottling up and then shut up and let me rest. I don't feel very well' I said.

Rose looked quizzical and asked me one last time. 'But what happened? Did you fall?'

I didn't answer and for once in her life Rose showed a modicum of concern for another human being, for her only sister. 'If I didn't know better,' she said, 'I'd say that someone had done this to you. Look at the bruising on your wrists! I know we've not always seen eye-to-eye, but don't let him do it to you again.'

I stood to go into my bedroom. 'Thank you, Rose, for your concern,' my unbandaged hand upon the doorknob. But she just shook her head at me.

'Don't let him do it to you again,' she repeated. She was not so stupid, no more so than was I.

twelve | the beggar boy

November 1953

Craig had been told of my accident by Rose. He sent me flowers and hard taskmaster that he was, had written on the note, I'll collect you in three weeks on Saturday morning. I had a hospital appointment on that particular Saturday afternoon at two o'clock and hoped Craig would manage to take me round as I was unable to drive my car as my left hand was still bandaged and painful on movement.

He collected me very early, explaining we had a backlog of work. The streets were fairly quiet and he managed to get a parking space at the side of the office building under some trees and out of the heat of the sun.

As I walked towards the entrance the small boy who begged there, and who we gave money to each day, was sitting at a strange angle on the steps. He was moaning and seemed to be propped up rather than sitting. I noticed some blood on his shirt. I bent down and asked him, 'kia hua? He was unable to answer me. He seemed badly hurt. There must have been panic in my voice as I called for Craig. He came running towards me.

'We have to take this little fellow to hospital,' I shouted. I ran up to the office changing rooms and collected a couple of towels. Craig had already gone back to where he had parked the car and driven it in front of the steps and left the engine running. A crowd was starting to gather and together we realised we had to do something quickly otherwise we would be mobbed and wouldn't be able to help the child. They would obviously think we had knocked the child over with the car as many such accidents happened not infrequently.

He picked up the small boy. I was already sitting in the front seat of the car with the towels on my lap. He put the child in my arms and we drove off at speed, Craig blowing the car horn for the crowd to disperse. The child in my arms was so thin. He weighed so little. He was covered in mud. Who had propped him up on the office steps? I repeated to him as we were driving to the hospital '*kia hua*?' He managed to whisper '*lathi*.' It looked as if someone had beaten him with a large stick. Who would hurt such a tiny child and for what reason? Surely not for the small amount of change in his pocket, that is if he even had a pocket in his ragged clothing.

On arrival at the hospital I carried him, wrapped in the towels, to the accident department. The receptionist looked at me and phoned through to someone before we had even exchanged a word. Everything now moved amazingly quickly. I had envisaged sitting in the waiting room with a badly injured child in my arms for hours. A junior doctor came out of a side room and took the child from me. The receptionist asked me to fill in a form and answer a few questions. I had started to smell rather badly and was pleased everything was taken out of my hands. She said there would be a charge for his treatment and I readily agreed to pay.

Throughout this emotional turmoil, where was Craig? He was sitting quietly in the waiting room out of the way, observing the tableau. I went and sat beside him.

'Phew, you don't half stink, Josephine,' he said.

My clothes were stained with mud and blood from the little boy's body and through fear he had wet himself. Many people were waiting to be seen, some with cut limbs wrapped in unclean bits of cloth to staunch the bleeding. My own state was bad enough so I didn't take much notice of what was going on around me. I was starting to feel decidedly sick.

My appointment at the hospital was at two and it was nearly that time. I asked Craig if he could wait for me and he just nodded. I walked down the corridor to the treatment room. The blood and mud had dried on my dress. The nurse looked at me with some distaste; took me into the shower room and gave me some disinfectant soap and a clean white gown. She took the bandage off my wrist and put on a fresh sterile dressing. 'You'll have a jolly good scar now my girl,' she said handing me an old but freshly laundered nurse's uniform. Barely looking at me she continued speaking, 'You had better go home in that and return it. We are very short of everything in this hospital. You can't save every beggar child on the street. You British come to India and think you can save the world.'

She stopped and looked at me closely.

'Oh, yes. You are that Adrian Greene's fancy piece. He's on study leave. He needs it with you wrapped around him morning noon and night.'

'Not night, and I'm nobody's fancy piece,' I retorted.

I walked down the corridor in the baggy old uniform which was at least two sizes too large for me, with a fresh bandage on my wrist and smelling of strong disinfectant. Craig was standing waiting for me with a grim look on his face.

'They want you in the small room near the reception desk,' he said. He pointed to the end of the corridor.

A doctor, dressed in an immaculate white coat, was standing near the receptionist and when I went up to him he presented me with a bill for one hundred and fifty rupees. Craig was holding my bag and he came over and handed it to me. I wrote out a cheque and then asked, 'What is his treatment likely to cost? I'll pay what I can.'

The doctor didn't answer my question but asked me to follow him into a small room which was sparsely furnished and contained a desk, a few chairs and a filing cabinet. He sat at the desk. I sat opposite him. He questioned me about the child; where I had found him and what I thought had happened to him. He gave me a short form to fill in and sign.

'Can you tell me what arrangements have been made for his discharge and is there anything I can do for him?' I asked. The doctor didn't speak for a moment and then said quietly shaking his head, 'I'm so sorry Miss Willis. I'm so sorry, the child died before we could do much for him. He seemed to have been beaten badly and possibly had internal injuries.'

I thanked him for his help, rose shakily, and walked towards Craig. There was nothing more I could do. Who had committed this dreadful act and for what reason? It was barbaric. He was just a little beggar boy, totally alone. I left the room with the smell of death and disinfectant, forming a dual cloak around me. The receptionist said they would take care of everything and would also inform the police. I walked down the corridor with Craig. We got into his car. What could I say to Craig who had been dragged into this hideous situation by me?

'Thank you for your help and consideration, Craig,' I said weakly and then started to mumble almost incoherently, 'Oh, God, why did this innocent little child die?' I questioned. 'How could he deserve this terrible death at such a young age? Where was his mother?'

'*Chup row,* 'Craig said sternly.

I was stunned at Craig's reaction, and being told to shut up, but he then spoke with emotion in his voice. 'Millions are born and millions die, and you, Josephine, are not the custodian of life and death. I don't do "Holy" so ask your boyfriend Adrian Greene to comfort you; he does "Holy" and let's put this day behind us.' Craig too had been visibly upset at the strange and harrowing turn of events.

I sat silently the rest of the way home and thought, Is there such a thing as reincarnation? This is what the sadhu had taught me to believe in as a child. I could only hope that if his words were

true, the small boy who had lived his short life in miserable circumstances would now be a free and beautiful spirit reincarnated into something pleasant and without pain. It had to be.

I heard Craig say, 'Today has been wasted, can you come in tomorrow?' His voice was low and there was a tightness in his demeanour. He didn't want to show any emotion but I knew he had a certain sympathy for the little boy who begged on the steps each day, as he had occasionally said, 'Be sure and see the wee lad has something to eat,' and had often laid down money on my desk for him.

This then was the day I promised myself no child I bore would go hungry; no child I bore would live in fear or be maimed in spirit or bruised in body.

thirteen | adrian's apology

Mid-November 1953

It was early on Sunday morning; mid-November and the cooler weather seemed to have improved all our temperaments. I was sitting having a cup of tea when the phone rang.

'It's Craig, Josephine. Sorry to bother you so early. I'm meeting Mr Rooter about our trip to Ranchi. I take it you're still eager to visit your father?'

'Thank you,' I said gratefully. Can I suggest we leave very early as it gets dark very quickly and the roads, after the monsoon, are dangerous and full of pot holes. We should stick to the Grand Trunk Road and not try any take short-cuts down side roads.'

'Point taken.' As usual he spoke decisively.

'That's fine, Craig, thank you once again. I'll take that as definite and let my father know.'

Mother and Rose were having a late lie in, the house was comparatively peaceful and I felt my heart lift with joy at the thought of seeing my father again. Today would be a good day, I hoped.

But, it was not to be. Half an hour after Craig's phone call while I was reading the morning papers the doorbell rang persistently.

I opened the door to a highly agitated Ranjit.

'Josephine, you really must come with me now. It's about Adrian. I'll sit in the taxi outside until you are ready.'

'What's the matter, has he slit his wrists to keep up with what he did to me?' He shook his head saying, 'Please don't joke.'

I dressed quickly and went with Ranjit to his flat. Adrian Greene, unshaved and dishevelled, was sitting on the couch. He rose and offered me a seat beside him. Ranjit left almost immediately.

'Well, what have you to say for yourself?' I spoke positively trying to keep my voice free of the pain I felt at the strange churning sensation within me. I continued speaking saying, 'I'll wait till you shave and shower and then we can talk.'

He left the flat without speaking while I took stock of my surroundings. It was a pity that this flat kept so clean and tidy by Ranjit was in such a poor area, the only view being a garbage-strewn courtyard. Children were kicking a tin can to each other; two stout sticks embedded in the mud represented goal posts. They were laughing and playing happily. How easily they were pleased in their poverty-stricken surroundings. How lucky I had been to be given so much in life and taken without thought of the poverty of others.

I must have been looking at the children playing for a good fifteen minutes and had not heard Adrian enter the room. A voice behind me said softly, 'Sorry is not enough, my Missy. Please forgive me and let me explain.'

I sat on the couch and he sat crossed-legged on the carpet in front of me. He tried to hold my hand but I pulled back from him. Again I spoke first and this time what I said was charged with emotion.

'Adrian, it's time we parted. Put your arms around me for one last time and let's say goodbye sensibly. Everybody I know says we are not meant for each other.'

He got up and started to pace the floor.

'I can't accept that, Jo.' he said. 'It's like this, Missy. A month before I met you I had been invited to join a religious order after I qualified, to tend to the poor. How can I when you made me fall in love with you. Yes, Jo, you encouraged me.

'Secondly, as I told you in the cemetery, my mother during her lifetime had ambitious plans for me. Your peers and family look down on me even though I am on the brink of qualifying as a doctor. One day people will look up to me. I will qualify and take part in important research. I have a great desire to succeed in life. I'm not accepted by your family or your circle of friends, nor in your clubs. You must be aware that even though the British Raj is over there is still a pecking order. I'm not a business man and even when I qualify, how many junior doctors do you know who can afford a club membership?'

He paused and with a look of anger on his face continued. 'Jo, there's another matter which is of greater importance to me. Jeb has constantly said you are a good time girl and will never be able to commit to one man. Is this true? I have been told by him you have a fondness for an American, Dean Mitchell among others.'

I didn't answer him immediately, shocked at the persistent allegations made by Jeb and he continued, saying, 'Speak to me. I will now believe you and not Jeb. This is the reason I was so angry on the day of the barbeque.'

The tears were welling up in my eyes. I felt ashamed. Why had I, so stupidly, chosen a man of such intensity of emotion for a casual flirtation? And now I couldn't explain my feelings for him, even to myself. He had hurt me, so why was I here. It was an accident, I told myself yet again. Desire, love and pity whirled within my heart and mind. Which was it? Was it an amalgam of all three? And was it wise for me even to be here, with him, at this time?

He paused and shook his head.

'Why are you crying, Jo? Is it the truth? You were so light-hearted when we met. You raised my spirits. The world suddenly seems a brighter place. It's not easy to live on the borderline of poverty. I fell in love with you from the time you slept so trustingly in the back of the cab when I drove you home from the airport. You were like an innocent child in my care. Any other man touching you is abhorrent to me.' He dropped his voice. 'Show your true feelings for me, Missy.'

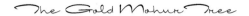

I was silent for a while and then answered him honestly. 'Dean Mitchell will always be a special friend. I knew him before I met you and we shared laughter and fun, dancing and music together. The only other man I know is Craig Mackie and he is my employer, and pays me well for the work I do. It's shameful that you don't trust me. Why should I justify myself to you? We aren't partners in love.'

He came towards me with an open palm to hold my hand. 'Don't touch me,' I said, afraid he might hurt me again.

'I wasn't going to hurt you. I wanted to hold your hand and put my arms around you.'

He sat on the couch beside me and did just that holding me comfortably in the crook of his arm.

'You might not be lying to me, but you surely are lying to yourself, my Missy.

How often have you said to yourself, I don't love Adrian Greene, knowing you were denying your true feelings? We do love ach other and I, for one, have a special passion for you.'

I looked at him in amazement.

He stopped and then spoke to me almost in a whisper. "You're sexually attracted to me. Don't deny it. I'm a man not a child, so stop playing games with me. I desire you, Jo, but I also love you. There's a difference. Commit to me.'

He knelt in front of me. 'Please forgive me for my bad temper. Forgive me for thinking ill of you. Forgive me for hurting you. You know it was an accident. I promise it will never happen again. Give me another chance, Missy. I will try and curb my jealousy.'

He picked up my hands and kissed both my wrists saying, 'How could I have done such a thing.'

Common sense told me I should end this relationship. Was his violence towards me a mistake – an accident - or was he violent by nature? What disturbed me was the intensity with which he viewed everything. Would there be a response within me?

'Commit to me, Jo,' he said.

He had wound himself cleverly round my heart but as I nodded my head in agreement and he kissed me, and I replied with tenderness for him in my voice saying, 'I do love you, Adrian, please be gentle with me,' a strange uneasy spark still lingered within me.

I told him I was going to Ranchi to see my father and offered him the use of my car which he accepted gladly. He had his final exams ahead of him and transport would be helpful for him.

I heard the taxi outside and realised Ranjit had returned.

We agreed we would try again with our relationship. Adrian drove me home and before I got out of the car he said, 'I trust you, Jo. You belong to me.'

These were the words that should have struck a note of fear in me, but instead they gave me a false sense of security. Someone really loved and wanted me.

fourteen | farewell my beloved father

End of November 1953

Heavy, menacing dark clouds had hung over us from mid-morning, waiting to unleash much-needed rain onto the city. Why couldn't we be sprinkled with cooling drops and gentle sprays of water instead of the drenching continuous downpours, accompanied by thunder and lightning. The constant fussing of Mrs Rooter who had never been in the Indian countryside had done nothing to improve Craig's temperament.

He arrived early on Saturday morning and I was surprised that we were to go to Ranchi in two cars. One car, driven by their driver, carried the Rooter's luggage much to Craig's annoyance as it would, to some extent, slow down our progress and he didn't want to arrive late at night.

'No wonder everyone dies in this wretched climate,' he groaned as he mopped his face repeatedly with a small hand towel.

'Not everyone, Craig,' I commented, trying to jog him out of his morose mood. 'You're still here.'

As we left Calcutta behind us his temperament seemed to improve with the cooler, fresher air. Not wanting to annoy him, I curled up in the front seat and dozed.

Thoughts of my early life in the factory kept flitting through my mind. The fun and laughter with my father when I had eventually learnt to swim. He had taught me with such patience. The grazed knees he had tended to before I had learnt to ride a bicycle. The tears he had wiped away. He had taught me not to fear life. As I dozed I recalled the most frightening episode we had shared together.

My father often visited the districts to buy lac for his factory. He often took me with him on these trips. On the grand trunk road he had come across a Marwari who had his Chevrolet car, which had broken down, pushed to the side of the road by some villagers. My father had stopped and helped him get it started. The Marwari whose name was Pokur had a mustard seed processing factory.

Both men were interested in cars and a close friendship developed between them. I often spent the day with Pokur's family. Two daughters and a young wife, who taught me Indian dancing, were always good company. They plied me with aromatic pilaf for lunch and Indian sweets made freshly on the premises.

We were late in leaving Pokur's house one evening. The night was dark and the incessant rain prompted my father to stop overnight at a Dak Bungalow.

My father asked the rest-house *bearer* to prepare a meal for us. A couple of hours later he managed to serve a delicious chicken curry and chapattis. One large room passed as a bedroom. The furniture consisted of two *charpoys* and a couple of cane chairs which had seen better days. There was no electricity. A hurricane lantern sufficed. It cast strange shadows on the walls as the light flickered.

Dak Bungalows and strange stories went hand in hand. Tales of lonely young bachelors hanging themselves; suicides over unrequited love, and the inevitable stories of man-eating tigers were often repeated. On this night, the tiger was no tall story.

It was some time after midnight. The strange heavy smell of a tiger, the clawing, growling and grunting, together with the noise of shattering glass had already roused my father. He shouted to raise the alarm. '*Koi hai! Ko hai!*' There was no reply. The large cat

grunted and roared and threw itself against the outside walls and clawed at the flimsy brick-built building, plastered over by a thin coating of cement and then painted white. Bars at the window kept the beast at bay.

My father moved my *charpoy* with me in it, into the corner of the room and turned the one he had been sleeping in on its side, making a barrier to protect me. He always carried a gun but the bullets he had would never have killed the tiger. He fired several shots from the bathroom window to frighten the animal and to alert anyone on the premises. Again, no one responded and the big cat continued to claw at the brickwork. My father sat with his back to the wall for the rest of the night, with a loaded gun. The tiger circled the flimsy building, its heavy smell wafting towards us, time and again, reminding us of his presence. It had dislodged one of the bars at the window. The opened space was too small for the tiger to get into the room. It did however manage to put its paw and forearm through, hoping his outstretched claws would touch the prey it so desired.

My father put out the hurricane lamp and we sat in the darkness while the animal growled, prowled and clothed us in its stench.

In the morning a nervous bearer appeared, shouting '*bagh, bagh!*' Apparently a man-eating tiger in the nearby forest came out occasionally and stole goats. There was no talk of it ever having attacked a human being. On this night in particular, it had taken a goat from an adjoining hut and had eaten part of it on the premises. We didn't wait for breakfast.

Throughout the night I never felt any fear. I knew my father was there to protect me.

In my half-awake state I thought, Wait till Craig sees the factory. I wondered what he was expecting. No, I wasn't going to tell him about the tiger. He would either scoff and say, 'Rubbish, is that another of your tall tales, Josephine,' and laugh, or believe me and say his usual, 'Bloody hell.' He would have been even more distressed had he seen the living conditions when I was a child.

There was no water supply for the house. The toilets were 'thunder boxes' as they were commonly called. They were seats with potties in them, regularly cleaned and emptied by low-ranking servants. What a disgusting job for anyone.

The water for washing was brought from the well in the garden in buckets, and an old-fashioned boiler called a salamander in an outside courtyard provided hot water in winter. The lights in the evening attracted a variety of small insects and little lizards, grey in colour, which Rose called chick-chicks. They too were attracted to the light and a feast of insects awaited them. Over many years, my father had put in plumbing and the lights ran off a generator.

My eyes were still closed as I thought of these things when Craig tapped me on the shoulder and said, 'Lunch.' I looked at him and smiled. It had not been an unpleasant meander through the past.

'Thank you, Josephine. You rarely smile at me.'

Smiling, no! Laughing inwardly, I thought. What would he have made of the almost primitive living conditions? I think he would have packed his bags and left on the first available passenger liner back to Scotland. Craig liked his creature comforts, which was apparent in the delicious lunch he had arranged for us. There was cold chicken and plenty of salad and fruit, plus a large thermos of steaming hot coffee. It was well past noon before we stopped for lunch. It had been a long tiring drive for Craig.

'Thank you for your good driving and the delicious lunch,' I said.

He looked at me in astonishment. 'Are you feeling well, Josephine? Your politeness astounds me.'

'I'm softening you up, in case you end up as a feast for a tiger. There are quite a few around here.'

'Don't be idiotic, Josephine,' he said laughing.

We had made very good time and our mood had lightened and as we progressed on our journey the weather became cooler and not so sticky and humid. The road was clear for the most part. I had slept comfortably in the large front seat. Usually, lorries and bullock carts blocked the road at intervals; the bullock carts often having shed their loads. Today we had been lucky.

It was early evening when Craig dropped me off at my father's factory, promising to spend a few days with us. I walked up the stone stairs into the flat above the factory where we had always lived. Everything was still the same. It brought tears to my eyes to think how the years had slipped away. I had never noticed the harsh noise of the machinery. I was saddened to see how unkempt the entire place was looking. The old cook Tuku came out of the kitchen when he heard someone coming up the stone steps.

'Ah Jo *ba ba*,' he said excitedly.

He ran out of the room and shouted over the balcony.

'*Sahib, Sahib, Jo ba ba ah ghia.*' (Jo is here).

I went out onto the veranda and heard the whirr and whine of the washing barrels closing down. My father was always in the factory for the evening shut down to see everything was in order for the next day. The workmen were filing out of the gates and the *durwan* (watchman) was waiting to close up. My father was standing in the middle of the drying areas. He noticed me on the veranda and started to come up. In years gone by he would have run up, lifted me off the ground and twirled around with me laughing in his arms. This was now a strange tired man I was observing. He walked slowly and waved his hand.

I stood waiting for him to come up to the flat. What had he done over the years when I was away in boarding school? We had been such good friends during the holidays. He loved me so much as a child. I was always around him and the reason I had few inhibitions was because of his indulgences. If I had faults, and there were many, surely he could see that some of them were attributable to him. How had he coped with Rose? He had nothing in common with her. She had been a prissy little girl.

I heard his footsteps as he came up to the flat. There was not going to be a great welcome for me as I knew my mother had written to him constantly complaining of my supposedly bad behaviour. He did, however, put his arm around me and hug me to him. I knew he would always love me despite my shortcomings. He looked a little older but had not changed much. 'Hello, Josephine,' he said, as if I had just gone out for a walk and was returning. 'We will eat first and then we can talk.'

Tuku had made curry from fresh garden vegetables accompanied by rice. Baked custard and fresh fruit from the garden was the sweet. My father got up and poured himself a stiff whisky. Food costs little or nothing here, I thought. You either grew it, or caught it or shot it. I was struggling to put food on the table in Calcutta.

'Thank you, Dad, that was a very nice meal,' I said appreciatively. We sat together in the sitting room while I told him, excitedly, about my trip to London and the different way of life.

'Yes, I know, Jo,' he said nodding and smiling at my enthusiasm. We spoke of the different flowers and seasons. He had always loved his garden. I also told him about Vali and Aunt Ruth's generosity to me.

'Living conditions are difficult since your Uncle Edward died, poor chap,' he said. 'I haven't met the new manager. I'm told he's a very educated fellow. He's Indian.'

'Of course. Why not? This is an independent country now, and it should be that way,' I replied.

'So, is that then the basis of your uncontrolled behaviour?' he said.

I was distressed that my father should make such a remark. He had always considered India his home. He had many Indian friends and he loved the way of life it had given him. He opened the writing

desk and threw across a bundle of letters held together with a rubber band. 'This is, I suppose, something you were not going to tell me?'

I read a few of the letters he had passed over to me, picking them out at random. I started laughing and didn't finish reading the pile of letters. They were all the same, written by Rose, spelling errors and all and full of exaggerations.

'The ungrateful bitch,' I said.

'Jo, that's another thing. As a young woman your speech should not be interspersed with swear words.' He reprimanded me but he was smiling. He had always thought it amusing that as a child I was able to swear in Hindi. I had held his hand and walked round the factory with him and copied his every word.

I looked at him and shook my head. 'Dad, most of what she has written is untrue. I'm not an immoral young woman. I work hard. Mr Mackie, whom you will meet in a few days time, is my employer and he pays me well. My mother had hinted in her letters that I obtained money from men. I honestly don't know where this idea has come from. When I was in London, Aunt Ruth, Vali's mother, put money into my account in London and gave me five hundred rupees in cash. She knew I was struggling. I didn't tell Mother and Rose how much as they would continually ask for more.

'My mother gambles, playing bridge in the evenings and Rose spends her time making one dress after another for herself. Why has my mother not mentioned that I work and give her most of my wages? You must realise that what you send her is not sufficient. They take from me and blacken my character at the same time.

'Did Mother tell you that Rose keeps company with a man twice her age, with Mother's permission? No. It's only Jo who's wrong.'

'What? Is that so. I'll shoot the swine if he hurts her,' my father said angrily.

He then turned his questioning to the fact I dated Adrian Greene saying, 'I'm glad you think it's funny, Josephine. You laughed at the letters. Your mother says you are constantly seen in the company of an Anglo-Indian taxi driver. Whatever are you thinking of, my baby? Don't do something that will make me ashamed to call you my daughter.'

'Dad, I would ask you to take time to think carefully about what I am going to say to you. The name of the person I am involved with is not 'that damn taxi walla,' as Mother puts it; it's Adrian Greene. His mother was French. He is well educated and is in the final year of his medical course. He should qualify this year, and possibly, I will marry him. He is poor. That I agree. He drives a taxi to help with his finances. And how did I meet him, you are going to ask? It was Adrian who drove me back from Dum Dum airport when I arrived back from London. He is registered with the Airport and the Police, so I considered it safe.'

'French and Indian,' he said, ignoring my remarks. 'That's a hell of a mixture. I can't approve.' He stood up to go to bed. I noticed he had another drink in his hand as strong as the one he had poured himself before dinner.

'Doctor or no doctor,' he said, 'I will not have such a 'mixter-maxter' of blood in this family. What you actually mean is that you picked up an Anglo-Indian taxi driver at the airport and you are now trying to justify your behaviour to me.'

He turned and left the room.

I went to the room I had always used as a child and as a young girl, and was saddened to think that my father, without knowing or seeing a person, could be so judgmental. Over a quarter of a century is a long time to live in a country and still hold prejudices, I thought.

Together with a woman worker from the factory, I spent the next three days tidying up the mess the flat was in and cleaning

and washing couch covers and curtains in all the rooms that had not seen soap and water for quite some time. My father seemed to be viewing the bottom of his whisky glass more often than was really necessary, I thought sadly.

He was not the loving father I had expected to meet after a long absence. The years had not been kind to him and he was becoming a bitter man, struggling financially. He only smiled when we recounted incidents of my childhood.

fifteen | the sadhu. my mentor

Early on the Wednesday morning of my visit, Craig's car drew up outside the factory gates. I was still in bed. I hurriedly put on a pair of shorts and an old shirt and ran down the stairs bare-foot. I told him where to park the car and showed him the bedroom he could use. He looked at me and said. 'Good heavens have you not even washed yet?'

'No. but I will before we have breakfast. Don't you ever dress casually, Craig?'

'I do casual, but rarely savage,' he answered smiling at the state I was in.

I collected some eggs from the hen-house, showered and changed into heavy trousers and a shirt. This was the outfit I wore when I went out into the small forest with my father to shoot snipe. I usually wore wellingtons because of small snakes but today I was not going to the forest. My father as usual had been down to the factory early in the morning and came up to join us for breakfast. I then was able to introduce him to Craig and the two men took to each other well.

Tuku cooked fried eggs and tomatoes for breakfast and there was the usual toast, jam and fruit.

I was good-naturedly teasing Craig about the fact that he never wore shorts. We were still sitting casually at the breakfast table drinking several cups of tea and Dad too seemed relaxed, while Craig was recounting to him the reason for his short stay in India.

I butted in saying that Craig didn't understand India and mentioned his constant refusal to wear shorts, so I teased him saying, 'Craig, I bet you have skinny legs; that's why you never wear shorts.'

My father couldn't help smiling, but Craig, not to be outdone left the table and went to his room. He was out in a minute or two with shorts on.

'There you are, Josephine. Rugby players never have skinny legs.'

It was just a silly incident but it seemed to break the tension between my father and myself, for a short while, as he laughed, and to me his deep pleasant laughter which I had known so well as a child, was a relief and a pleasure for me.

I had decided to go up Monkey Hill to see the sadhu. So many worrying things had happened to me. I needed a time of peace and comfort with him. I thought my father might have objected but he never said anything. The sadhu had taught me about spiritual manifestations. I had discussed my dreams with him. I now needed help.

We had called the hill Monkey Hill because, years ago, there had been a surfeit of small monkeys living in the trees on the hill, but with the passing years they had abandoned their home as the trees didn't bear much fruit. Quite a few of the plum trees on the hill had either been cut down by the villagers for firewood or had died off because of dry weather. My father reluctantly informed me that the sadhu was still living on the hill somewhere. I would have to find him.

I was packing some lunch for myself. Fruit, some sandwiches and bottled water. My father gave me a basket of fruit and some money to take to the sadhu saying, 'I often give him fruit and money, Jo. I always tell him it's from you. Sometimes he can't be found. He came down from the hill in April, asking for you. He said he wanted to warn you of spiritual danger. He probably just wanted some money. What is spiritual danger anyway? It's a load of bosh, Jo.'

My father, like Craig, dismissed anything that was either spiritual or mystical. He did, however have a certain regard for the sadhu and I knew he would never let him starve alone on the hill. April was the month I had returned from America and had met Adrian. It made me feel decidedly uneasy.

Craig asked if he could accompany me and I reluctantly agreed saying, 'It's not your thing, this is personal.'

We walked slowly up the hill, Craig carrying the basket. After we had walked, following an old path, for about fifteen minutes we could find no sign of the sadhu.

'He isn't here today, Josephine. I think we should go back,' Craig said, a note of relief in his voice.

' He'll be higher up, but if you feel uneasy, you can return now. I don't mind. I'll be perfectly safe continuing up the hill on my own. I know this area like the back of my hand.' Craig continued to climb with me, silently and sullenly. I noticed some shallow steps had been hewn out of the side of the hill with a sharp turn to the left. A smell of burning wood and herbs guided me. Turning the corner I saw a somewhat larger hut than I remembered. I retraced my steps to get a drink of water before meeting the sadhu.

A large flat stone was visible and Craig had stopped by this stone. It had been used as a resting place as a few empty *dhabs* were piled on one side. Craig and I sat down on the stone, glancing at the coconuts. It was out of sight of the sadhu's hut. Once again, I asked Craig if he would like to return to the factory but he insisted on staying. He had a book with him. The stone we were sitting on was near a banana tree, its green leaves forming a shaded area. Large unripe fruit hung from it in bunches.

I walked up to the hut. The sadhu was sitting with his eyes closed. I put the basket of fruit down beside him. 'It's Jo ba ba,' I

said. He was sitting in the lotus position and beckoned to me to take off my sandals and sit opposite him. I did as he asked.

'I know who you are, you never have to tell me, Jo ba ba. I saw you arriving wearing a blue dress.'

I was always amazed at him. How did he know I was wearing a blue dress when I had arrived at the factory? I handed him the money I had brought for him. It was very much more than I would ever have considered giving him in the past. It was fifty Rupees as I knew he was finding it difficult to manage. Possibly I would never see him again. The sadhu didn't speak English, but my Hindi was good and we had always communicated well. He spoke slowly and distinctly to me.

'Jo ba ba, I went down to the factory from this hill to see your father in April. The signs were so bad for you. You should have been warned. Your father just laughed at me as usual. I know he never gave you the message. I wanted to see you then. Now is too late. Jo ba ba, your father gives me money and laughs at me. He has had a very hurtful time in his past and cannot believe the spiritual forces that surround us. I'm sorry. He's very sad in his heart and mind. He's been like that for a long time.'

He paused. 'You're now a grown woman. I had hoped for a good path for you. Unfortunately, I saw three paths and you have taken the wrong one. I thank you for bringing me offerings to the gods, they're generous. May blessings be with you and may calm return to you. There's hope. The evil I see for you will pass but with great difficulty and, unfortunately, over a long period of time. It saddens me to tell you this and I will have to pray daily for your spirit to be strong.

'Today I wish you to receive from me a spark of my spiritual energy to help you through difficult times you're about to face. I can only do this if you are still pure. Answer me truthfully. Have you known a man, Jo, ba ba? Are you *sadah*? I hear the ways of the West are different, and your father tells me that you have travelled much recently.'

I looked into the sadhu's amber-coloured eyes. They held my gaze. I answered him truthfully and in his own words. 'Yes, I am pure.'

He had difficulty in asking me this question and had used the word *sadah* which really means white or unblemished. He was asking me if I was still a virgin which I was, although I had often enjoyed feelings of intense arousal, which had left my body floating, and my tummy flooded with butterflies. I had strong urges but could not discuss them with anyone, least of all my mother.

He rose and went into the hut and came out with a small bundle of twigs and dry herbs and two very small clay pots; one was filled with yellow ointment, the other with a brown powdered substance. He had a brass container of water with him and a small scroll of paper, tied with a string of jute from which hung a talisman; a small prickly seed the size of a marble.

To the left of the hut there were several steep uneven steps of rough stone. He asked me to follow him. We came to a small flat area where the earth was packed hard. A small hole in the ground lined with clay had a few coals smouldering in it. He added the twigs, herbs and the powdered substance.

'Take off your shoes and outer garments, Jo ba ba, and stand on the earth.'

I did as he asked. The ground was warm beneath my feet. He joined me standing half an arm's length away. 'Close your eyes and hold out your hands and stand very still.'

He cupped my hands in his upturned palms. He had never touched me before. His hands were soft and very warm. He had rubbed them with a fragrant substance. The herbs smouldering in the clay oven gave off a heavily scented smoke which swirled and enveloped us. The pungent smell was making me feel slightly dizzy.

'Try and chant with me the way I have taught you,' he said.

He chanted ceaselessly with a strange intonation, very different from what I had known before. I couldn't feel the earth

beneath my feet, although I knew it was there. I was weightless. I felt a strange vibration from his hands and a warmth enfolding me. A soft cloud of smoke seemed to wrap us together, lift us off the earth for a moment and put us gently down again. The chanting grew softer and more monotonous. He stopped suddenly. I gasped and opened my eyes. I had come out of a trance and I was in a bath of perspiration. How long had I been in this state I wondered. .The sadhu was motionless. I stood silently.

When he spoke it was with a hollow ring to his voice. 'A faceless woman will be the source of fear within you. I can't make it pass. It has been written in her stars. Tragedy will befall the faceless woman. Pray for peace within yourself each time you see it.'

He opened his eyes and handed me the scroll. 'Jo ba ba. I know I will not see you again' in the flesh. However, I hope my spirit will be able to reach out to you in troubled times. I have written down all the things I taught you as a child. In these pages I have also advised you how you should live as a young woman. Maybe you can get someone to read and translate them for you. Even better, one day you may learn to read this language you love and speak so well. I know you believe a lot of the things I have taught you. They are not harmful. You will be blessed with children. They will be your joy. Shiva is a god of death and regeneration. The white bull Nandi, the river Ganges that you know and, of course, the full moon, are only part of some symbols that prove Shiva is a fertility deity.' He stopped and looked at me earnestly.

'You have been hurt.'

He put some of the ointment from one of the small clay containers on my index finger and massaged it.

'This is medication that the West doesn't know about yet. It's healing oil from the petals of yellow flowers. You have a lot of tension in your hand. Massage it gently every night with just a very little of this ointment. Life will come back into your finger. Put the ointment into a pot with a lid. I'm sorry I don't have one to give you.'

He asked me to keep standing. He poured the water from a brass container over me. It was rose scented and cooling. I dressed and took my leave of the sadhu.

I had noticed with sadness that he had become gaunt since I had last seen him. His silver-painted arms and the red streaks on his forehead and his long matted hair would, I suppose, frighten some people. I had accepted his painted body as part of his religion.

I started to walk down the hill towards Craig. Gathering dark clouds together with vultures circling above me formed a menacing scene. What dead and disgusting feast were they anticipating? Probably the corpses of bandicoots. They had become a danger to health in the area and were killed off in quite large numbers by the villagers. My father had repeatedly joked that these rats made a tasty treat. I wasn't so sure that it was entirely funny. I feared that in hard times there was an element of truth in what he said.

Craig rose from the large flat uncomfortable stone he had sat on, waiting patiently for me. Together we walked a little further down the hill for our picnic lunch. We found a shady spot where the ground was flat and we unpacked our picnic.

We ate in a strange silence until Craig spoke his mind in worried tones.

'What are we doing here, Josephine? This is a heathen place. I get the distinct impression that there was something coercive in this mysticism today. Be careful of what you're doing. You're no longer a child and sadhu or no sadhu, he's a man of a very different faith. These mystical attractions can lead to strange happenings.'

I had never felt uneasy with the sadhu before, but was I being sucked into a different faith of which I knew very little and which had always held a great fascination for me. Craig always turned everything into something base. I had felt slightly dizzy when I left

the sadhu. The food revived me. Craig was overawed. I thought, well he came of his own volition so I will have to tell him what it was that brought me here.

'Craig, I'm sorry you're upset. There's something very strange about me. I don't know what it is. I feel sometimes there is a veil of secrecy around me. Laugh as much as you like like. I have strange dreams. Repetitive dreams of a woman I don't know, dancing with me when I was a small child. Strange, I like wearing blue and the woman in my dreams wears blue. I get a feeling of not belonging. What is it Craig? Why am I so odd, so different?

'As a child I came up this hill and sat and cried at the lone-liness I felt. The sadhu found me and befriended me, com-forted me and taught me to read and write a little in Hindi. My ayah used to be petrified of him. I always brought him fruit and money and sometimes pictures that I had drawn for him, always of a woman in blue with red hair. Who is she? Is she a visitor from the spirit world and why have I been chosen? He merely said I was drawing myself in later life. My ayah Minnie constantly reported me to my mother for visiting the sadhu. She stopped sneaking on me when I told her I would get the sadhu to cast a spell on her and turn her into a snake and then my dad would shoot her.'

We laughed together. 'Quite a clever threat,' Craig said. It broke the tension.

'Were you not afraid of him as a child?'

'No. He taught me many things, the basic rules of life really. A sadhu is a holy man, they live austere lives. They are mainly her-mits, celibate and chaste. The Hindu religion is a very old one. Hin-dus don't eat meat as you know. This religion has a deep respect for all forms of life. You should not cause harm to any living thing.'

Craig butted in here.

'It's a pity that you didn't teach that to your boyfriend. Why are you continuing your relationship with Adrian Greene?'

He stopped speaking, didn't wait for a reply, then said, 'I'm tired. Let's go back and have a nice cup of tea with toast and jam and re-enter the real world.'

As we started to go down the hill a sharp heavy shower of rain drenched us.

'I hope the roads won't be flooded on our way back,' I commented.

We hurried down; as the path we had come up would be very slippery once the hard packed clay-like earth was wet. It had started to rain heavily by the time we left the hill and the walk back to the factory was difficult.

Small rivulets of water formed at the sides of the road, which was the overflow from the open drains, and we carefully picked our way through floating garbage, snagged on small twigs, dead mice and myriads of dead cockroaches and insects. Coconut shells floated amongst them like miniature coracles from some forgotten land.

By the time we returned to the factory, we both looked as if we had showered with our clothes on.

We dried ourselves and changed and I made tea and toast and we sat and talked about work, the monsoon and India in general. Craig had not long been in India and didn't have a feeling for the country. He couldn't see beyond the teeming masses, the dirt and the poverty.

'I'm here to do a job of work and I'll finish around October or November and return to Scotland. I'll always feel like a visitor here, Josephine and you'll always look on it as home.'

The next day was dull and pouring with rain. I wanted to go to the bazaar and asked my father for the use of his car and driver as I had decided to buy provisions for our return journey on Friday.

I told my father I was going to see the old potter who lived in the village and spend a little time with him. Craig said he would accompany me. The driver stopped at the potter's shop. The old

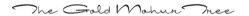

potter was at the wheel making *chatties* and water jugs as he always had done. He was surprised and pleased to see me.

'Ah, you have come to learn to draw, Jo ba ba.' It was his little joke. He had taught me to draw when I was a child, always in charcoal. He had acquired a couple of chairs and offered one to Craig. I sat on the floor on a mat just as I had done when I was a child. I had brought with me a large range of coloured crayons and pencils and some really good drawing paper. I gave them to him as a gift. He thanked me and said, 'I can draw wonderful things now, trees and flowers in their proper colours, how good it will be for me,' he said excitedly.

He offered me tea in one of his *chatties* which I willingly accepted. Craig refused. The potter showed me some of his recent work and then went to the back of the shop and brought out a sketch he had done of me as a child.

'This is a special present for you. Hang it on your wall and remember me a little each time you look at it. As for me, how can I forget the small red-haired child that brought a light into the dim world of an old man?'

I had tears in my eyes for him. It was such a good drawing. I was looking back in time as I saw myself as a child.

Craig was fascinated with the potter's wheel. I had never managed to throw a pot no matter how hard the potter had tried to teach me. No tourist visited the area but the old potter had his pictures on display and many a traveller stopping for tea bought one. Craig was taken up with two portraits of children. I recognised them as the twins I had played with as a child. They had sadly lost their lives in a fire in one of the huts when an oil lamp had overturned and set the hut ablaze. I remember my father writing and telling me about the tragedy when I was in school. I had been very distressed at the time. I hoped that Craig would not buy the sketches of the two dead children, but he insisted, bought them and gave the old man fifty rupees. The potter was astounded at the amount of money he had received for his sketches. I thought it was some sort of bad omen to buy pictures of dead children, especially in view of the tragic circumstances. He had been very interested in the potter and the artistry of his work and I was touched by his generosity.

Craig looked at the portraits of the children on our way back to the factory and commented casually. 'Who are these children? Are the portraits of the same child, drawn differently or are they twins? They have an ethereal look to them.' He paused and was strangely emotional as he spoke again. 'Beautiful! Maybe one day I will father such a pretty little girl.' I didn't comment. How could I sour his dream, telling him they had perished in a fire?

We were home by late afternoon and my father took Craig round the factory. He also showed him how everything functioned in the making of shellac. Craig was far from enthusiastic. Later he commented to me. 'It's really a cottage industry, is it not? It will be increasingly difficult for him to continue to make a decent living if he doesn't modernise.'

Dinner consisted of grilled wild snipe that my father had shot a couple of days previously which had been marinated in a delicious sauce by Tuku. We had vegetables from the garden and fruit. I told Craig I had organised food for our journey back the next day.

'The boss expects everything to be done for him. I don't suppose the Rooters even thought of what they were going to eat or drink on their way back,' Craig said irritably.

He needed an early night as the drive back to Calcutta the next day would be long and hard. He thanked my father for his hospitality, said goodnight and went to his room. A final shock awaited Craig. I had told him earlier there was a lantern in his room as the lights would go off for the servicing of the generator. He hadn't expected near darkness.

Later on in the week when we were back in Calcutta he was to comment to me, 'What a hell of a way to live, the jungle is certainly not for me.'

After dinner my father asked me to walk with him in the garden. It was dark but we took a couple of hurricane lanterns with us. They would ward off some of the mosquitoes. We sat on the bench near the well, which had always been our supply of drinking water. We talked of the old days when I was a child and this seemed to cheer him up a bit. This was the spot where Rose and I played together and jumped about and laughed under his watchful eye. We had played here as it was cool near the well in the shaded area of the garden. He remembered it and then asked about Rose. 'There's nothing much to say.' I lied. 'She spends most of her time sewing and at coffee mornings with Mother.'

I wasn't going to sadden him with the fact that Rose and I lived in separate worlds and now quarrelled constantly.

I turned to him sadly. 'Dad, why don't you arrange for Mother and Rose to return? I can't manage to support them much longer. The money I earn is barely enough and my savings and the money Aunt Ruth gave me is dwindling. After October, I may not have a job as Craig says he is keen to return to Scotland.'

We sat silently together and I then blurted out, 'Is it true Mother wants to divorce you? From various comments on her part, that's how it looks to me.'

He jumped up from the bench and started pacing about smoking his cigarette.

'It's nothing to do with you, Josephine. Nothing at all. Your mother and Rose can't cope with the life here any more.'

He started to speak quietly, so quietly that I could hear the buzz of the mosquitoes.

'Please, my baby, please give up this man you have set your heart on. You have always been my special child. Why do you persist in such a downward path? You are vibrant and clever. You can do so well in marriage.'

I too spoke very slowly and quietly,

'I am committed to him. I can't change my mind.'

He looked at me and in the glow of the lantern he looked much older than I had at first noticed. I put my arms around him.

'Please forgive me, Dad, but I have to choose for myself. He loves me and will look after me.'

'No, Jo,' he said sadly but firmly. 'I can't accept him into our family. No matter what you say, others have a different opinion of him. I even spoke to this chap Craig and he was non-committal. It seems to me that you will not give him up,

and in my opinion such a marriage for you will be disastrous. Even that daft sadhu, who would have starved himself to death but for the fact that I give him money and supply him with fruit, says you have chosen the wrong path in your life. Jo, you have been the one bright spot in my painful and difficult life. I have loved you so completely. Think hard of what you're about to do. Don't destroy yourself. Your hurt will be my pain.'

We sat together on the bench while he finished his cigarette with the smell of ripening fruit around us and the drone of the mosquitoes in their dozens singing a requiem for our long dead past.

It was the last time I was to see my father.

sixteen | an uneasy final parting

December 1953

Mine was a long and sad journey back to the wretched place I called home where I was unloved and unwanted.

I noticed the paddy-fields as we drove past and was pleased there had been some rain. Hopefully there would be more to ensure a good harvest of rice. Oh God, I prayed, please don't let there be a drought this year. I couldn't bear the thought of starving children with their swollen bellies and their sunken eyes. The picture I conjured up filled me with dread and I remembered with sorrow the little beggar boy who had been abandoned and beaten and still found the strength to smile at me, and who had virtually died in my arms.

We had another sharp shower before we stopped for lunch. Craig seemed to be tiring and was driving a lot slower. I looked at him sitting beside me. He was a good looking man, dependable and a fine colleague. Today I felt comfortable with him. Neither of us spoke much and there was no banter between us. A feeling of regret at leaving my father seemed to cover me like a shroud.

It was very late before we arrived in Calcutta. It had, in many ways, been the saddest week of my life.

I entered the flat as quietly as possible hoping not to disturb my mother and was astonished to find the sitting room strewn with some of my clothes. In disgust I put a couple of cushions from the sofa on the floor and fell asleep, physically and emotionally exhausted.

I awoke to Rose speaking to me with a cup of coffee in her hand.

'Jo, what are you doing down there? Why didn't you sleep in your bed?'

I sat up and took the coffee from her.

'Thank you, Rose, I got fed up living in Government House so I thought I would sleep on the floor of this less than palatial establishment,' I answered sarcastically. 'What are my clothes doing strewn about here? Are you having some sort of a clear out?'

'I suppose you could call it that. Mother is going to ask you to clear out.' She tried to laugh at her rather silly joke but burst into tears.

She sat on the couch and I was still sitting on the carpet drinking my coffee. 'Why, Rose, whatever is the matter with you.'

She wiped her eyes and said. 'I really don't want you to go. Why can't you do as Mother asks and give up this Adrian fellow.' She dried her tears and then said slowly and distinctly, 'Mother is putting you out.'

'Putting me out! What are you talking about, Rose?' I got up and put an arm around her to soften her distress. What is this all about?' but she shook her head and wiped her eyes and didn't answer.

I went through to my bedroom and noticed most of my clothes had been packed into two suitcases. The wardrobes were empty. I showered and changed and made breakfast. My mother came into the dining room, still in her dressing gown.

'What's going on here, Mother?' I asked, while we were having our breakfast, still not wholly believing what Rose had said.

She took a swallow or two of tea before she spoke.

'During your absence last week, I thought long and well about our future together as a family. I'm sorry, Josephine, you will have to leave this flat as I cannot tolerate any longer your association with Adrian Greene. My friends now look down on us. You are a

young woman now, no longer a child, so you should leave and follow the path you have chosen – your way, without involving us.'

She spoke in clipped tones, leaving me in no doubt what she had decided.

I was emotionally fragile. The long journey from Ranchi had also taken its toll. Now, as an adult, I was coming to the conclusion that my mother was unable to think logically. Why had my father married her? She should be trying to help him through difficult times, not spending her days playing bridge, gambling and gossiping worthlessly and considering a divorce.

I looked at her and shook my head saying, without raising my voice, and genuinely trying to plead with her. 'Mother, please; we, as a family, are facing difficult times and we need to hold close and ride the storm but you seem to be hell bent in blowing us apart. You want me to leave and you want to divorce my father.' I sighed before I spoke again. 'Think well, even Rose is distressed.'

She didn't answer, but merely sighed. I continued.

'I'll leave, Mother, but can you answer me first? Who will pay your rent and who will give you money every month? Do you have the funds to take over the lease? Of course not,' I said, answering my own question. She looked at me with her mouth half open in surprise. She hadn't, for one moment, thought out the results of her actions. I looked at her and spoke sadly without any venom in my voice, trying to reason with her.

'Mother, can't you think again? It's you that will destroy this small family for your own selfish pleasures. Let's put our differences aside and try and bond together. We need to support Dad. He's slowly going bankrupt and is drinking heavily.'

It was as if I had never spoken. 'I want you out of here, you're a thorn in my side,' she said and got up and left he room.

Though it was early on a Sunday morning I knew Juliana Burton, who ran a small guest house, would be awake and preparing breakfast for the residents. I had often booked visiting personnel into her guest house on behalf of Mr Rooter. I phoned her and she immediately recognised my voice.

'Juliana, do you have a single room available for a week?'

'Yes, but as usual I'll need a deposit.'

'Book it for me, I'll be around as soon as possible this morning.'

I packed the rest of my belongings and went to see if there was anything of mine in the room that Rose used. She was sitting on her bed and had been crying.

'I really don't want you to go,' she repeated, paused to wipe her eyes and continued, 'and I'm so sorry I destroyed the letters from Dean. Mother made me do it.'

'And the sly letters to Dad?' I asked, but she had no reply for me. Still, I felt sorry for her and a deep regret that we had not been loving sisters in adulthood. Her personality had been warped and smothered by her mother.

The perfumes Vali had given me were lined up on her dressing table. I went across and sprayed myself.

'Are you taking them,' she asked, her voice barely audible.

'No, you can have them.'

I wrote the telephone number of the guest house on a slip of paper and handed it to her. 'This is where I'll be if you want to contact me.' She took it from me and put the slip of paper under the bottles of perfume I had given her.

'Well, goodbye then, Jo,' she said, tearfully.

Once we had romped together, swam together, held hands together in our childhood days and laughed together. Now it was time for tears, but still sadly, I couldn't forget or forgive her sly behaviour in the not so distant past and the pain she had caused me, so unnecessarily.

I turned and left the room leaving Rose still sitting on her bed. What were her thoughts I wondered. How different it could have been.

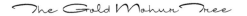
I went down to the taxi rank and asked a taxi driver to come up and help me with my cases. One last look at the dingy flat I had shared with my family. One last look at misery, and then perhaps a step too far, a step, not of my own volition, but the path kismet had chosen for me – a step which now would surely encourage me to seek the arms and promises of Adrian Greene. I had no other anchor.

It took all of ten minutes to arrive at Juliana's guest house.

'What's all this about, Josephine?' she asked as she opened the door to me.

'If I can get my cases into the room you've reserved for me I'll tell you.'

She realised I was upset and spoke gently. 'Come on into the lounge. We'll have coffee and you can tell me all about it. I'm guessing it has something to do with Adrian Greene.' I nodded my head.

She had coffee and biscuits ready for me. I gave her a cheque for the full amount for a week's bed and board.

'Well, what's the story?' she persisted.

'This morning my mother asked me to leave the flat we shared, and, yes, it's because of my friendship with Adrian. She's so disorganised regarding money. I have struggled to pay the rent and food for them. She asked me to leave without any thought of who would provide for her. I really fear for their future, Rose especially. She has little education and won't be able to fend for herself. There's a small matter I would like you to help me with. Adrian has my car. He was supposed to meet me some time this afternoon at the flat. He won't know where I am. Can I write a note and ask a bearer to drop it round to him?'

'That's no problem. You look exhausted, girl,' Juliana said with concern.

'I returned from Ranchi last night. It was quite a journey. Can I have a rest.'

She nodded. 'Would you like to join us for a curry lunch? There's plenty.'

I thanked her and went to the room she had prepared for me. I slept fitfully until midday. The bearer had come back with a message from Adrian. He had scribbled on the bottom of my note. 'Can't come now. See you at four o'clock.'

I asked Juliana if we could sit in her guest sitting room when he came to see me.

'Yes, as long as you don't kiss and cuddle and embarrass the other guests', she said half in joke and half with a certain concern in her voice. 'We Anglo-Indians are a close-knit community, you know. Your affair with Adrian, if I can call it that loosely, has astonished some of us as there was some gossip about him wishing to join the priesthood after he had qualified as a doctor. He never looked at girls until you came along. What on earth did you do to him? Your behaviour with him is blatantly sexual. It's not proper. You'll rue the day, child. He's not the marrying kind. You seem to have acted on him like some sort of heady drug. He's always been serious minded, even as a child he seemed to have been a solemn little fellow, always reading books of one kind or another. Josephine let him go. Your worlds are too far apart.'

I smiled at her and replied rather frivolously to break the seriousness of our conversation.

'I'm not so thoughtless. I know he's religious and I respect that. It doesn't mean he wants to join a monastery. Anyway, he doesn't look like a monk to me. He's too young and has too much hair. Monks are usually bald old men, are they not?' She laughed with me saying, 'Don't be so silly, Josephine.' and then became serious again, repeating, 'Let him go.'

Adrian came round soon after four. He decided we should go out in the car rather than sit in the guest sitting room.

'We have important matters to discuss, sweetheart. I don't want the whole of the guest house to know our affairs,' he said.

We drove to the maidan. Tennis matches, hockey and football were being played in small outdoor clubs. We found a shady spot

under a tree. Even in the open air there was a still, oppressive humidity. I had a rug in the back of the car and spread it between the tree and the car. He spoke anxiously of his own affairs, not realising the turmoil I was in.

'I have the results of my finals, Jo. I have merits and passes and now I have to face the orals for recruitment abroad. I thought they might have taken place in Calcutta as in past years, but this year the venue is Delhi, so this looks like the end of my career, or shall I say the career I had hoped for recently. I can't afford the fare to Delhi. I have tried for a loan the last two days but nobody wants to know. I suppose I should be grateful for even a junior post in the Presidency General Hospital. If I don't appear for the exams in Delhi, I will be considered a failed candidate. Not so good for me, eh! Jo?' He held my hand and raised it to his lips, kissing the palm.

'That's excellent news about your exams,' I said.

There was silence between us for a few moments before he said softly, 'Jo, aren't you listening to me. I don't have the money to go to Delhi, let alone support myself in a hotel there for two to three nights.'

'It's not such a serious problem, I can....'

He interrupted and spoke with a certain amount of annoyance in his voice, but also laced with a certain amount of sadness.

'I have lost the opportunity of a lifetime.'

'Adrian, I know you are upset but please let me finish what I was about to say. I can let you have sufficient funds, so let's go and sit in the car and I will write out a cheque for you.'

Balancing the cheque book on my bag I wrote out a cheque for four hundred rupees. It was a deep dip into my savings, part of the extra money I earned working for Craig on a Saturday, but I had to do it for him. I couldn't let his career be cut off at this crucial stage.

I handed the cheque to him saying, 'I hope that's enough, it's all I can manage just now.'

For a moment he was speechless. He shook his head in disbelief at what I had done for him and spoke with a tremor in his voice. 'Why do I never trust you, sweetheart? Why do I keep thinking you don't care? Why am I such a fool?' I put my finger to his lips to stop him.

He paused and then exclaimed, 'Good heavens, Jo, forgive my stupid selfishness. I should have asked immediately when I collected you. Why are you at Juliana's. What has happened?'

I told him briefly about my father, and then I tried to tell him without emotion, and tried harder still to sound casual and uncaring, saying that my mother and Rose had virtually thrown me out of the flat. I had held back all feeling but now with Adrian, the man who surely loved me, holding my hand, the floodgates opened and I let myself weep for a short while. He put his arm around me, comforting me, but there was really nothing he could do about my changed circumstances.

Trams thundered past where we were sitting and then came to a grinding, screeching halt, spewing out their human cargo intent on refreshing themselves after a large curry lunch and an afternoon nap. For them, nothing would change as day after day and week after week, it would be the same; hoards of humanity, swaying to and fro in an overcrowded tram going about their business; the same chaotic scene.

Adrian and I sat quietly taking in the atmosphere.

'Look at this carry on,' he said smiling, trying in some way to comfort me. 'Why does everyone need to do the same thing at the same time? I can't understand the herd instinct.'

And then sitting together in the old Morris 8, we were silent, under the boughs of a Gold Mohur tree, giving us a modicum of shade. The heat haze made the distant Victoria Memorial shimmer, and the grass seemed greener than it actually was, and I sat

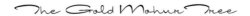

contentedly holding the hand of the man I loved. We were in our own bubble of time while the world swirled around us.

Before he started the car to take me back to the guest house he spoke passionately, not really asking for a reply.

'Love me as I love you, sweetheart.'

On the spur of the moment I wanted to be light-hearted and giggly with him and say, 'of course I love you,' but at twenty-eight he was not a man for joking about our relationship so instead, as I got out of the car, I said to him, 'God be with you Adrian, and help you in your endeavours. I'll see you next Saturday.'

seventeen | a proposal

Early December 1953

On Saturday the driveway in Juliana Burton's guest house was flooded. To get into my car I had to remove my shoes and wade through filthy water, avoiding stepping on dead cockroaches floating in their watery grave. Even the two lower steps to the office block, where the little boy had sat each day, were flooded, not from monsoon waters but the result of blocked and overflowing drains. The stench was overpowering Miniature rivulets at the side of the pavement carried their fetid cargo of garbage and the pavement was strewn with curry-stained banana leaves used for snacks eaten round the vendors' trays.

Craig was already at work, humphing and mumphing.

'I hate this bloody constant flooding,' he said as he noticed I was bare-foot and carrying my sandals. He said it as if it was my fault.

He looked at me with some concern before continuing, 'You'd better wash your feet with some disinfectant. Heaven knows what diseases lurk in that water.'

Craig had a considerable amount of mail and I had two air cards from Vali. I read them before starting work. The contents were disturbing Vali's mother, Ruth, had been taken to hospital with severe breathing problems. The second air letter card was garbled. I couldn't understand what she had written. She had repeated herself several times and ended the letter with a plea for me to return to England.

I handed the letters over to Craig for his comments. He read the letters twice and passed them back with a single word.

'Drunk.'

'What do you mean, Craig?' I asked.

'She was drunk when she wrote that garbage. I assume your friend is well-educated and sane, so what other explanation is there? Anyway, keep them and show them to your boyfriend. He's supposedly a doctor, he may know what to make of them.'

'He's in Delhi just now doing exams and should be back today or tomorrow. I hope he does well. It's been a hard struggle for him, despite the fact that you think we just spend our time flirting and kissing in the taxi, which is far from the truth.'

We settled down to work and I decided I would write to Vali more often. There was no way I could go to London at the present time. Paying for a return fare was totally out of the question.

We had eaten the sandwiches and finished the coffee, and it was almost time to go home. It was well past noon as the paperwork we had to deal with from Friday was complicated and disorganised. We continued working. It was nearly three o'clock and we still hadn't finished.

'Don't swear under your breath and throw your pencil across the room, Josephine, I can do it for you today. These accounts are hellish. I'm a chartered accountant, not some sort of company accounts nanny,' Craig commented.

I got up and decided to get a drink of water. As I was returning to the room I heard someone banging on the office door. The premises were always shut on a Saturday for security reasons and Craig had his own set of keys. He went down to open the door.

I heard voices and then Craig accompanied by Adrian came into the office. Flustered and embarrassed I asked, 'What are you doing here Adrian?'

'It's well past three, Jo and I couldn't find you at the guest house or at the flat – got an earful from Rose,' he said smiling. He turned to Craig and apologised for the intrusion saying, 'I'm sorry, but I wanted to share my joy with Jo. I have passed my tests in Delhi and have been offered a junior post in a hospital in London. It's not great but a start is better than nothing.'

I introduced the two men formally. Craig congratulated Adrian and stood and shook hands with him. I wanted to shout and sing and dance around with Adrian to show him my appreciation of his achievement. It would have to wait. I handed him the car key saying, 'I'll join you in a few minutes.'

Craig had never met Adrian. He had only seen us from a distance mostly walking together, Adrian casually dressed in khaki shorts and sandals, but today he had on a suit, his one and only suit. He had his hair properly cut and Craig had shown surprise as he had shaken hands with this well-built young man with the grey eyes, whom I had fallen in love with. I had noticed an expression of surprise on Craig's face when the two men shook hands. They were about the same height. I always thought Craig Mackie was a much taller man.

I apologised again to Craig for the interruption.

Craig was uneasy. He had never really believed me when I told him that Adrian was in the final year of his medical course. He thought I had merely invented it to make our friendship, which Craig termed my ridiculous obsession, look acceptable.

'I apologise, Josephine, for not believing you,' he said, ' but then you do have a habit of making up daft stories – note, the man-eating tiger story you told me on our way to Ranchi.'

'Well you know, Craig, both stories are true, I promise.'

What could he do but laugh and say, 'You win, so let's pack up, it's gone four o'clock.'

I put away the papers I was working on and closed my desk and left the office. I hadn't realised that Adrian had come straight from the airport to find me. He held my hand and we sat quietly in the car before he spoke.

"Jo, this achievement is yours as well as mine. If I didn't have the money to attend the interview it would have been the end of my career. As it so happens, look.'

He took out a cheque from his pocket. The money was much more than the amount I had given him. It was a little over a thousand rupees. The note with it said it included subsistence allowance and incidental expenses for the time he was in Delhi.

'I can pay you back and then I'm going to take you out on a proper date tonight, Jo. I know you have scrimped and saved for so long. I owe you a happy evening out. I will collect you round about nine. Be glamorous for me, sweetheart. I will hire a monkey jacket.' That is what he called an evening suit.

He dropped me back to Juliana's guest house and took the car. We had never been out on a date in public before. We had bickered and wept; prayed, quarrelled, kissed and cuddled and met in strange and awkward places. Not any more. We were going to have this date in the public eye.

Amongst the clothes that Vali had put in my case in London, a green chiffon dress was my favourite. I had never had the occasion to wear it. This was the dress I would wear to please Adrian.

He drove to the dance club and restaurant which had opened recently. We managed to get a place to park but it was a short distance from the club itself. I looked at the handsome man beside me. Gone were the worn-out clothes and with it the perpetually worried look. He smiled and held my hand as we walked up the steps to the restaurant. This was the man I loved.

'Tonight, sweetheart, nothing is too expensive for you, especially as you look so sensational,' he said as we walked towards the tables. We selected one further back in the room, away from the edge of the dance-floor. Large groups of men and women on a night out were talking and laughing loudly. The waiter suggested we order quickly as we were already late for the meal. We dined on savoury omelettes with salad, followed by jumbo ice-creams.

I noticed Craig was sitting on the opposite side of the room with two young men. He came across when he noticed I had seen him and asked if he could join us for a few minutes. Adrian seemed pleased to have him sit with us. The band was playing a slow number and Craig asked Adrian's permission to dance with me. I was surprised Craig was such a good dancer. I had expected a shuffle across the floor. He complimented me by saying, 'You look sophisticated and attractive tonight, Josephine. Green suits you so well.'

The band stopped playing. I returned to our table and Craig went back to his companions. I had never danced with Adrian. The only person I had danced with was Dean. I thought of him now, a little sadly. The band then played a waltz and I hoped I could follow him and not make a fool of myself. Adrian and I did, however, dance well together and as the evening drew to a close the lights were dimmed on the dance floor. Adrian held me close and said, 'Jo, we will dance until the end of the evening.' I put my arms around his neck as we danced and he kissed me.

'It's been quite a day for us hasn't it, Jo?' he said.

I could barely see his face as the lights had been dimmed, but I could see his grey eyes looking into mine. We were moving slowly on the dance floor when he whispered to me, 'Jo, marry me.'

I didn't know if I had heard him correctly.

'Jo,' he said again a bit louder, 'did you not hear me. Marry me.'

I answered him saying, 'Adrian Green ask me again properly.'

'Josephine Willis, I love you, please will you marry me?' he said earnestly.

'Yes, I think it might be a good idea,' I said letting him kiss me again. He stopped dancing, took off the ring he always wore on the little finger of his left hand, lifted my hand and put it on my engagement ring finger.

'It's all I have, Jo. It was my mother's ring. Wear it with love.'

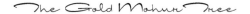

The three small diamonds that were embedded diagonally in a wide gold band had a bright lustre under the artificial light. Had love danced and sparkled in his mother's heart? He never spoke of his father.

The music stopped and we went back to the table. The band packed their instruments and left together with the revellers of the night. We waited for the crowd to thin out. Craig had obviously been watching us and came over and took a seat.

'Are congratulations in order?' he asked.

I nodded and Craig offered his congratulations. 'Well done, Josephine,' he said.

The whole day had been too much for me. I was almost beyond speech. I held out my hand for Craig to see the ring.

'It's very pretty. Look after it carefully,' he said.

He sat with us and made small-talk with Adrian until the crowd thinned and we left the club together. My car was blocked with several vehicles both in front and behind us by inconsiderate parkers. We had to wait until the traffic cleared. We were sitting holding hands, waiting for the traffic to clear.

'Well, Jo,' Adrian said with a sigh, 'Today I feel as if the ropes that have bound me for so long have been cut forever. With your love and understanding I can progress in life feeling a certain amount of freedom. The ambitions I have can hopefully be fulfilled.'

I touched his face tracing his jaw line with my index finger. 'Who said I love you?' I said smiling, 'I just adore you.' He looked at me quite astonished and for once we laughed together without restraint. 'You're really something,' he said gently.

And as the traffic cleared, amongst the shouts of rickshaw men and the honking of the horns of impatient motorists, a good-natured cloud enveloped us, all the way back to the guest house.

eighteen | a painful parting for jo and dean

Juliana congratulated me reluctantly when I told her of my engagement to Adrian asking, 'When's the wedding and where are you going to live?'

'I'll make arrangements this week and let you know as soon as possible. Can you let me have the room for another week?' I asked.

'Yes, of course. I let rooms, that's my job,' She commented.

Dean had my passport. I needed to get in touch with him urgently. He was in Delhi and the only point of contact was Jenny Mason, a colleague. I phoned her; informed her of my engagement to Adrian and asked if she could remind Dean he still had my passport with him. I gave her my address.

It was Thursday evening when Dean came to see me. I asked Juliana if we could use her guest lounge.

'Who's this then, Josephine?' she asked.

'I have some work with him. I won't be long,' I said evading her question.

The lounge was empty. Dean and I sat in a corner of the room. He seemed upset.

'Jose, how could I forget your passport was still with me? I'm not happy about what you're about to do. His world is not yours. Think hard honey. Jose, you have cut yourself off from your father. How hurtful is that? Does Adrian Greene realise how much you have given up for him? Why doesn't he try and contact your father and explain or even go up to Ranchi and see him. It's not at the

other end of the world. It would be the right and decent thing to do.'

I took his hand and held it between mine. 'Now don't you worry about me Dean, I'll be fine. Adrian loves me.'

Dean changed the subject. 'I'm so very tired. I'm here to clear my flat, spend a short time in Delhi and go home.' He smiled ruefully. 'I'll go and look at your England before returning to America.'

'Dean, can I ask one last favour? I have a friend, Vali Finlayson, who lives in London. I've spoken to you about her in the past. We were close school friends. I've always been made to feel a sense of responsibility towards her. Can you visit her for me? She doesn't seem too well just now. She'll show you the sights of London if she's fit. She's a happy person but at the moment her mother is extremely ill. She seems to have had some sort of problem of her own but she's not been clear in her letters as to what's really wrong with her.'

I wrote her Kensington address on a piece of paper and gave it Dean.

'I'll look her up. Jose, I had hoped you would come to America with me. I'm real cut up to think we'll never meet again. Christmas cards will be all we can exchange now. The fun and laughter of our friendship will always be with me.'

He handed me my passport and an envelope. 'My address is in there. If at any time you're in trouble, write to me. I'm not saying this lightly. By the way, what are you doing living here?'

'I've been put out of the flat by my mother. I need something small until we leave for Britain. I can't afford to stay in this guest house. Adrian has a post starting in April 1954 in London. I need a flat for a few months.'

'You can have mine. 'The rent is paid for another six months. I'll put the keys in the mail box in your office the night I leave. Hand them to Jenny when you leave or tell her to collect them from your office, whichever is more convenient. I need to go now, Jose. God bless you.'

He stood up and walked to the door holding my hand as if he didn't want to let go of me. I had a strange hollow feeling, almost as if I needed to be sick. My life had taken so many strange turns. I was losing Dean.

When he had left I opened the envelope with the address he had given me. It also contained a Christmas Card. He had remembered. A cheque for five hundred rupees was also enclosed. In the card he had written the words he had said to me several times,

'I'll hold you in my dreams and Jo will always kiss her Dean.'

This man was truly special for me. Why had I let him go so easily?

I thought of the flat he had so generously let me have and immediately remembered I had to cancel the rent I paid on the flat my mother and Rose were living in.

I phoned Mr Chakrabarty, the landlord of the flat, and made an appointment with him for Saturday afternoon. He was about to have his lunch when I arrived at his office.

Mr. Chakrabarty spoke very broken English, but well enough for me to understand him. 'Well Willis. Why you come?' he asked.

'Mr. Chakrabarty, I am giving you a month's notice. I am vacating your flat. You can use my deposit as the rent due. I will not be paying the rent. My mother and sister are still in the flat. You will have to move them out if they don't pay.'

He had understood me and nodded his head saying, 'Ah ha, putting your mother on road. We Bengalis don't put mother out on road. Not good.'

'Mr Chakrabarty, she has put me out of the flat,' I explained.

"Ho, ho, so you do naughty things? Mummy throw you out. Never mind, you come have lunch with me. Come, come, have curry and chapatti lunch and fine mangoes,' he said. 'I give you new flat. What you want?' he said hoping to do some business with me.

'I don't want a new flat. I'm getting married and leaving for England. I'm staying in a guest house.'

'Guest house,' he almost squeaked with amazement. 'How you got so much money for guest house? I give you flat. Small flat. I have trump cards now. No British. I do all business. You no proper British, Willis,' he said shaking his head and laughing. 'You stay India. Why you want England? You good for here. England too cold for you, Willis.'

I laughed at him.

'No, I go,' I said to him in broken English. 'I know you have trump cards. All the flats are now yours. You have a hand full of aces.'

I got up to leave.

'No, no, you stay and have lunch,' he urged. 'You *sadhi* (marry) with rich English man and you never eat delicious pakoras again,' he said in mock sorrow.

I sat and ate with him. I listened to him grumbling about the government, the refugees and ultimately and inevitably the monsoon that for him seemed worse each year.

I smiled at him as I started to leave saying, 'Don't grumble, you have lots of money now Mr. Chakrabarty.'

As I was leaving I heard him say once again.

'You stay in India Willis, good for you to stay.'

It was a fortnight before I got the keys to the flat from Dean. Adrian was delighted that we now had a place to sit in and talk to each other without constant interruptions. He had always been in correspondence with an aunt he had in England. She was his mother's sister and now she had written generously inviting him to stay until he got settled. He had also written to her at length, at my request, about Vali and asked his aunt to befriend her.

'I am starting to feel civilised,' he laughed. 'Sweetheart, we badly need some time together. I am tired of this business of courting in cars, taxis, park benches and walking endlessly. I love you and want to be with you. We need to adjust to each other in many ways, including sexually. It's very important for a good marriage. I think we should marry soon. Say the first of February. Will you agree with that date, Jo?'

'Yes but we will have to book a church or registrar office. If it doesn't upset you, I'd like to marry in the small chapel your mother used to pray in, the one you've told me about. It's scarcely going to be a marriage with many guests, flowers and all the paraphernalia of a large wedding. There will just be a handful of people.'

'Our marriage is nothing to do with other people,' he said irritably. 'It's our vows to each other that are important, Jo. I'll make arrangements. Thank you for suggesting the chapel. It will be just a month before we leave for England. Jo, I'm deeply worried. How are we going to pay these fares? I'm now working full time in the hospital and have most of the money from the interview left but, still, I have only enough money saved for one fare.'

'Well, you can just go on your own then,' I said.

'What! Are you serious?' he said in an agitated voice.

'No, silly, I'm just joking. I can make up the balance. Don't worry so much, Adrian.'

Each night in the flat on my own I wondered what life was going to be like for me in Britain. The words from Mr Chakrabarty, 'you stay in India Willis,' kept repeating themselves to me. He had obviously meant I was a child of India and belonged nowhere else.

nineteen | the wedding

February 1954

And so, at the age of twenty-three on the first of February 1954, I married Adrian Greene.

This was my wedding day, a special day to hold in my memory for all time, but yet a sadness found a corner of my heart. No cathedral filled with fragrant flowers. No smiling, approving guests with beautiful clothes, hats and gloves; no carpeted aisle and sadly, and most importantly, no father to give me away to the man I had chosen and loved. No relations and only but a handful of friends.

I had on a simple cream-coloured lace dress ending just above my ankles with satin high-heeled shoes to match. An orchid adorned my hair and I carried an ivory coloured prayer book in my hand. It had been given to me in school by the nuns as a prize for something mundane like a progress prize. .

Children from an orphanage in white dresses with pink ribbons in their hair sang a hymn, accompanied on the piano by an elderly nun who seemed to miss a few notes.

Adrian was waiting at the altar for me in a new dark blue suit. The tension I felt made me tremble. He had to steady my hand before slipping on the wedding ring. I remembered our first meeting when I had slept in his taxi, trustingly. I could almost hear him say, 'it's time to wake up, Missy.' Today I was marrying him. I heard him speak so softly and tenderly.

'I will love you forever, Missy.' It was not part of the service.

The register was signed and the certificates made over to us. Small pouches of coins in pretty floral sachets chinked as they were handed out to the children who had sung for us. We were truly man and wife. I was now Josephine Greene.

It was late in the afternoon and Craig drove us to the flat. We had sandwiches and coffee together. Craig had invited the few people assembled in the chapel to a celebratory dinner in his flat. The Rooters were there as were Juliana and her husband who had kindly taken me to the church in his car and acted as photographer. It was late by the time we were back in the little flat, decorated with flowers by Juliana. I went into the bedroom to take off my dress. Adrian was sitting on the couch having a cold drink. I half expected him to get up and go home. By the time I returned to the sitting room he had fallen asleep on the couch. I left him there and went to bed. Some time during the night he must have woken up as I felt him in bed beside me.

I awoke early and showered and dressed. We needed bread, milk, eggs and fruit for our breakfast. I was in the New Market as the stalls were opening. I looked at my left hand as I drove the car. My wedding ring sat neatly with my engagement ring. Well they can shout and howl and call me names. I am Mrs Greene now and that's all there is to it.

Adrian had showered and was in his dressing gown when I returned to the flat.

'What are you doing sweetheart. Why are you up and dressed? This is our honeymoon.'

'I went to get bread and milk,' I said, rather sheepishly.

I felt shy for some reason. It seemed strange to have him in my bed. This was the man I had kissed so passionately and wanted and desired. Why was I feeling shy? I was lost for words.

'Oh! there has been a baby elephant born in the zoo. The market stall holders were speaking of it. Shall we go and see him today?'

Adrian looked at me and started laughing.

'Now, why would I want to go and see a baby elephant on my honeymoon? Come here Mrs Greene.'

He put his hand out and unzipped my dress. His smiling eyes widened appreciatively at the contrast between my willowy slim figure and shapely full bosoms. He drew me to him tenderly.

'Come to bed with me, Jo.' I had my arms around him and his body was warm against mine. He started caressing me. 'Your body is so feminine – it's like silk against mine, my darling. I will be very gentle with you.'

We never did go to see the baby elephant.

It was a special time for us. We enjoyed each others company and our evenings were precious and calm before we launched ourselves into a different life-style. I sometimes wished during those heady magic days that time could have stood still for us. We spoke and laughed together without any strain in our relationship. He held me close in his sleep as though I had always been there for him. He was a passionate lover. I adored him. Surely I had done the right thing in marrying him.

There was one very dark cloud on our horizon, however – a cable from Vali. It told of Aunt Ruth's death. She was distraught. We sent her our condolences and said we would be with her in London very shortly. Adrian sent his aunt a cable asking her to contact Vali and see if there was anything that could be done for her.

Further letters from Vali were a bit more cheerful. She said she was happy at meeting Dean Mitchell and that Aunt Eileen – Adrian's aunt – had been a tower of strength for her so soon after her mother's death. The last letter I had from Vali, before we left India, annoyed me. She had written 'Dean's a great guy. He looks after me very well.'

'I don't like Vali's comments about Dean,' I said to Adrian.

'Jo, mind your own business. You're married to me and Dean Mitchell's affairs have nothing to do with you.'

The time came for us to leave the cocoon we had built around ourselves. It didn't seem that long since I had met Adrian beneath the boughs of the Gold Mohur tree on that humid June night. He had said to me then 'You'll be safe with me, Missy.' Would I? Superstitions of both prosperity and disaster surrounded meetings under this most flamboyant of trees. Which of the superstitions would come to pass? Would we prosper or would disaster stalk us? We were now leaving India to go into the cold fresh air of spring in England.

I was leaving the father I loved and the land of my birth to live in a cold and foreign land whose food and the habits of its people were strange to me. Who would guide me? I only had Adrian Greene and he had never lived in the West or in a cold climate.

Craig insisted on driving us to the airport. He had a folder for me with his address and the names of several companies that might employ me in Britain. He had already written to a few telling them that I had worked for him. The references were excellent. He seemed quite upset at our parting and shook Adrian's hand firmly, saying 'Be sure and look after her.'

It seemed as if he didn't want us to go. A few minutes before we were due to board the aircraft he did what was for him out of character. He put his arms around me, hugged me and said, 'Take care of yourself lassie.'

twenty | a dazzler for adrian

April 1954

The international flight took off on time after the usual safety drill. The air hostess handed round wet scented cloths and barley sugar sweets. Adrian settled down and dozed, still holding my hand, relaxed and at ease. I had married a man who was still a relative stranger to me and who didn't have a penny to his name.

The flight touched down at Heathrow airport half an hour late. As we disembarked the gods of excitement held Adrian in their embrace.

'Jo! Have a look at the size of this building. How many Dum Dum air ports would fit in here?' he said with amazement in his voice.

We walked slowly looking for his Aunt Eileen. A small solitary figure was standing waiting for us. When Adrian saw her he rushed forward and picked her up off the floor in his embrace. I stood back. He held her hand and came towards me and introduced his sole only living relative.

'Aunt Eileen this is my wife, Josephine,' he said with a hint of pride in his voice.

She looked at me for a moment or two before speaking.

'So, you're Josephine. I've heard so much about you in all the letters that Adrian has written to me. I had no idea you were English.' She held my hand and kissed me lightly on the cheek.

Amazement and a tinge of jealousy was rising within me as I noticed Vali walking slowly towards me holding Dean Mitchell's hand, a hand that I had held so often with love, and then I felt Adrian's arm around my waist and introduced Vali and Dean to him. Vali was unusually subdued. She kissed me. 'How wonderful to see you again,' she said tearfully, as she hugged me.

'Well Jose Greene,' Dean said kissing me on the cheek, 'You didn't expect to see me here,' and as he did so the buzz between us was still there.

We left the airport together, Dean helping to carry our luggage. Aunt Eileen took us in her car and Vali and Dean followed, Dean driving what used to be Vali's mother's car.

Adrian was looking out of the window pointing out things he found exciting, and kept on asking, 'Where's the hospital?'

'Adrian,' Aunt Eileen almost shouted, amazed at his enthusiasm. 'You can't see the whole of London in one hour. As the magicians say: all will be revealed.'

I was pleased he liked what he saw I had often worried about what would have happened had he disliked his new surroundings.

We were welcomed into Aunt Eileen's flat which was not far from where Vali lived in Kensington and Vali made coffee and sandwiches. It was obvious they had formed a close friendship in the short time they had known each other.

I apologised to Vali for not being able to leave India earlier and visit her and offer her my support during the time leading up to her mother's death. She put her arms around me emotionally for a few moments before replying.

'She loved you so much and asked for you towards the end. Such a shame you couldn't come and see her before she died. Incidentally, Jonathan our lawyer wants to see both of us regarding her will. I think it's pretty straightforward. She was such an organised person. I think mother has left you a little something

as a token of her affection for you. Do you remember Jonathan? He was the chap who came and asked me for a date when you were last in London with us.' She smiled and then giggled a little. I remembered she had turned him down. 'His company is Marsden & Watson,' she continued. 'he's the Watson half. You should appoint him as your lawyer. He's very particular and extremely efficient, though a bit of a bore.'

I had a vague idea that the reason why the lawyer wanted to see me had something to do with taking care of Vali. Aunt Ruth and Uncle Edward had both mentioned it to me many times.

We were all in Aunt Eileen's sitting room. Everyone seemed to be talking at once. I turned to Vali who was sitting near me and said quietly, 'What's this about you being unwell? You mentioned it in your last few letters to me. Are you fully recovered?'

'Don't fuss like a mother hen. I'm fine,' she smiled. 'Besides, Dean is here to look after me now. Mother always wanted me to be happy. Look!' she said holding out her left hand. She was wearing a very pretty diamond ring. 'Dean and I are engaged. We're to be married very soon. You're to be a bridesmaid. No, Jo darling, that's silly. You aren't a maid any more,' she giggled.

Aunt Eileen interrupted. 'Josephine can be matron of honour, Vali.'

Suddenly aware she was causing some embarrassment Vali said, 'Anyway, we'll let you have a rest. We'll come round tomorrow.'

Dean and Vali left soon after.

At last, Aunt Eileen got a chance to speak to us privately. She handed Adrian a cheque.

'This is a wedding present for you. I would like you both to buy some good warm clothes. You'll need them. The weather is still pretty cool.' She handed me a tray with a flask of hot chocolate to take to the room she had so generously let us use in her house. 'Have a hot drink before you sleep. It'll do you good after the long journey Josephine. I've also put hot water bottles in your bed.' I thanked her for her kindness and thoughtfulness.

We slept well into the morning as the flight had been exhausting for us. When we awoke Aunt Eileen had already left for work. She had laid a table in the kitchen for our breakfast.

'Just look at this,' Adrian exclaimed. 'Look how soft and white the bread is and fantastic strawberry jam too, and as for the flat, sheer luxury for me after what I've been used to. Everything dazzles me.'

'Well, there's plenty for us to do. What shall we do first?'

'I've already made up my mind, sweetheart. We can start with going back to bed. I'm dog tired after that flight.'

It must have been past midday when there was a loud banging on the door. Adrian was still in his dressing gown when he opened the door to Vali and Dean.

'Don't you pair have anything better to do than to come and wake us?' he said to Dean.

'You obviously have something better to do judging from the state you're in,' said Dean, laughing. 'Come on, Jose. Vali is here to take you shopping and I'll show Adrian some of the sights and introduce him to my tailor.' He was trying his best to please Adrian.

'An American is to show me the sights of London. How about that?' Adrian joked.They left together soon after.

Vali had several expensive-looking carrier bags with her. 'These are for you. See if anything fits you. They're new and can be returned,' she said. I selected a couple of sweaters and a skirt. We visited her hairdresser and she seemed to pay a small fortune for my cut and style. We shopped for shoes and boots and lunched and laughed together, and even though rationing had recently ended, the selection in the shops was not plentiful, but Vali managed to select well but expensively for me, saying, 'these

are your wedding present, Jo.' We returned to Aunt Eileen's flat in good humour in time for an evening meal. She had put together a substantial casserole for all of us.

Vali and I spent a lot of time together during the following weeks, but she was anxious and nervous about the wedding, so on a particular afternoon when her nerves seemed to be getting the better of her I tried to put her at ease saying, 'Why the rush to get married? You've known each other only for a very short time.'

She looked at me saying almost in a whisper, 'Darling, please understand, we have had a strong attraction for each other from the day he came to see me saying you were his friend. We sleep together, we have to get married. Besides, he needs to return to America shortly. He can't hang around here indefinitely and I must go with him as his wife. His parents are coming for the wedding and I want everything to be just so; perfect.'

Where were the words love, fun, laughter? A strange uneasiness came over me and I almost said, please don't harm him with you selfishness, but would I dare? She could be very short-tempered. I was married to the man of my choice, so she too had every right to be responsible for her own behaviour. It should have nothing to do with me, except I felt a sense of foreboding; perhaps it was some form of jealousy on my part. Dean Mitchell had been my first love and she was marrying him and she now had a wedding to arrange.

The dress she had ordered for herself was outstanding and extremely expensive. What she chose for me, a deep burnt orange lace dress, was a little short of ghastly considering my red hair. It was spring, so why not pale green or blue. I didn't argue with her as she was already jumpy.

Adrian was excited by his new career and spoke continually of how much he loved the work, the wonderful equipment in the hospital, the congenial colleagues, the orderly wards and all he saw and was learning. Each night as I was about to fall asleep he said 'I will have to catch up with my colleagues. I must do some research. They are all ahead of me in my training and I'll need a good subject to enable me to excel.'

I took no notice and put his remarks down to nothing else but enthusiasm for his new surroundings, but I should have been more cautious.

On Thursday evening I was late getting home. The final fitting of the wedding dress had upset Vali. She was irritable and felt the dress didn't look quite right. It took a great deal of persuading, pinning and tucking before she was pleased. Vali dropped me at the door of the flat and Adrian and Aunt Eileen were waiting for me so that we could have our evening meal together. I apologised for being late and laughingly described Vali's silly concerns. Aunt Eileen accepted my apology.

'It's just a case of pre-nuptial nerves, Jo. Most brides are like that,' Aunt Eileen said in a comforting tone, but not so Adrian. He was in the sitting room having a cup of tea and reading the newspapers, moody and out of sorts. I interrupted him saying, 'Oh, darling. It's nice to see you home early.'

'Is it now,' he said sarcastically. 'What have you been doing while I've been working?' he said folding the papers. 'Have you made even the slightest attempt to get a job? No, of course not, you've been gadding about spending someone else's money. You shouldn't let Vali indulge you.'

I tried to make light of the situation and replied happily, 'All the shopping for the wedding is done now. It was great fun. The shops are wonderful. We are due to see the lawyer first thing tomorrow morning. Oh, Aunt Eileen, it was so good having Vali's company, after such a long time.'

Adrian, determined to vent his ill-temper on someone, said rudely to me, 'Fun, is that all you think of? I'm not here for fun. I need money and a good career. They do go hand in hand, you know, so stop gadding about with Vali and try and get yourself employed,'

There was really no need, but he became increasingly irritated, determined to argue with me.

'You and Vali are all dressed up running around London, lunching out and shopping. That's not all. Men are looking at you and Vali with more than a passing interest. I noticed the glances when you both went out of the building yesterday. Why are you dressed like a tart? You're a doctor's wife. In just a few days you've changed your whole personality. Your hair, your clothes, everything about you. You're becoming so silly and giggly, just like Vali Finlayson. I suppose you're taking a drink like her. I noticed she had two large glasses of white wine with her sandwiches while we had coffee. You and Vali are much too fond of male attention, together you're a lethal cocktail.'

I had spent a happy time with Vali and was pleasantly relaxed. His last sentence annoyed me. We had a few wonderful weeks before we left India. I had hoped we had built a strong foundation to our marriage and once again we were in a situation of confrontation and jealousy. The little flat in Calcutta had been a haven for us. We had relaxed in each other's company, laughed a lot together, and made love eagerly. How could he dare think I would look at another man?

'Adrian,' I said angrily, 'I have worked very hard to get us here and out of the dark tunnel we were in. Have you forgotten? I now need a little laughter and light in my life. Just stop this obsessive jealousy. Don't keep on digging up the past like some rotten skeleton that needs to be dangled in front of me from time to time.'

I was speaking loudly and panicked as he strode towards me. Aunt Eileen had left the room as our conversation had turned into a quarrel.

'What did I say to you about your jealousy and bad temper and the promises you made to me. I swear I'll leave you if you so much as touch me in anger.'

A sudden fear had risen within me. His right hand had been clenched as he came towards me. He turned away from me and went into the bedroom.

Adrian didn't join us for his evening meal. In the sitting room after Aunt Eileen and I had eaten she brought in coffee and biscuits.

'What's all this silly arguing about?' she eventually asked.

'He's impossibly jealous and thinks I'm going to jump into bed with every man that looks at me. He has a bad temper and he needs to curb it.'

'Oh dear,' she said sadly. 'I had no idea. He seems to be following in his father's footsteps. Adrian's father nearly destroyed his mother with his jealousy. She was so beautiful. She was almost a prisoner in her own home. He rarely ever let her go out of the house without him.'

'Well, he can forget that,' I said sharply. 'I'm much too strong willed to put up with bullying. I love Adrian. It took a long time for me to commit to him because of his temper. I wanted to be sure that when he said he loved me and would never harm me that he meant it. He shouldn't do this to me. "Lethal cocktail." What an expression. He is dazzled by the West and seems to want everything all at once.'

Aunt Eileen was distressed about the whole episode, especially as it was so soon after our arrival and so early in our marriage. Aunt Eileen rose and went to bed. I sat near the fire in the sitting room and turned my thoughts to the past. Many people had commented on his mother's beauty. Nobody had said anything about his father. It was almost midnight before I switched off the electric fire and went into the bedroom. Adrian was kneeling by the bed with his prayer book open, his lips were moving silently. I undressed and got into bed without speaking to him. He lifted his head. and looked at me.

'Oh, Jo! I was merely going to take you in my arms to calm you down. You were shouting.'

He was lying.

'If this continues, I will leave you,' I said, stressing the word will, 'as you are not fulfilling your promises to me. I'm not putting up with temper tantrums. Children have temper tantrums, not grown men. If you were going to put your arms around me then why was your fist clenched? Don't lie to me.

I turned my back on him in tears and slept fitfully throughout the night.

When I awoke next morning he had already left for the hospital. Aunt Eileen was still at home. She put the kettle on when she saw me in the kitchen.

'I need to speak to you,' she sighed. 'Adrian was so upset. Forgive his outburst. He says his colleagues at the hospital are better qualified and younger. He is having difficulty adjusting. Give him a little time. Try and understand.'

I looked at her and shook my head. 'I do love him very much, and he knows it, so why is he jealous and unable to control his temper?' I showed her my wrist and told her briefly what had happened between us in India.

'And you married him?' she said solemnly, shaking her head.

twenty-one | a strange legacy

And now it was time to visit the lawyer.

Vali came into the flat later in the morning as we were to visit the lawyer together. She was in good spirits, not so I.

'What's the matter, Jo darling?'

'Nothing, I just didn't sleep well,' I lied.

'You can't expect to sleep when you have the gorgeous Adrian beside you,' she teased. I wasn't in the mood for her banter.

We managed to get a taxi to the lawyer's office and were seen shortly after we arrived. Jonathan came into the reception area and ushered us into his room where a tray of coffee and biscuits was waiting. He chatted informally to put us at ease and then produced a large manila envelope from which he removed several papers. He said he would deal with our legal affairs separately although they were linked by Vali's mother's will.

He then read Aunt Ruth's will which was straightforward, and handed a list of bonds and shares to Vali, which was her inheritance, together with a statement of a large sum of money which she could have credited to her account. She was delighted at first, but when Jonathan pointed out she would have only the interest of the bonds and shares until her twenty-fifth birthday, she showed a great deal of displeasure, pushing her chair back and rudely saying to Jonathan, 'We'll leave now. What a waste of time, just credit my account and send me the papers.' She then turned to me saying, 'Come on, Jo, let's go for lunch and drinkies.'

'You can go now if you like, Valerie. I have further business with Josephine,' Jonathan said firmly.

She sat down again, pouting like a child.

'Well then,' Jonathan said kindly, smiling at me, 'you have been left a large plot of land in Perthshire. I don't know the exact area at the present time. All this will be gone into at a later date. There's a lodge and a bungalow on it at present and planning permission has been granted for a house to be built. Apparently a large house once stood on the land. It was in a dilapidated condition and had to be demolished for safety reasons. I don't know the story behind the buying of this land as it was a fairly recent purchase. There are separate funds for the building of the house and refurbishment of the lodge and cottage. I'll be in touch with you about this later. I can, of course, make the necessary arrangements for you.'

Vali interrupted.

'What! Land and a house. I know you were close to Mum and Dad, but this should be mine. Ridiculous! There must be some mistake.' Jonathan held up his hand to silence her and continued, asking me for my account number as twenty thousand pounds had also been left to me and he was to arrange to have the money credited to my account.

I was amazed. All I could find to say to Jonathan was, 'Thank you. I will leave all these matters in your capable hands.'

Twenty thousand pounds was an enormous amount of money for me and I knew nothing about building houses. Jonathan paused, looked at both of us and said, 'Please be patient and listen.

'There's a strange request in regard to the building of this house, Josephine. You are to give help and accommodation to Vali should she ever need it. You are in a position of great trust here. This house cannot be sold after it's built. It's for your heirs after your demise. The bungalow and lodge are almost habitable. You should be able to move into either of them with minor alterations.'

Vali was getting increasingly agitated. 'Huh,' she exclaimed loudly, and turned to me saying, 'As if I need you to look after me. I can look after myself, and Dean will take care of me.' Vali was not prepared to listen any further. She jumped up out of her chair, pointed her finger at me and said, 'She was my mother, it's my money, all of it, and the house will also be mine. You build it if you want.' And with that she flounced out of the room and banged the door.

Jonathan, realising I was upset, ordered more coffee for me and he spoke at length, calmly explaining that the will was sound and that he would proceed with the arrangements in regard to the property on my behalf.

He then asked me about the relationship between Vali's family and mine and voiced his concern about Vali's behaviour. I told him not to worry unduly explaining that Vali had been a much-loved only child from a rich family and a trifle spoilt, and recounted one particular incident when her mother had given us sweets, a particularly delicious type difficult to obtain in India, and Vali had grabbed the few I had saying, 'they're mine, all mine,' and later had cried and hugged me realising her selfishness.

'It's just a shock to her, she's vulnerable just now and pretty nervous over her wedding arrangements,' I said trying to reassure him.

Just before I left he asked me to contact him after my twenty-fifth birthday as there were other important matters he had to discuss with me. He said he would contact Valerie. I thought it had to do with the current situation and just nodded.

I thanked him and decided to walk part of the way home and then take a bus. I was disappointed in Vali and her sudden change in attitude. Only a couple of days before she had appeared to be her old fun-loving self, and showing me the generous side of he nature, appreciating the difference in her wealth and my poor circumstances.

I wondered if she was dragging Dean to endless parties and could he curb her drinking habits or had his fascination for her blinded him?

I had tried to reassure Jonathan all was well with Vali, but who was there to help me calm my troubled spirit. Was there something wrong mentally with this beautiful girl, or was she spoilt and obsessed with the trappings of wealth? What need had she of a house in Scotland when her tastes were for the bright lights and the sophisticated lifestyle she had adopted in London.

Adrian was sitting in the lounge tapping his feet to some music on the radio when I got back to the flat and I went into the bedroom to lie down. My head was pounding with the stress of the events of the morning. I took my clothes off and lay down on top of the bed in my dressing gown. As I was dozing he came into the room, put the covers over me, took off his clothes and lay down beside me.

'You'll catch cold, sweetheart' he murmured.

'Don't touch me, Adrian.' I said. 'I love you, but sex doesn't solve everything. You promised to trust me. I can't live with your constant jealousy and bad temper. It's making me miserable.' I turned my back on him thinking he would leave me alone but instead he put his arms around me burying his face in my hair.

'Forgive me Jo, please. I do love you. Everything is so new for me. It makes me unsettled. Each time you leave the flat a strange sense of fear grips me. I panic, thinking you aren't coming back.'

I turned towards him. I really needed to understand this man whom I had married and loved so passionately.

'Please don't destroy my love for you,' I said as I lay in his arms wondering if he would be able to control his temper. How was I going to cope?

Late in the evening we were in the sitting room having coffee after our evening meal when there was a persistent ring at the doorbell. Aunt Eileen opened the door to Vali. She flounced into the room and bounced herself onto one of the chairs like a petulant child. She had a large carrier bag with her.

'It's Josephine I have business with. Anybody can listen,' she said, pointing her finger at me.

I hadn't had a chance to discuss Aunt Ruth's will with Adrian. I thought I would speak to him privately before letting Aunt Eileen know of my inheritance.

It was Aunt Eileen who spoke to Vali. 'What's happened to you, Vali dear? Why are you so upset? Where's Dean?' She didn't reply, instead she sat clutching the large bag in her arms for a few moments and then again childishly pointed at me saying, 'Josephine is not going to have any of my mother's money or my house.' She looked at me angrily and continued, 'You'll not get the land or the money. It's my inheritance, my house, give it back or else I'll tell everyone you influenced my mother unfairly when she was sick. It's all mine!'

I was not about to give in to Vali Finlayson's petulance and selfishness. Money and a home had legitimately been left to me, and I shook my head at her. I had only one word for her and this time it was a definite 'No.'

She threw the contents of the carrier bag onto the carpet. It was the dress she had bought for me to be her Matron of Honour. It had been reduced to shreds. 'I don't want you anywhere near me,' she said, bursting into tears.

I pitied her. She looked so tragic and vulnerable despite her outburst. Where was Dean? Why hadn't he taken charge of her affairs in a positive way? I had loved Vali like a sister. What was happening to her? Her manner was not normal and she had thrown my day into turmoil with her erratic behaviour.

Neither Aunt Eileen nor Adrian spoke. They didn't know what she was talking about. Vali got up and left the room slamming the front door in temper with Aunt Eileen in hot pursuit, and I assumed she would be taking Vali home.

I waited until Aunt Eileen returned and then explained, at length, the morning's events, Aunt Ruth's will and my strange inheritance.

Adrian was pleased about the money, immediately assuming he would take control, saying, 'It'll be a cushion for us. We mustn't dip into it. It could help in financing a research programme for me. That's my ultimate goal as you well know. As far as the house is concerned, it looks as if it will be a long haul. What was Vali's caterwauling about? Everything is legal surely?'

Aunt Eileen looked annoyed. 'Vali obviously feels the will is flawed. She spoke to me about it when I dropped her home. Could she be right? Why should you inherit part of her parents' money?'

I was annoyed with both Vali and Adrian. They were like vultures; hovering. The money and property had been left to me and not Vali, and certainly not Adrian. Furthermore, what right had Aunt Eileen interfering, and thus my voice in anger, taut and strident, was turned on her.

'I'm not prepared to discuss the reasons for my inheritance as you know nothing of my family and the close connection I had with Vali's family. The will is sound. Jonathan has already explained this to her and there is nothing more to be said. The actual money left to me is small in comparison to the real wealth Vali is inheriting. The house and land is another matter and too complicated to tell you about at this stage.'

I rose from my seat and walked towards the bedroom door, Adrian following me. He turned to his aunt saying, 'Not only is Vali unstable and showing signs of psychological problems, but she might possibly, and very sadly for her, become an alcoholic if she continues drinking unchecked. Please try and discourage her drinking habits. The telltale signs are there. Mark my words.'

Eileen was about to contradict his statement but, walking behind me, he entered the bedroom and closed the door without giving her a chance for unnecessary argument.

For the next two weeks I tried to contact Vali several times but she refused to speak to me, and where were the apologies this time? Dean made excuses for her saying his parents had arrived from America and Vali was frantically busy. 'She'll call you later,' he said.

The phone never rang.

twenty-two | fear, a vision and a wedding

June 1954

It was the first of June, Vali's wedding day.

Warm and bright with wisps of fresh air playing amongst the green leaves of summer, making them flutter gently, but soon they would turn to gold and darker autumn shades, and the wind would strengthen and then surely fly them off the trees like small kites, and dash them down to earth for humans to trample their beauty underfoot, leaving bare branches, like skeletal arms pleading for the sun to return, and spring to give them new life.

What of Vali's beauty when age robbed her? What of our life-long friendship that had crumbled so cruelly? And the reason? For greed? For money, or a strange aberration?

Aunt Eileen had tried to persuade me to attend the wedding as a guest. I declined, knowing the embarrassment it would cause.

There would be no place for me at Vali's table. I tried to imagine the scene, which I had been deprived of. Vali, beautiful Vali, the centre of attention, as all brides should be and Dean, stalwart, waiting at the altar to promise to love forever a beautiful and rich young woman of his choice, and it was I, who had unknowingly, put this prize before him. What more could he want? Had I offered him a tainted chalice filled with a bitter draught?

I dressed and decided to start looking for work, and as I left the flat I noticed clouds were gathering, almost like old grey-haired men standing in groups, bowed and whispering together.

My thoughts kept turning to Vali and Dean. They would be married by now. How would Dean cope with Vali's selfishness, her mood swings, her constant greed for money and worst of all her drink problem that he didn't seem to notice? Were the clouds gathering for him? A sense of unease was churning within me as I walked and took a wrong turning.

I was now in a small dark lane, having walked a considerable distance. The fear that started in the pit of my stomach was threatening to overwhelm me and wrap me in its invisible shroud. The day seemed to darken and in the lane the shadows were long and menacing.

I hurried, but there seemed to be no end to the lane and felt I was lost, and then I noticed a woman walking towards me slowly. I would ask her the way I thought. I kept observing her and as she came up to me, she had no face, only a hazy light shining where her face should have been. Terrified, I turned and ran back the way I had come, stopping only to take breath. I slowed my step as I left the lane behind me. Strangely, the day was not as dark as it had first appeared.

A nearby small cafeteria was full of noise and light and chattering people. I found an empty table, sat down and asked the waitress for tea and a bun.

The horror of my vision was back. The sadhu had said not to dwell on it, a strange mirage, borne of stress in difficult times, he had said it was nobody, and not a haunting from the spirit world. What was it then? I had asked him several times, but he had withdrawn from my questioning and made me sit and chant facing him in the lotus position adding to the herbs in his brass urn, the smoke of which while pleasant, seemed to life me out of myself, dizzy and weightless.

But I had come out of the dark tunnel today, and surely I should leave all dark thoughts behind me. It was then as I sat in the cafeteria waiting to be served amongst the chinking and clinking of

cups and saucers and the buzz of conversation, that I saw him. He was looking for a seat and my eyes met his and I indicated he could share with me. He came over slowly on his crutches, his trousers folded over one leg, where no limb now existed, and as he lifted his cup to his lips, with a trembling hand, I noticed his little finger and his ring finger were missing.

This then was the legacy of war which we, in India, had never thought about. As we sat silently facing each other, unable to communicate over the shrill laughter and the loud buzz of conversation, thoughts of the little beggar boy who had died in my arms came to me in a wave of sorrow, and I knew then I would also grieve for this unknown young man who had given so much for the chattering crowd around him, who hadn't even noticed him. Did they really care?

This was a different kind of poverty, a poverty of spirit and the ache for the lack of a whole body, brought on by selflessness and the results of serving King and Country. I had a crazy notion to stand him up straight beside me and shout to the tea drinkers. Look! This is what he did for you.

Instead, I merely smiled at him, rose from my seat and paid the bill, his and mine.

A day of sadness, searing my being, tormenting me.

I returned home, mentally and physically exhausted, and still I hadn't looked for employment. I made myself sandwiches and sat quietly in the sitting room, listening to music, ultimately going to bed quite early.

At least today I hadn't heard Adrian's voice carping on about *his* money, *his* house and *his* career and the dreaded subject of medical research. Much to his annoyance, I had pointed out to him that he should wait about five years to get established and that he still had a lot to learn, and then I had said foolishly, Junior Hospital doctors don't lead important research projects nor do they wear designer suits.' He had shrugged his shoulders and replied, 'You'd be surprised what money can buy.'

It must have been late when Aunt Eileen and Adrian returned from the wedding. They didn't wake me and were considerate enough not to mention Vali or the wedding in the days that followed.

twenty-three | life in london

July 1954

The dreary days now seemed endless for me. The confines of the small flat and Adrian becoming less enthusiastic about his post at the hospital were an added worry. I longed for space, and though it was summer it rained and I longed for the real warmth of the Indian sun.

I managed to get employment with a small firm of chartered accountants as a dogsbody to a rather uninteresting and disorganised woman.

Jonathan paid us a visit in regard to the building of the house, and with much hesitation I left the discussions to Adrian as he had insisted he was to take charge of our financial affairs. At one point Jonathan corrected Adrian irritably as Adrian continuously referred to the property development as *his* house and the money as *his* money. Jonathan pointed out succinctly that he had no call on the money or the property as both were willed to me solely.

I had started to feel very unwell and had little enthusiasm for the project. Aunt Eileen said she would like to rent the bungalow that came with the land. She was getting older now and was looking on us as her family. She was keen to retire and move out of London. Living in a bungalow in close proximity to the house we were to build was an attractive proposition for her.

At this point my health took a downward turn. Each morning I dragged myself to work with little enthusiasm, even though it was summer and the sun shone with warmer days and Adrian looked drawn and tired. We lacked privacy and I was lethargic and often sick. I thought the food didn't suit me. I bought fruit for my lunch each day which for me was an expensive indulgence. I longed for the lush and juicy tropical fruit so easily available to me in India.

The woman I worked for, Margaret Reid, was not a clever accountant like Craig, and I was bored with her ineptitude. My energy was at a low so there was no incentive to get myself another post. Apart from the boredom of the work, the pay was poor. I managed to pay Aunt Eileen her rent adding to the shortfall from the money Jonathan had put into my account. Adrian didn't have a car and his walk from the bus stop to the hospital was long and tedious. I felt sorry for him. This was the man who had driven for most of his adult life.

We badly needed transport. One Friday evening, after our meal together, I suggested Adrian apply for a driving licence. At first he was reluctant to agree and said irritably, 'to drive what?' but Aunt Eileen thought it was not only a good idea, but essential for our well being, if nothing else. We were 'legging it' as she called it, too far and too often.

'I'll let you have the money for the car. I'll give the garage a cheque,' I said quite innocently to Adrian.

He didn't speak for a few moments and then replied angrily, 'Do you want my colleagues to think I'm under "petticoat rule"? That money you inherited should by rights be in my account and I could then write a cheque for what I require. I'm your husband, not some sort of gigolo getting money doled out to him at your whim.'

I refused to argue and let the matter drop. I was at no time going to let Adrian have control of our entire finances. I knew I couldn't trust him to use money wisely. He had made no attempt to pay his aunt for our board and keep. It was I who paid Aunt Eileen each month. Adrian could never account for what he did

with his money and was testy when I suggested he give me a monthly allowance from his wages. I had noticed, however, that he indulged himself in expensive and well-made clothes.

It was the weekend but Adrian said he was on duty. Aunt Eileen and I took a walk in the park after lunch on Sunday and then returned home and sat drinking coffee in the sitting room and chatting.

'How big is Perthshire?' I asked. 'You see, a friend of mine who used to be my employer, Craig Mackie, is a Scotsman and when I worked for him he constantly mentioned he lived in beautiful Perthshire. I know he must be home from India by now as when he saw us off at the airport he had only a few months left to complete his contract in India. I have his address and telephone number somewhere among the papers he gave me. Perthshire is stated as the address of the land I've inherited.'

'Oh my, your geography is poor, Jo. Scotland is small compared to India and the land might be motoring distance from your friend. Find the correct address of the land and we'll look up the map of Scotland I have somewhere.'

I just nodded.

I relaxed by the fire with her and she spoke of Assam and her marriage and what a good and kind man her husband had been. She had lived a fairly stress-free life with little argument between them. She did say, however, that she regretted not having any children.

Eileen stopped speaking and looked at me with concern saying, 'You are right not to let Adrian gain control of your money. From the little I've heard and seen of him I don't think he has any idea of the financial world. I noticed he was confused as far as accounts were concerned when you spoke with the lawyer.'

I agreed with her saying, 'Even if I wanted to let him have control, the lawyer won't agree. As far as the house is concerned, once built it can't be sold. It's to be for my use as well as for Vali's, should she ever require a roof over her head. Ultimately, it's to go to my heirs. Trust me. I will always look after Vali.'

'I'm pleased,' she said changing the subject. 'You've been sick a lot recently. Do you think you might be pregnant?'

'I don't know, it's possible. I would need to be checked. Don't mention it to Adrian, though.'

It was late September before Adrian passed his driving test. One of his colleagues Ian Ross seemed to know quite a lot about second-hand cars and Adrian took his advice and bought a second hand Ford from his own funds.

'The old Fordie will go forever Adrian,' Ian had advised him.

At last we were mobile again. Adrian was able to drop me off at work each morning. I had been to the doctor who had referred me to a clinic and I had confirmation of my pregnancy. I was elated by the news. The baby was to be born sometime at the end of March or early April. Another human being within me was amazing to me and I had a strange desire to keep my secret forever. Each morning when I woke I murmured softly, 'Hello bump, try not to make me sick today.'

And then, of course, I told Adrian and Aunt Eileen, both of whom were delighted.

Now followed a short time of halcyon days for me and I hoped our marriage could sail into calmer waters.

Adrian often smiled saying, 'Oh! Sweetheart, what a funny shape I've made you. He was in such good humour over the baby it amazed me.

Dean had written to us to say that Vali also was expecting a baby in April. Our children would grow up approximately the same age. She had phoned Aunt Eileen several times.

And then came the cold weather with a vengeance and Christmas arrived, with all the fuss and decorations, the pot-bellied old Santas, bells and carols, tinsel and sweets and sights we had never witnessed in India. I bought Aunt Eileen a slim gold necklace and

Adrian a ring, large and square with his initials on it which suited his hand. Aunt Eileen cooked and we spent a peaceful afternoon together.

twenty-four | jo and frances

April 1955

Just before my baby was born Vali wrote me a letter wishing me well. She said she was coming to England for her confinement. 'I don't want an American baby,' she had written, which seemed a strange comment. She asked me to see that her flat was cleaned and aired for her. She ended her letter by saying 'Jo, stop being angry with me and forgive me. You know I behave stupidly sometimes. I do love you'

I replied saying we were all looking forward to seeing her. I didn't enthuse as I was now wary of her dramatic mood swings. This was a different woman to the happy girl I had known. I would have to tread cautiously in my dealings with her.

March was windy, clear and cold but the sun gladdened our hearts. Swathes of early daffodils amazed Adrian. He had not seen a daffodil or a tulip growing in a garden. 'If we ever get the house completed, Jo, we must have some of these,' he commented frequently.

Aunt Eileen had helped me buy baby clothes and re-arranged the furniture in the bedroom we used to house a small cot. The date the hospital had given me was the end of March or the first week in April, and on the twenty-fifth night of March 1955, I went into labour. Adrian drove me into the hospital and took control, calming my fears, mopping my forehead, and soothing me. It was a difficult birth and I knew I was losing a lot of blood. I sensed an anxiety in those attending to me, and suddenly the voices around

me seemed to be coming from a distance and I couldn't make out what they were saying. Someone was giving me an injection into the vein in my arm, but all at once I was sinking into a strange open place devoid of anything, a large hollow drum, but there to my surprise the sadhu was seated on a rush mat, a great deal of ash on his body, almost a totally white figure, praying and chanting softly, his palms touching in an act of intercession to his gods. Where was his urn of burning coals and fragrant herbs? Only disinfectant and the smell of death surrounded me as line after line of women walked past him one at a time, clothed in white, their heads bowed, carrying small dead children in shrouds adorned with the flower of both death and celebration, the marigold. I waited to see if I was to be in the rows of passing dead, looking closely, trying to pick out the faces of the women, but I couldn't find myself. And still I watched, starting to float towards them, a strange force pulling me silently and endlessly towards the rows of white clad-figures.

Then a voice seemed to boom from the hollow I was in, calling out to me from a distance, unclear but real. I had to somehow move from this dreadful place so I forced my eyes open with great difficulty only to see with such joy Adrian by my bed, red-eyed, his face tear-stained, and now I heard him distinctly, repeating over and over again like a chant, ' Open your eyes, Jo, for God's sake open your eyes.' And then I passed my free hand over my body slowly and realised I had given birth.

'Adrian, where is our baby? I want my baby.' I whispered anxiously. I noticed Aunt Eileen was also in the room. She came towards my bed and held my hand. 'Shush, shush, Jo,' she said. You have had a difficult time. The baby is big, over eight pounds but unfortunately she is not taking her bottle. We are waiting for the consultant to come and see her.'

As weak as I was I tried to sit up. 'Her,' I said, 'I've had a girl. What bottle? I want my baby.'

I sensed all was not well and started to panic and sob and cry, insisting they brought my baby to me. The nurse not wanting to upset me further in my weakened state went out of the room and came back with a tiny bundle in her arms. I stretched out my arm to her and she put the child beside me gently. Aunt Eileen was crying.

'Don't upset yourself, Jo,' she said through her tears. 'The baby is too weak to suck Cuddle her and give her back, child.' She obviously thought my baby would not survive.

With trembling hands I put her to my breast. She whimpered a little and having found my breast started sucking slowly. As she sucked my milk started to flow. Adrian helped me to lift her on to my shoulder to burp her. She took more milk from my breast before falling off to sleep on me. I cried with joy. This was the child who was within me. She must live. She was warm and had a special smell all of her own. I felt I could hold her against me forever. The sadhu had said I would be given children. Surely his gods would not take this one away from me. Surely we would both live. I had not joined the line of the dead infants.

I asked Aunt Eileen to bring me the old-fashioned Indian drink for increasing milk flow. Well-cooked sago, warm milk and honey. She brought in a large flask of it for me each day. She knew exactly what I wanted because she had heard of it herself.

I was home within a week, tearful, weak but joyful. There was such tenderness within Adrian for his baby. How was it that he also had violence within him? Why was it that I couldn't understand his moods? Why did he get strange ideas into his head? He was stubborn and lacking in creature common sense. Yet, I loved this man. He sat with me a long time the day we took the baby home. He stroked her gently, his large hand covering her head.

'I can't believe we're so lucky. She's ours, Jo,' he said emotionally time and again. I laughed saying, 'Of course she's ours and

she's very special to me. I'll never part with her.' It was a time of great harmony between us. Would that it could always be like this, loving and free from argument and anger.

Aunt Eileen started worrying that we would never stop calling our child, baby. It was after dinner when she broached the subject.

'Josephine and Adrian, what is this about? Nice baby; pretty baby; good baby; my baby. Is she to be called baby until she is twenty-one and chooses a name for herself?' she said jokingly.

I looked at both Adrian and Aunt Eileen and laughed. 'She has a name, Aunt Eileen. Her name's Frances. It was decided a long time ago. I hope the gentle spirit of her grandmother will live within her.'

It was Adrian who spoke emotionally. 'Darling, thank you for your love and bearing my child. Beautiful and elegant Frances, just like my mother.' When he was out of earshot Aunt Eileen said dryly, 'I only hope she doesn't have a similar cruel fate in life.'

We heard nothing from Vali about the birth of her baby. We eventually had a letter from Dean saying Vali had delayed arrangement for her flight to London to such an extent the airline had refused to take her on the plane in an advanced state of pregnancy. She had her baby in Boston much to the delight of his parents. He sent us photographs and she was to be named Vali-Jo. I was, however, disturbed with the rest of his letter which said that Vali was ill after the birth of the baby and that his mother was looking after the little one until Vali recovered.

I sent a congratulatory card as did Aunt Eileen, and still we heard nothing from Vali, all we had were photographs of the little girl and a few hastily written lines on postcards from Dean, saying they were progressing.

twenty-five | a house yet to be built

Summer 1955

The lack of positive action in regard to the building of the house was a source of worry. Jonathan had sent us drawings and even to the untutored eye, Adrian and I found them wholly unsuitable. Jonathan had not been able to get a builder to take on the project. Frances was three months old and still there was no progress. I had spoken to him several times. His answer had been the same.

'Don't worry, Josephine. These things take time.' I was not convinced.

On a morning when Frances had been particularly fractious and I was feeling cooped up and lacking space, I took matters into my own hands, after hours of careful thought, and phoned Jonathan to inform him I had decided to put the building of the house into the hands of a Scottish agent. He seemed annoyed at first but eventually agreed, pointing out that he had control of the expenditure and was to be advised of the arrangements I was making, step by step. I asked him for the papers he had in his possession.

Adrian was horrified.

'That's put the lid on it, Jo. What are we going to do now? I suggest you take a course in bricklaying and get yourself up to Scotland. Maybe Frances could help. Get her a tin hat.'

Aunt Eileen's comments were less flippant. 'You're quite right, Josephine. Apart from unsuitable drawings and dodgy paperwork, nothing's been done.'

Craig Mackie was now constantly in my mind. Before leaving India he had always said I could contact him if I was in difficulty. He had stapled a card with his name and address in Perthshire in a folder he had given me. Surely he could help me now? Perhaps he would be able to advise me. When I broached the subject with Adrian he shook his head and commented. 'I won't have anything more to do with this. Be it on your head. I am busy enough with my own work and I certainly have no idea how to build a house!'

I hadn't seen Craig Mackie nor had I communicated with him since the day he drove us to Dum Dum airport. After several telephone calls I eventually managed to speak to Craig at his house late in the evening.

'What's up?' was his comment at hearing my voice.

He explained he had been busy setting up a chartered accountant's business of his own. I heard his story and then told him mine. He was pleased to hear of my inheritance but shocked that nothing constructive had been done for over a year regarding the building of a house for us.

'Bloody hell,' I can't imagine you letting things get so out of control. Have you gone soft or something? What's up with you?'

He agreed to come to London within the next few weeks for preliminary discussions and I offered to pay him consultation fees, his train fare and put him up for a week in Vali's flat.

'By the way, I have a baby,' I said during the course of our conversation.

There was dead silence for a moment, so much so that I thought we'd been disconnected.

'The young of the human race has never particularly attracted me.' He paused, disregarding the subject and gave me the train timings.

Adrian collected Craig at the station early in the morning and took him to Vali's flat. I dressed particularly carefully and put up my hair neatly as I didn't want to make a poor impression on Craig. Aunt Eileen had the day off and had agreed to look after Frances for me. I had, with me, all the papers Jonathan had sent and managed to meet him by late morning. He seemed pleased to see me and had made coffee and sandwiches. Just like old times, I thought.

In his usual bluff but efficient way, Craig took control. After two days of meetings with Jonathan he came to dinner. Aunt Eileen cooking a delicious meal as usual, and later in the evening, and much to my surprise, he handed me a cheque for seven thousand Pounds which was the interested that had accrued on the money Jonathan was holding on my behalf. He also had with him a large package of tastefully selected clothes for Frances.

Before he left he stood quietly near the cot where Frances was asleep, looking at her with a smile on his face. 'Nice baby,' he whispered as we left the room.

At the end of the week, Craig, Jonathan and I had a final meeting regarding the building of the house and Craig offered us some advice on our circumstances advising us that Adrian could work in Scotland saying, 'We are not entirely in the sticks. We do have hospitals in Scotland and damn good ones at that. I think you really must come up to Scotland and see this land and then make up your minds about letting the house when it's built. The generous funds available will give you a very attractive property. What a shame it would be if you didn't live in it and enjoy it yourselves. Think about it. It's worth a go.'

Adrian took him to the station the following morning, and I was confident that now in his capable hands we had nothing to fear and the building of the house would progress well.

Craig Mackie, as promised, moved quickly in regard to the property in Perthshire. He sent us two plans for the house asking us to

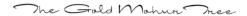

select one. He was insistent that we see the land before choosing. Craig had decided to have the small bungalow already on the land and the Lodge, refurbished.

Aunt Eileen now confirmed she would like to live in the bungalow while we had use of her flat. She had now made up her mind she definitely wished to move out of London. She moved in the late spring of 1956 and Craig helped her settle in, giving us the full use of the London flat and some much-needed privacy.

Adrian, on the insistence of Craig, took a week off work and visited Perthshire. He travelled by train and enjoyed the views of the open countryside. He stayed with Aunt Eileen.

I was left with one-year-old Frances to entertain me. It was the first time we had been parted since our marriage and despite arguments over money I missed him terribly. I promised myself I would try harder to please him and bond with him. How was I to control his temper tantrums which were mainly triggered off by his frustration at work? Now that Aunt Eileen was in Perth there would be little constraint on his behaviour. On one occasion he lost his temper when I had no answer for the solution to 'his problems and smashed his fist against the wall, grazing his knuckles.

A crazy but worrying thought stayed in my mind after he left for Perth. Would I be the wall next time?

Adrian returned to London early on Saturday morning having taken the overnight sleeper. I was still in bed. Frances, unwashed, started bouncing about in her cot when she saw him come into the bedroom.

'Oh, you're whiffy, Frances,' he laughed, picking her up out of her cot. He washed and changed her until I showered and dressed. I made breakfast and then there was no stopping Adrian in his enthusiasm.

'Craig has an attractive house opposite the South Inch. A large area in front of the house goes down to the river. An attractive bridge close by glinted in the sunshine making the whole scene suitable for a picture postcard. It was so clean and fresh. The pure air made you want to gulp it in. Our house will be bigger than Craig's. The plot is near Bridge of Earn which is not far from Craig's house. He had some beautiful flowers coming out in the garden. You know the ones, Jo. What are they called?'

'You mean tulips and daffodils, don't you, darling?' I answered.

'Yes, yes, he said. 'We definitely must have some of those in our garden. Craig thought the house would be ready for us to move into during the following summer or autumn, but there's nothing to stop you moving into the Lodge until the house is habitable.'

Craig now phoned often always insisting that I should visit Scotland and see the land I had inherited. He was a proud Scot and said to me on one occasion, 'It is a great honour to own such a piece of land in Scotland.'

Adrian wasn't able to get a further week off work until mid-July and we scheduled our visit accordingly, but by June 56 I was three months pregnant and hadn't told Adrian.

It was a warm Sunday afternoon and I had made curry for lunch but all of a sudden the smell of it made me rush and be sick. I laid down beside Frances for a rest and Adrian who had been reading books on Scotland, loaned to him by Craig, decided to make some cool lemon tea. He then continued reading in silence while I dozed.

'Sweetheart,' he said softly.

I wondered what was coming next.

'On Craig's recommendation I've started applying for posts in Scotland. I really think we should live there. I know this is a bit of a shock for you. You will agree to live there, won't you?'

'Adrian, I'm sure I'll cope. Here's a shock for you though, I'm pregnant.'

The joking went out of our conversation. He put his book down and came over to me.

'I've always wanted more children but don't you think it's too soon after the difficult time you had? Are you sure you're well enough to bear another child?' he said anxiously.

'I'll be fine, I hope you're not going to worry continually,' I said putting my arms around him.

'When are you due?' he asked.

'Some time after Christmas. Frances should be toddling by then, so it won't be so difficult.'

He picked up Frances and put her in her pram. 'I'll take her for a walk. You have a rest,' he said.

Adrian was given an interview for a hospital post in Perth. He was taking the idea of living in Scotland very seriously. I phoned Aunt Eileen to see if she could accommodate us for a few days in July. While he was not hopeful of obtaining the post, as there was a strong local candidate, he thought he should attend the interview to get himself known. He was also to be interviewed for an opening in a GP Practice.

Aunt Eileen was pleased I was eventually going to visit Scotland. The journey was long and tedious and Frances was fractious by the time we arrived and an enthusiastic Craig met us at the station, ready to show us his neck of the woods.

We were immediately aware of the cooler air as it was evening before we arrived at Aunt Eileen's bungalow. She had prepared a hot meal for us, Frances enjoying mashed potatoes and gravy and some pureed stewed fruit. Though Aunt Eileen had never had any children of her own she seemed to know instinctively what to give Frances.

I awoke early next morning to make the most of the day. I looked around the tastefully furnished bungalow before anyone was awake. I walked slowly round the grounds, coming upon mounds of rubble and large stones of various hues left abandoned from the demolition of what must have once been an imposing building. I wondered if some of the larger stones could be blended into the new house. Pieces of granite formed an arch lying on its side.

Who had abandoned such a place? Had they all perished, taken by some unknown dreadful disease? Were they murdered? Had the family died off with no heirs? The mystery remained unanswered. I would like to find out who had owned this land previously as I had often wondered why Aunt Ruth had bought it and willed it to me. She had left no letter of explanation for me.

As I walked back to the bungalow fanciful notions of children laughing and carriages arriving full of guests and friends filled my thoughts. How pleasant a thought. The darker side too came to mind. Had a recluse lived here and had he died alone, and been found years later, his body petrified and swathed in cobwebs? No. I had to put such thoughts away, but real people had loved, laughed, quarrelled and died here. How was it that an obviously once imposing building had become abandoned and derelict, and for a moment I felt as if I was not alone and was being welcomed by the spirits of the past, as I walked on this land, now mine. Were they willing me on to rebuild their long-lost heritage and why had it become mine?

I returned to the bungalow only to find Aunt Eileen had already given Frances her breakfast. As she saw me she said, 'Good heavens child, you'll be frozen. Come and have a hot drink and something to eat.'

Craig collected Adrian to take him for his interviews for the two medical posts. Later Aunt Eileen and I lunched together at the bungalow while Frances took a nap. The conversation turned to Vali. It was a mistake.

'Well, my dear,' she sighed, 'Vali will be coming to England shortly, I had a rather scribbled note from her saying you're both to see that stupid lawyer Jonathan again.

You know I'm fond of both of you but please speak to me honestly. Is there any truth in the assertion Vali makes constantly

that you have in some way influenced Jonathan to have a substantial portion of her funds put into your name? She insists this
is the case. I'm not accusing you. It's what Vali says. Has Jonathan
made a mistake? Lawyers do make errors. If you're even vaguely
aware of such a slip-up, give Vali back her money Josephine. It's
not right.'

I was furious with Aunt Eileen for raising the subject of my
inheritance yet again and even considering believing Vali.

I spoke sternly. 'This type of foolish and inaccurate statement
is ridiculous. It's slanderous. How could a lawyer of good repute
like Jonathan do such a thing? It's all nonsense. Vali has a large
inheritance and a substantial income. Vali's mother, who I knew
and loved as a small child, left me this land and the money to build
a house on it. I've taken nothing from Vali. Aunt Eileen, I've grown
up with Vali and I know her better than you do. She can be a very
selfish and greedy girl and at other times absurdly generous. The
will is sound, so please don't insist on raising this subject with me
again and again.'

She didn't seem to believe me. Why was she taking Vali's word
against mine when such an accusation could not possibly be true?

Later that day we decided to have another look at the land
left to me.

We tucked Frances snugly into her pram and were able to take
a slow walk with her. I couldn't believe the extent of the land left
to me by Aunt Ruth. We arrived at the Lodge where the workmen
were completing the inside plaster work. The overall condition of
the Lodge had not been as good as the bungalow and a considerable amount of money had been spent to bring it up to stand-
ard. Jonathan had, however, agreed the expenditure as we were
well within budget, and with the exception of the land around the
Lodge which needed to be cleared and planted, possibly with some
of 'those flowers' to please Adrian, the work was almost complete.

While we were looking at the Lodge a workman came out and spoke to Aunt Eileen.

'Excuse me Mrs,' he said, 'you *shouldnae* be on these premises. Visitors are *no'* allowed. The Finlaysons would *no'* like people on their land. This is private property.'

Aunt Eileen pointed out that she was living in the bungalow.

He nodded and as we were about to leave he spoke enthusiastically. 'Don't you think it's wonderful that the Finlaysons will be back in Perthshire?'

'What's he talking about?' I asked.

'Blethers.' She laughed.

Aunt Eileen suggested that we move to Scotland and live in the Lodge until the main building was finished. It was within walking distance from the bungalow and we would be company for her without crowding her out. I only hoped Adrian would not continue to be bad-tempered with her as, together with Vali's nonsense which I was sure she still believed, it was bound to cause a rift in our relationship.

Posts and temporary wire fencing surrounded the area of land which now belonged to me. In due course a more substantial fence was to be erected. The Lodge had two spacious bedrooms and a large sitting room and a kitchen with a dining area. Yes, it would be more than adequate for us but I was not going to contemplate a move until Adrian found employment in Perthshire.

Just as importantly, how could we bear the sight of someone else enjoying a large new house and open spaces that had been willed to me, perhaps foolishly, by Vali's mother? If the house was to be let, then I didn't want to know about it. I would treat it as an investment and try to obtain a property close to the hospital in London.

Craig and Adrian came home late in the afternoon. We had tea and Craig talked about nothing else but the house and how things

were progressing. I walked him to the door as Adrian was busy entertaining Frances.

We said our goodbyes and I asked him to let me have an account for settlement of his fees. He turned to me at the door and said, 'I hope that's only weight you're carrying, Josephine.'

Craig had guessed I was pregnant so we had to tell Aunt Eileen.

Even though they were born of concern, her reactions surprised me.

'This is just nonsense,' she said irritably. 'It's far too soon for good health. One doesn't have to keep on producing children nowadays. There are ways of preventing multiple pregnancies and considering you're married to a doctor, he should know better. Your life could be at risk here. You do know you had a very difficult birth with Frances.'

I didn't answer her, but Adrian spoke to her gently, reassuring her and saying we did want another child.

'Aunt Eileen, its God's will,' he said.

'If it's God's will, Adrian, you certainly have given him a jolly good helping hand,' she replied tersely. It now seemed they were never to agree on anything, even if it didn't concern her.

She dropped us at the station the next morning. Adrian was particularly silent on our return journey. He had not been given either of the posts at the interview.

As the days passed in the small London flat he became increasingly despondent. I was carrying my second child very clumsily and my size seemed to irritate him. He continually arrived home late and had no explanation for his behaviour. One afternoon it was just past lunch-time when he came in. He was in a hurry and very excited.

'I'm invited to a seminar and reading weekend. I'll have to leave now. You'll be fine here. The flats in this building are secure,' he said.

He started packing feverishly. Before I could argue or object he kissed Frances and was gone. I found his departure strange. A sudden seminar? Surely it took time to organise such events. How was it he hadn't known about it beforehand? I phoned Aunt Eileen as I was anxious at being left alone in London, pregnant and with a small child to look after. I had neither friend nor relation near at hand.

'Where is that great know-it-all doctor then,' she asked sarcastically.

'He packed a case and went off to a weekend seminar in quite a rush,' I explained. 'He's to be away until Monday.'

'What do you mean all of a sudden? Nobody decides to have a seminar all of a sudden. He shouldn't be leaving you on your own,' she said with concern in her voice.

Adrian returned on Monday afternoon. He seemed self-satisfied. He picked up Frances and kissed and cuddled her.

'Was the seminar rewarding, Adrian?' I asked.

'Rewarding, phew! Yes, new faces, new ideas, happy intelligent people. It was very good. I feel refreshed.'

For the next few weeks he always left early for work returning late and telling me he had been given extra duties. He never mentioned research again during that time which surprised me. On a few occasions he didn't return home at night and phoned to say he had overnight duties as there were many emergencies coming in.

It was two o'clock on a Wednesday afternoon when the phone rang. Frances was taking her usual afternoon nap and I had been resting. A pretty light voice with a cheeky giggle in it said, 'Is Ad there?'

'You have the wrong number, I'm sorry,' I replied.

I put the phone down, but it rang again persistently. There seemed to be laughter in the background.

'Is Adrian there?' the same voice said. She never waited for a reply from me but continued, giggling and speaking quickly and

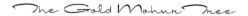

excitedly, 'Tell him he's left some of his clothes in my flat. What a sexy guy. Sorry, I shouldn't speak like this to an elderly aunt. It must be a burden for you looking after a small child after his wife died in childbirth in India. Poor chap. I've promised faithfully to look after his babe. Poor darling. I must...'

I was astonished but quick to interrupt her prattle.

'Just a moment,' I said firmly. I'm not an aunt and not a dead wife, and if this is some sort of bloody silly joke it's far from amusing. You have the wrong number surely. I'm Josephine Greene, Adrian Greene's wife'

There was a pause, total silence.

'The lying bastard,' she screamed down the phone. The line went dead.

Was this some silly dare or joke by young medical students or junior house officers who would have our telephone number for emergencies? The girl had a giggle in her voice which gave me only a glimmer of hope that it was a stupid sick joke, but in my heart I knew he had cheated on me. The signs were there. The continuous early mornings, staying out at night saying he was on duty, night after night. All night – what? Surely no hospital ran that way.

The choice was mine. I could have a hysterical outburst and challenge him or pack up and leave and go to Perthshire and live alone in the lodge. No. I would do neither of these things. I would have to ignore it and sadly bear the pain. A small part of my spirit died within me that day. I could no longer trust his love. There would ultimately be some sort of confrontation between Adrian and the girl concerned. I would play a waiting game. How was he going to handle his misdemeanour? After all I wasn't a dog to roll over and play dead. Dead indeed. I wanted to cry, scream and hit out but I had a small child to look after and I had the responsibility of carrying his second child.

He came home as usual and behaved as if nothing had happened to him. After a few days he asked, 'Do you get any calls from the hospital for me? I have asked the switchboard not to ring the house unless it's very important. I don't want you disturbed, especially in the afternoons when you're resting. Have you had any recent calls?' he repeated. 'No, darling, but I often get wrong numbers and sometimes calls for Aunt Eileen. I give the genuine callers the Perthshire number,' I too could lie.

I never mentioned the giggling girl on the phone, but his moods and temperament darkened towards me. He was highly irritable and seemed to have little time for Frances now and stopped taking her out for walks.

twenty-six | a frail vali and my identity

Autumn 1956

Autumn was upon us and my concern at not hearing from Vali was growing. The few short sketchy letters from Dean saying Vali-Jo was being looked after by his mother perturbed me. Why couldn't Vali look after her own child? Jonathan had persistently reminded me by letter that it was important that I see him soon after my twenty-fifth birthday. He had written the same letter to Vali. We were now both over twenty-five.

Her flat had been aired and cleaned and a pretty cot bought for Vali-Jo. The room had been fitted out with little girl toys and furnished prettily by me. I phoned Jonathan asking if it would be possible for there to be a deputy for Vali but he refused. I did, however, insist I have an adviser present at the meeting, remembering Vali's last outburst.

Eventually Dean wrote to say they would be arriving in London on the fifteenth of October, late in the afternoon, and planned to spend a short while in London before returning to America. He asked if I could arrange a nanny for Vali-Jo on a temporary basis.

This proved difficult for such a short period but I managed eventually to obtain the services of a very pleasant woman who had recently retired. On Dean's insistence a cook/ housekeeper was also arranged. 'All in that one small flat – ridiculous,' Adrian had commented very sensibly.

Even with all our differences I was looking forward to Vali's arrival, hoping she had recovered from her strange nervousness and that Dean had persuaded her to stop drinking in excess, especially now that she had a child to love and care for, so a meeting was arranged with Jonathan, and Craig had agreed to attend on my behalf.

'What's all this about and why are you so uneasy?' he asked.

'I don't know,' I had replied, 'but maybe it's because I'm pregnant and feeling unsure of myself.' It was not the whole story; for some reason I had a strange sense of foreboding.

Adrian collected Dean, Vali, and Vali-Jo from the airport. I arranged to meet them at Vali's flat. I had laid on sandwiches and hot drinks for them. Frances was with me and I wondered how the little girls would react to each other. They arrived at the flat with Dean carrying the luggage and Adrian carrying Vali-Jo. She was a beautiful child and had inherited her parents' good looks. I was amazed at Vali. She was quiet and just put her arms around me and said, 'Hello Jo, pleased to see you.' There was none of the usual exuberance about her. She took Vali-Jo from Adrian, giving Adrian and Dean some time to speak to each other while they had coffee and sandwiches.

'Is there a cot for her?' she asked.

I took Vali into the room I had arranged with such loving care. Unlike the girl I knew she didn't even bother to offer a word of thanks. She put the child in the cot roughly saying, 'Now just you stay there.' There was no kiss or cuddle for her from Vali.

I was now to become the observer of a nightmare. The child didn't seem to know her mother.

'Where's the staff I asked for,' she said speaking to me in a high-pitched voice. 'I'm not here to wash and scrub. Jo, and first of all I need a proper drink, not endless coffee and sandwiches.'

'Vali, dear, I have arranged a nanny and a housekeeper for you,' I said quietly and ignored her request for a drink. I thought it might have been the journey that had made her bad-tempered and continued by saying, 'they'll both be here tomorrow morning for you. By the way, our appointment with the lawyer is the day after tomorrow.'

I tried to speak reassuringly and kindly; she seemed unhappy and under so much stress for some reason. Again in my mind I excused her behaviour.

Dean in the meantime was trying to hold a conversation with Frances. He was smiling as she prattled on in her own language. He was down on his haunches beside her. She was pointing to herself and trying to tell him her name.

'Yes, honey,' he said laughing, 'I know you're Frances.'

We took an awkward leave of Dean and Vali. Adrian was upset at the manner in which Vali had handled her child. We drove home in silence. I put Frances to bed after a warm drink and a goodnight kiss and cuddle. Adrian made a hot drink and brought it through to the bedroom. He propped up my pillows for me. His behaviour was almost like an apology. It was quite a while since he had been tender with me. Vali's attitude had upset him. He had always been very caring towards children and had noticed more than I had real-ised.

'Shaking his head, he said sadly 'Vali Mitchell is not a well woman. Dean told me she had post-natal depression and was treated by doctors in America. She should have got over it by now but she's still not right, in a depressed state, difficult, and unable to cope with her child and now refuses medical help.

'Dean is extremely worried and asked me to try and per-suade her to see a psychiatrist. He's fearful of what she might do to Vali-Jo, as Vali openly dislikes her own child and it's his mother who has been looking after the little one. We'll have to be very patient until we can get her some help. Dean didn't say much, we didn't have time to speak at length but I can guess she's possibly still drinking, cleverly and secretly. He's banned from her bedroom. She literally barricades herself in at night and doesn't come out of her room to attend to Vali-Jo. She refuses to feed or change her. Dean is doing all he can.'

He was asleep before I could gather my thoughts to answer him.

He was caring about so many things and I prayed silently that his violent temper and stubbornness would not wreck our marriage and more importantly our lives.

I was almost sure he had had an affair and wondered how faithful he would be to me in the future as I was not the kind of woman who would put up with a philanderer.

So, where was the man who had wanted to join the priesthood and be celibate? Would he be unscrupulous when it came to strange unfulfilled ambitions?

And now it was the day of the meeting with the lawyer. It was up to Vali whether or not she appeared at the meeting. Craig arrived early at Jonathan's office and as we sat in the waiting room I had the opportunity to warn him about Vail's condition but he brushed my concerns aside.

'Stop fussing like an old biddy. Valerie Mitchell's a grown woman. She can look after herself. If we finish early we can go out for lunch and have a discussion about the building of the house. It's a long time since I had a good going argument with you. Goodness only knows why I'm stupid enough to want to take a pregnant woman out to lunch,' he smiled. 'The refurbishment of the Lodge is almost complete. What do you want to do about it? In my opinion it's time you moved to Scotland. Why do you want to live in a pokey flat in London?'

'Give me a month or two,' I replied. 'Let's see if Adrian is successful in obtaining a post in Perth.' He took out an envelope from

his briefcase saying, 'Give this envelope to your Adrian. He might be interested. It's an advertisement regarding a post in a GP practice. I know two of the doctors as we sometimes golf together. I'll put in a word if Adrian's interested. Now be sure and give it to him, Josephine.'

As we were speaking Vali appeared alone looking extremely attractive and fashionable as usual. She nodded to us and walked into Jonathan's room without being asked. We followed. Craig and I sat opposite Jonathan and Vali sat to one side near me.

He addressed Vali first saying he had papers for her signature which were straightforward. He passed over a slim folder to her showing the extent of her inheritance and informed her that as she was now twenty-five she was to gain control of the entire estate left to her by her father. This was obviously unexpected and I heard her sharp intake of breath. Jonathan then advised her she could leave the investments as they were, accruing a considerable amount of interest, reinvest, or spend as she wished. The choice was hers and he would act on her instructions. She looked at him for quite a few moments before saying quite sensibly and distinctly, 'Leave everything as it is, Jonathan. Change doesn't agree with me. My life was happy until I decided to change it.' She answered every question Jonathan asked with the words, 'Leave everything as it is. I want everything the same as before.'

Jonathan then asked her to sign papers to this effect and congratulated her on her good sense to leave the money invested. He didn't realise she was trying to go back in time. She kept getting increasingly agitated. I put my hand out to calm her as I had done when we were children. Strangely enough after the aggravation between us, she clutched at my hand and interrupted the proceedings by saying, 'Look after me. I don't feel very well just now.'

I had to hold back tears. Poor Vali. She now realised all was not well with her health.

Craig rose from his chair and left the room. He nodded to me on his way out now knowing something was amiss and fearing the worst during this meeting. I apologised to Jonathan for the interruption.

I held Vali's hand as I had done when we were children saying to her reassuringly, 'I'm here for you. I'll do all I can to see you're well looked after.'

It was becoming clear to me that Aunt Ruth in willing me property and money had put a veritable noose around my neck in the form of Valerie Finlayson, now, unhappily for me, Valerie Mitchell.

Craig came back into the room and Jonathan restarted the meeting. He tried to put Vali at ease.

'Valerie, don't worry so much. All your monetary affairs are in good shape. You can speak to me about your investments at any time. Now, what I'm about to say to Josephine has nothing whatsoever to do with your Estate. It is neither your money, your mother's money nor your father's money. I hope you can understand what I am saying to you. You can leave now if you wish'

She nodded her head saying 'I'll stay and see what you have to say to Jo.'

Jonathan then addressed me.

He passed over a sealed letter to me saying, 'It's up to you to break the seal, Josephine. The letter is from your Uncle Edward and is of great importance and will possibly have a bearing on how you will view the rest of your life. I broke the seal and gave the letter to Craig to read out loud to us.

The letter read:

Dear Copper Knob

I am very sorry if this is a sterile way of giving you this shatter-ing news. I have to write this letter and lodge it with the lawyers. If, however, I am alive on your 25th birthday, you will not have the pain of seeing this letter. I will have explained it all to you gently and you will have been able to ask me questions about your past.

Your real mother was my sister. Her name was Rosamund Finlay-son. She came out to India one winter to stay with me as she wanted to see something of India. Your father is your father. He was a young handsome fellow. He was an engineer on a three-year contract at the plant where I am manager and set up a lot of the machinery. He is an excellent engineer, Josephine and has the proverbial 'clever pair of hands.' To this day I don't know much about him or his parentage. The war shattered many lives. He and your mother fell in love. They met at a club dance. I can remember her to this day, laughing with him on the balcony with her curly auburn hair bouncing as she laughed. She had on a blue dress of some light material. Try as I might she would not be put off marrying him. They were very much in love. Your father adored her. At the end of his contract he persuaded her that they should stay on in India and buy a factory and live in India. As you know, many people did this in the past. They loved India and made it their home. She, of course, had some money of her own; she was a great saver of money. You have taken after her in that respect, Josephine. She gave him her savings and they were happy together. Her father, of course, had tied up her inheritance and she couldn't use it. She got the interest and I think, basically, they lived on it initially. They were very careless about a lot of things and your mother developed malaria. Your father was not very careful about the housekeeping of the factory and the place always seemed to be infested with flies and mosquitoes. She had a few bouts of malaria and he took her to Cal-cutta. They both refused to go back to England despite the doctor's advice about your mother's worsening health. You were just a tiny child, Josephine, when your mother died of malaria.

As you can imagine, the death of your mother caused me great agony. I had a falling out with your father as I felt he neglected her health. That's why the relationship between your father and me was always strained. I'm so sorry. I don't even know where your mother's buried. He repeatedly told us he would tell you everything when the time came.

Your education was paid for by the interest on the money that was left by your mother. Your father didn't inherit after her death. I saw to that at your birth as I had your interests at heart. I had control of the family fortunes, such as they were. Your father's handling of money, to say the least, was poor. I can only assume that with the interest that will be added to the capital you should inherit a tidy sum. There are to be no strings attached to this money, some of which is in bonds. You are to get it all on your 25th birthday.

The woman you call mother was a nurse your father met when he took your mother to Calcutta when she first got ill. The speed of the marriage after your mother died astounded us, but all I can say in his favour is that he had a small child and he needed someone to look after her.

The money you are about to inherit was initially left by your great-grandfather. He made his money in trading in indigo and bought land in Perthshire and built a house there. I don't know what became of the property. It was so long ago. Rumour has it that it was sold either to pay taxes or gambling debts. The rest of the money stayed intact thankfully Money devalues and what you will inherit is nothing like what old Mr Finlayson made out in India. Apparently after the house was sold nobody thought he had any money. The house was eventually derelict and had to be pulled down. I am sorry to say what I know is very vague. I never took much interest in family history. Vali's mother knows more about it than I do.

*One thing is not in doubt. Your father loved your mother dearly,
and he loved his little girl.*
Use the money wisely.
Love from your Uncle Edward

Silence, tears and deep sorrow.

I bowed my head and let the tears drip down my face. I then
heard Jonathan clear his throat and say, 'We'll take a short break.'
The slow ticking of the clock seemed to have its rhythm broken
as I heard his chair scrape the floorboards behind him. Craig and
Jonathan left the room leaving Vali sitting quietly beside me.

She sighed and eventually said, quietly, 'You're my cousin, Jo.'

A childhood memory, deep in the hidden crevasses of my mind
stirred, and I saw myself running up Monkey Hill, a scrap of paper
in my hand on which I had drawn, in my childish way, a woman in
a blue dress and in a red crayon I had given her plenty of red hair.
This was my dream, the dream that had haunted my childhood
and I had cried and beaten the dry earth with my tiny hands.

And then I had seen him for the first time. His body covered
in ash, wearing but a red loincloth and sitting in the lotus position, coils of hair like snakes piled high on his head. I was fascinated but not afraid. He had beckoned to me and I approached
him cautiously, Minnie, my ayah, standing back in fear. He had
gently asked me to sit, showed me the lotus position, sprinkled
my soiled palms with rose water and in an urn beside him coals
burned. He had asked me to copy his mantra with my eyes closed
and my palms held together, and I felt a great peace but in the
end, and after our friendship had developed, he still didn't tell me
anything about the woman of my dreams.

But now I knew, and combined with my sorrow I mentally
excused myself from the guilt I had sometimes felt at disliking
the woman whom I had called mother in all my childhood days,

and in my girlhood and who had not found it in her heart to be kind to a small motherless child.

Craig and Jonathan came back into the room with coffee for us and Craig's face was expressionless. I couldn't even guess what he was thinking. Whatever emotions he might have felt, he was certainly holding them in check successfully.

Eventually, after much explanation I was advised that my assets were in the region of a quarter of a million pounds and Jonathan then handed me a small sandalwood box.

Sad mementoes of a mother I had never known. A few bits of jewellery, amongst them what must have been an engagement ring. A solitaire diamond beautifully set. A lock of auburn hair and some dried rose petals were in a small sealed glass box. Had she loved roses and was that why my father had tried to grow, with little success, the beautiful Rosa Mundi, in memory of his Rosamund, so very beloved by him.

Our meeting concluded with Dean coming into the room to collect Vali, and Craig dropped me home reminding me to give Adrian the letter he had handed to me earlier.

twenty-seven / an unwanted child

Late Autumn 1956

Adrian had been delayed at work and as it was past nine o'clock I decided I would go to bed and see him in the morning. I left a note on the kitchen table in large black letters.

'How would you like to be married to a woman with a quarter of a million Pounds?'

I left the letter from Craig beside it.

He must have come in very late. I felt him get into bed and put his arm around me. I awoke with Frances crying in her cot. Adrian had already left for work. The little face with her large grey eyes, inherited from her father, was peering out at me through the bars. I put down the side of the cot, kissed and cuddled her and lifted her out. I was finding it increasingly difficult to lift Frances. She was becoming quite a big child. Adrian hadn't opened the letter on the table that Craig had said was so urgent. He had just turned over the note I had written and scribbled. 'Very funny, Jo.'

He was home by four o'clock the next day.

'Well, Mrs Millions, what's this about?' he asked. I handed him the envelope from Craig which, in his hurry, he hadn't opened. He read Craig's letter and then handed it to me. Craig had attached a newspaper cutting to his letter advertising a post for a junior member of a team in a new practice to be set up in Perth. The interviews were to be conducted in London. He seemed quite pleased and said he would apply.

I then handed him a large brown envelope containing the copy of my mother's will. He was visibly upset at the contents of the letter and the sandalwood box.

'I'm sorry, Jo, he said shaking his head. Why didn't your father speak of these matters to you when you went to Ranchi? There was nothing to stop him sitting you down and talking to you about your mother. It seems almost cruel to keep such a secret for so long; so Rose is only a half sister and Vali is your cousin.'

I nodded my head in agreement. This was a moment when I felt Adrian showed real sympathy towards me. He had had a mother who loved him well, a love which had been denied to me.

He then spoke of Vali sympathetically, 'Poor girl, she is her own worst enemy. If only she took her medication regularly the outcome would be good. As it is, her drink problem seems to be going totally unchecked, a problem that even my aunt refuses to accept and it's being swept under the carpet, so to speak. This is the result of heavy social drinking going unchecked.'

Tears were in my eyes for the girl that illness and her own folly had changed so much.

'Adrian, Vali is now of the opinion that as I'm her cousin I should adopt her child.' He was shocked at my statement and replied positively, 'No child of Dean Mitchell is being brought up by me or you for that matter.'

'What do you think of my inheritance' I then asked, 'Aren't you pleased?'

'Yes, of course, Jo. More than pleased, but I'm sorry it has come to you in such sad circumstances.'

It was a pleasant evening and Frances was full of restless antics so we put her in her pram and walked her along to a nearby park and while we watched the older children at play he commented, ' I want Frances to enjoy good health, to have our love and understanding, to have a garden and swings to play on. It's not too much to ask.'

For a few short hours we seemed to be at peace with one another. We were a family, a husband and wife with a little girl and a baby on the way. What more could I want. We also had a substantial amount of money. Could Adrian Greene be satisfied?

We returned home, had our meal and I put Frances to bed. It all seemed so perfect. I had tried hard to put the episode of the giggling girl on the telephone out of my mind, but the knowledge of his unfaithfulness hung over me as a rotting, swollen corpse, ready to burst forth and spill its evil stench over our lives. I knew I could never convince myself it was a prank. It had happened and he had been unfaithful, of that I was almost sure. Life is not perfect though, is it? I thought.

We were sitting having coffee when Adrian once again raised the question of research, dangling it in front of my eyes, like a matador swishing his cloak in front of an ill-fated beast. This time I had to lay this silly notion of his to rest.

'Jo, I need to fulfil myself. I need to do research. Ian Ross, my colleague has been offered a place on a project on Cancer. He is to lead the team funded by a large company for a three-year period. If I'm able to obtain a good project I too could organise and lead a team very successfully.' He continued in the same vein.

'I can't be an extension of you and the children. We have had nothing but family worries since we came to England. I need to form some worthwhile academic connections once I get a post in Perth. A lot of the chaps in the hospital have done a few years of research and it has helped their careers enormously. At my age I shouldn't be holding such a junior post. I need money, and you now have plenty of it. I can do better than Ian Ross. I am looking to you to do the right thing for me and fund a project. I can set up a laboratory with the money you have, hire a couple of research assistants and I can lead a small team. It will be good for my career. Will you do this for me now? '

I cut his remarks short and tried to keep my temper but I knew I had to be firm this time.

Still carrying the shock and grief of my real identity, I was in no mood for his constant desire to control all my money, especially as I knew of his unfaithfulness. What did he really want the money for, I wondered. Another mistress?

'No, I'm very sorry, but let's put this idea of yours regarding research on hold. I can't afford to fund such a grandiose scheme. The interest of my money is important for our well-being. It will take care of all our living expenses but nothing more. We will have two children to raise and the cost of running a home. Besides, I know and you know full well to finance medical research costs hundreds and thousands of pounds. Research on the scale you're thinking of is usually funded by large pharmaceutical companies or by multi-millionaires. I am not in either category.'

He didn't reply immediately and I continued, speaking softly, trying to persuade him his idea was flawed. I have never heard of a junior hospital doctor leading a research team. Surely this is done by Consultants and Professors of good repute and long standing experience? You are far too junior. In a few years time, when you're established, then maybe.'

He glowered at me and wagged his finger at me menacingly, but thankfully, didn't lose his temper or contradict what I had said; but what he did say cast a chill over me, mind and body.

'Very well, suit yourself, but I'll find a way somehow or other and Jonathan must release funds to me and I *will* have total control over our funds. Just watch me.'

I had to put this matter out of his mind and now spoke angrily to him.

'Adrian, they are not our funds, the money was left to me. You cannot have total control or any control for that matter, and I will not fund some hare-brained idea of yours regarding research.

Everything has its place and you have no experience of research, even in your own field.'

That night in bed, there was no loving arm around me, instead he turned his back on me like a small child who had been refused an expensive toy in a shop.

And so, November, cold and wet, with slippery, slimy steps, pavements and roads was upon us and I was eight months pregnant.

I was putting Frances in her cot for her afternoon nap, when I heard the doorbell being rung persistently. It was Vali with a large bag slung over her shoulder which she quickly flung on the couch on entering the room.

'Don't close the door just yet,' she said excitedly.

She ran back down the steps and appeared with Vali-Jo in her arms. Where had she left the child when she had come up with the bag? Vali-Jo could have wandered off into the road and been run over. Vali was not thinking straight.

'There you go. She's yours now, Jo, clothes and all,' she said putting the child down near the large bag she had placed on the couch. 'I will see Jonathan about you adopting Vali-Jo.' It's the right thing to do. She started to laugh saying, 'That's what cousins are for, and you're supposed to look after me, so start now.'

Distressed, I had no immediate reply for her and she continued saying, 'I'm divorcing Dean for adultery. I've told Jonathan.'

Ignoring her remarks I asked ,'Vali, where's the nanny?'

'To hell with the nanny, where did you find such a stupid cow? She left this morning. She said she couldn't work for me. Never mind about her. I've come to party with you. Do you remember the party we went to when you were on your way back to India? Don't you think it was fun? I'll need to contact my old friends and then we'll party, party, once I get rid of Dean.' She started to laugh again.

"Don't you love your child, Vali? Are you certain about Dean's adultery? I can scarcely believe that.'

What would Aunt Ruth have said I thought with almost a sense of fear within me, and whatever would she have been able to do.

'*Chup row*, Jo, I have to be free.'

She had remembered the old expression for 'shut up' we used when we were annoyed with each other as children. This, however, was no childish quarrel. She spoke quickly and in an agitated manner. 'I need a drink with plenty of ice. Come on, chop chop.'

Little Vali-Jo had fallen asleep on the couch, and I was not about to give Vali a drink. She went to the fridge and helped herself to lemonade. Opening her bag she took out a half bottle of Vodka and added a good amount to the lemonade she had poured for herself.

'Stop this nonsense,' I said angrily. 'Please see to Vali-Jo. I'm pregnant. I can't lift her; the doctors have told me to avoid lifting heavy weights as much as possible.'

'Ignoring my remark she said, 'If you won't party with me, I'm going home.'

She gulped down her drink, got up and left, banging the door behind her, leaving Vali-Jo asleep on the couch.

I then phoned Vali's flat and managed to get the housekeeper. I asked her to get a taxi to my flat immediately and she was with me in fifteen minutes.

The woman was visibly agitated and as I opened the door to her, her first words were, 'Please, do something. She'll kill that child in a drunken rage.

Mr Mitchell tried to stop her putting vodka into her tomato juice at breakfast. She flew into a temper and when the little one started crying she hit her. The nanny has left, unable to put up with this uncontrolled behaviour. Soon after your phone call I contacted Mr Mitchell. He'll be here soon.'

Dean phoned an hour later to say Vali on her way home had fallen down the steps leading to the flats. She had a broken arm

and disfiguring lacerations to her face. He had sent for an ambulance and she was now in hospital.

'I'll be there as soon as possible, Jose,' he said with anxiety in his voice.

The housekeeper stayed until Dean arrived. He barely had time to speak to me. He picked up Vali-Jo. The housekeeper went ahead of him with the large bag of clothes.

'Oh Jose, Jose, what on earth have we done with our lives. God help us both,' he said emotionally as he picked up his small child and held her close in his arms.

He kissed me on the forehead, said 'thank you' and was gone before I could speak to him at length.

I phoned Aunt Eileen telling her that Vali had been very drunk and fallen down steps and had injured herself.

'No, that can't be true, Josephine,' she said in a high-handed fashion. 'You're prone to exaggeration. Once again you're making a drama out of a simple matter. Anyone can fall down steps. You don't have to be drunk to fall.'

Dean Mitchell, in desperation, had packed his bags and taken Vali-Jo back to America and his mother. I, Josephine Greene, was left to pick up the pieces.

After several visits to the hospital and great persuasion on the part of Adrian, Vali was admitted to a clinic in regard to her drink problem. I was told her arm would heal well but it was her face that was the problem. She would need plastic surgery.

Aunt Eileen came to London, lived in Vali's flat and was soon back and forth visiting Vali, who, now sober and under treatment remembered only vaguely the incident of that fateful afternoon. I had broken the news to her, as gently as possible that Dean and left and returned to America with Vali-Jo.

Adrian kept a close eye on Vali and was pleased with her progress, and had made arrangements for investigations into her depression and extraordinary behaviour. All seemed to be going well until Aunt Eileen interfered. Her stupid actions were the downfall of poor Vali.

She convinced the clinic that the whole family would shortly be living in Perth and it would be better for Vali to be in Perth. In her own inimitable way she took charge, overriding any arrangements Adrian had made. The clinic informed Adrian that Vali had wanted to move to a hospital in Perth to be near to Aunt Eileen.

Adrian Greene and the aunt he had spoken of so frequently in India and whom he had loved as a child now had an irreparable rift between them. Unfortunately their quarrel had repercussions and Aunt Eileen saw fit to embroil me in their arguments.

Before Vali moved to Perth she had asked Jonathan to see her in the clinic. At that time she seemed to be responding to treatment, but was not really fit to make life- changing decisions. She wanted to ask him what arrangements could be made for me to adopt Vali-Jo. He was extremely upset at such a request. Jonathan phoned me asking for a response.

At this stage I pointed out clearly that the child had a father, Dean, who loved her and had taken her to America where she would be well looked after by his family, so there was no justification for such a request from Vali.

And so the matter ended there, or so I thought, but Aunt's Eileen's interference was like a large stone thrown into a pond; the ripples circled endlessly and were to touch us all in many ways.

twenty-eight | denigration and andrew

Christmas 1956

Vali was making progress, and on Aunt Eileen's insistence she was reluctantly given permission to take her home for a weekend. It had been very poor weather and on the Saturday night the rain and stormy conditions had woken Vali. She had got out of her bed, forced open Aunt Eileen's drinks cabinet and helped herself to a bottle of vodka. She had then walked out of the bungalow and lost her way in the dark.

The building site was a quagmire with the heavy rains and she had sat down among the bricks at the site and had drunk most of the vodka. She was in a stupor when found by the night watch-man. He had noticed the light from Aunt Eileen's torch while she was searching for Vali and gone to her aid. He had carried Vali back to the bungalow.

After this incident Aunt Eileen was unwell and took to her bed with a heavy cold for several days.

Doctors at Perth now decided that Vali needed specialist treatment and moved her to Edinburgh. In London we learnt of the problems when the hospital authorities in Edinburgh wrote to me stating Vali had given them my name as next of kin and asked me to make an appointment to see them. I asked Adrian if he could attend on my behalf. His reply was in the negative.

'I don't want anything more to do with Vali or her treatment. Let my so-called clever Aunt deal with it. It's a problem of her making. Besides I can't get time off to go to Perth.'

In desperation, once again I turned to Craig.

He sighed and then agreed to see the doctors on my behalf. This was a good opportunity to speak to Craig regarding my finances. Worriedly I said to him, 'While you're on the phone there's another matter I'd like to speak to you about. Can you and Jonathan go through the terms of my inheritance with a fine toothcomb and assure me that there is no chance of Adrian taking control.'

He was amazed at my concern and reassured me once again saying, 'Stop worrying, Adrian can't touch your money. You have total control of your finances.' He then invited us to Perth to spend Christmas with him. I laughed at the idea saying, I'm vast. I really can't travel. The baby is due round about Christmas.'

'Well, I'll bring Christmas to you,' he replied and continued, 'Listen Josephine, Alison Watson, a friend of mine, has refurbished my property beautifully. Perhaps you should consider her services. I'll get her to bring samples to you initially and if you're pleased, you can then discuss the décor of the house and lodge with her.'

'That's splendid. I look forward to that,'

'I'll leave you to tell me in your own good time what's really troubling you and why you're concerned about your money.'

Craig phoned me again a week later. Aunt Eileen had been hospitalised with breathing difficulties. She had a bad chest infection.

I told Adrian when he came home. All he said was, 'If you do stupid things you have to pay the price.'

I was saddened by his callous attitude to his aunt.

'Craig and his friend Alison are coming to us for Christmas, Adrian,' I said excitedly, pleased at the thought of having company. 'Alison will be bringing samples of furnishing for us to choose from. We don't have to do anything. They'll bring the food and do the cooking. Apparently Alison is a very good cook. It will be good to have company over Christmas, don't you think?'

'So; I don't have a say who comes into our home and how and where we spend our Christmas. What if I say no? I can manage to feed my own family, thank you. You have no right to make arrangements without consulting me. I am the head of this household and I call the shots. Just remember that Jo. Once again I would like to repeat to you, I call the shots.' He spoke loudly and pompously.

'Well, if that's how you feel I'll cancel,' I said, going towards the phone. 'The furnishing of the house will have to be put on hold along with other matters Craig needs to discuss with me.' He didn't answer and I didn't cancel.

On the fifteenth of December Adrian was offered the post in Perth as a General Practitioner, starting in early March, and now his arrogance reached its peak, constantly dictating to me how I should dress, how I should behave and the ultimate insult was when he emptied the contents of a drawer where I kept my perfumes and cosmetics into the rubbish bin.

I was not about to start an argument with him as I was too far gone in my pregnancy and tired easily, both mentally and physically, and that night I cried silently for the loss of respect and contentment in our relationship.

The snow graced us before Christmas but I still hung on to my baby. It was almost as if the child in my womb didn't want to be born to the father I had chosen. Christmas arrived and with it came a happy Craig and an elegant Alison Watson, laden with samples of materials, carpeting and wallpaper and a large hamper of Christmas fare and gifts for us. They would be staying in a nearby hotel and Alison would visit every day and discuss colours and styles of furnishing. She cooked a beautiful Christmas lunch and Adrian turned on his charm. It was almost as if he was flirting with her. Craig and I discussed the house and he was keen we move into the Lodge as soon as possible. He had arranged a gardener-handyman whose wife was to help me with cooking and general duties in the house.

'It will be too much for you to cope with on your own, Josephine, especially with two young children.' he said. 'You'll like her.'

Adrian commented, 'Craig, the question is will she like Jo? After she has this baby she's not going to be just flamboyant. She will be plump and flamboyant. Just look at the size of her.' He feigned a laugh.

Craig chose to ignore his remarks and Alison was embarrassed.

I had felt alone so often in life. This was different. I was not alone. I was unwanted. My self-esteem was reaching its lowest ebb.

Adrian was not at the hospital nor was he at home when I went into labour at night. I phoned for a taxi and took Frances with me to the hospital. I had no other choice as there was no one to look after her. I gave birth at two o'clock in the morning. Later in the morning I asked the nurse to phone Aunt Eileen to tell her of the new baby. She came back looking extremely embarrassed.

'I'm sorry, I'm so sorry,' she said.

'Well, what did she say?'

'I don't want to know about Adrian Greene's sprog,' the nurse said haltingly.

It was afternoon before Adrian came to see me in the hospital. The nurses had seen to Frances. No flowers, no kiss of congratulations. Had he really wanted this child? Where had he been all night?

He took Frances home and looked after her for three days. Each evening he came and saw me and sat on a chair in the corner of the room with Frances holding on to his trouser leg and the baby in his arms.

'I looked at him on the second evening sitting and rocking the baby and spoke to him quietly.

'Adrian, try and be happy with me and our little family, please. We can give our children a great deal in life. What's troubling you so much? What's the reason for your unkind behavior towards me?'

He didn't speak for a while.

'I married you, didn't I? That's what you wanted,' was all he had to say to me.

'What about a name for your son?' I asked.

He didn't give me an answer immediately. 'I don't know' he said turning away from me.

I phoned Craig and asked him to tell Alison I had had a boy. I knew she would be pleased for me.

'What's his name?' Craig asked.

"We don't know,' I replied foolishly.

'Struth, you don't know what the hell to call your own child. Well then, Josephine. You'll be living in Scotland. I suggest Andrew. It's a fine Scottish name.'

'Well then Craig,' I joked, repeating his words, 'Andrew it is.'

Adrian barely touched the baby in my presence. At night when he thought I was asleep he lifted him out of his cot and held him in his arms and looked out of the window at the dark night for long periods of time before putting him back. Why didn't he want me to see he loved his child? It was almost as if he was grieving for something else. I watched him one night when he thought I was asleep. His lips were moving as if in prayer and I was almost sure I heard him finish praying saying 'Forgive me Lord.' What was disturbing him?

'I've named our child Andrew.' I said to him after a week at home. 'Do you agree?'

He shrugged his shoulders. 'Suit yourself. You always do.'

twenty-nine | the lodge, death in the family.

1957

We moved into the Lodge in the early spring of 1957. The snow was still on the ground in Perthshire and the snowdrops were blooming in beautiful clumps around the door in attractive pots. The daffodils were not in bloom but their green shoots were apparent in abundance and I had asked for them to be planted to please Adrian as a special surprise as he had commented on their beauty when he had first noticed them.

The housekeeper arranged by Craig and Alison, Mrs Fellows, was a pleasant woman in her mid-forties. She was what could be termed as a comfortable woman. Frances took to her after a little initial hesitation. Mr Fellows was to help with the garden and general duties around the main house when it was completed. Craig had arranged what they were to be paid and I agreed.

'The kitchen is my domain,' Mrs Fellows informed me. 'Don't you worry yourself, the bairns are enough for you to cope with. Just tell me what you like and I'll cook it for you. Not too fancy, mind,' she said smiling.

I had vivid dreams when we moved to the Lodge, often dreaming of our life in Calcutta. The crowded streets, the noise and Adrian in happier times, holding my hand and laughing at some of my silly remarks. Now these same remarks irritated him. He had often bunched my hair in his hands and kissed it saying, 'My little Gold Mohur flower; you fell from the tree especially for me.'

Now in bed it was a different and sad story.

'Why don't you cut some of this damn stuff off, it gets in my face,' were his comments. We had been so happy then. Domesticity didn't appear to suit him. He seemed to want something more than I could give him, and this, in turn, made me lash out at him verbally.

Mrs Fellows was becoming confident with the children. Frances liked her and I decided I could leave the baby and Frances with her so that I could visit Vali.

I informed the hospital in Edinburgh of my visit and Vali had reluctantly agreed to see me. I arrived by train at about three o'clock and was ushered into a very light and pleasant room where Vali was seated alone on a seat near her bed, just looking into space. I was saddened at Vali's appearance.

She got up, hugged me to her emotionally and said. 'I didn't think you would want to see me like this.' She had put on a lot of weight which, I was told, had something to do with her medication and the scar on her face was disfiguring.

'Vali, I will always love you no matter how you look,' I said sympathetically. These were not happy times for us. As children how could we have foreseen the sorrows we now shared?

'Let's walk for a while in the garden and then we can talk in the large lounge together. It's nice and sunny there, Jo.' Here now was a woman, sad and full of disillusion.

We walked silently for a while admiring the well laid out grounds and then returned indoors. One of the nurses brought us tea. It was a pleasant afternoon and the sun warmed us through the large glass windows. The shine had gone from Vali's hair as had the sparkle of her personality. She seemed fairly peaceful within herself and she was able to speak logically.

'Jo, it won't be long before I'm out of here. I have stopped drinking, I promise. I also take the pills they give me regularly. I feel almost like my old self. Just once in a while when I get very upset I crave a drink. I'm what they now call stabilised. Where will I go, Jo, and what will I do?'

'Vali, first things first. What do you want to do about Dean and Vali-Jo?'

She started getting flustered and I knew I had said the wrong thing so I put my hand on her arm and steadied her, saying, 'You don't have to do anything you don't want to do. I'll see to that.'

In a very forceful way she then said 'I must divorce Dean and I've already spoken to Jonathan. I'm divorcing him for adultery. I have always felt there was someone else. Who do you think it could be? Even on our honeymoon I felt there was a lost love in his heart. I think his mother knows. She's never liked me. I've also spoken to Jonathan about Vali-Jo. You're to have custody of her. I can't cope with a child.'

I didn't want to argue with her in her fragile state and evaded the subject of Vali-Jo. In her heart she did want the child to be looked after properly and I was the chosen person. She had said 'where will I go,' so I hung on to those words.

'You must never worry about where you'll go. The house is almost finished and there is plenty of room for you. I will see you're comfortable and if you don't wish to stay in the main house, the Lodge is very attractive and private and quiet for you. The flat in London is also there for you. I will see it is well looked after'

She stretched out her hand and touched me saying, 'Thank you, darling Jo, look after me. I know that's what Mother would have liked.'

We sat and drank our tea and talked of our days in India and she smiled as she recounted the days when her father had taught us to drive and then laughed as I imitated him in a deep voice, saying, 'Now, girls, pay attention, this car is a lethal weapon and no laughing matter.'

'Yes, I'll come home with you when I get out of here,' she smiled. 'I'll heal in the peaceful Scottish countryside.'

She seemed so lucid. I had hope for her, even though I knew she was still very uncertain of herself.

She continued speaking with sadness in her voice. 'I just want to get out of here. How did we get into this mess? You don't look so great either. You're dowdy looking. Who did it to us? Will I be happy again? Will I find silly things to laugh at?'

How could I answer such poignant questions?

She smiled ruefully as I got up to leave. She came with me to the door. As I was walking down the path she opened the window and shouted out to me.

'Jo, don't forget to bring me cakes the next time you come and don't eat half of them on the way here.'

Yes, I had hope for her, though I saw merely a small glimmer of her former self.

It was early June. Craig hoped the house would be ready in autumn. The builders seemed to be tiring of the endless plastering and cement work. It had been decided we would have an area of field, between the house and the boundary fencing, and Adrian, when we had first looked at the drawings, had then said in fun, 'We'll call it the Shouting Field. The kids can scream and play their games there without disturbing us.'

The outside fencing looked onto large fields where cows grazed. Our strip was narrow and long. We could see the bungalow, where Aunt Eileen was now living clearly from this open area and from the Lodge. Arrangements were in hand to have it grassed over before the winter.

We tried to keep an eye on Aunt Eileen from a distance as we were told by Mrs Fellows, who often popped in to see her, that she was not keeping too well after the bad chill she had sustained, and for three or four days in a row there were no lights on so I asked Mrs Fellows to see if all was well.

Aunt Eileen was in bed with flu. I sent over hot food for a few days and asked Mrs Fellows to help her. She refused to see me or Adrian.

Adrian told me he was often on call at night and this I believed, but when he said he was on call every weekend, as the practice was reorganising itself, I knew it was not the truth.

He had stopped his golf lessons which he had enjoyed at first, laughingly saying to me at the time, 'Wait and see Jo, I'll be a better golfer than Craig.'

But now, even on a Saturday afternoon he was not home to play with the children, nor was he home for an evening meal with me.

Transport now became difficult and I arranged with Mr Fellows that we should buy a second car. I could no longer rely on Adrian's erratic timekeeping.

Mr Fellows and I talked about a second-hand car but he couldn't find anything suitable. A nearby garage had a new Ford for immediate sale. A customer had placed an order and then not been able to pay for it. I asked him to go ahead with the deal for me.

The day it was delivered was a Saturday and for once he was home early in the afternoon. He seemed to be in a hurry. I was admiring the car as he came into the driveway. He parked and came over to me.

'What's this?' he asked.

'I've bought a car for myself. Do you like it?'

He turned and walked into the Lodge without a word. I followed him only to be confronted by a volley of abuse.

'You've no bloody right to buy a band new car without my say so,' he roared.

'You constantly want to belittle me. I'll use the new car and you can have my old one.'

'You can't have the new car, Adrian. Everything to do with that car is in my name. It's mine. If you want a new car go and buy yourself one. You should have plenty of money in your account, considering you don't give me a penny from your salary. Why all the fuss?'

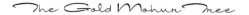

By this time we had walked towards the bedroom, arguing and bad-tempered as we entered the room together. The children were outside with Mrs Fellows.

He banged the door behind us and continued speaking with anger in his voice 'You don't need a car,' he shouted. 'Lady Muck. Chauffeur driven in a new car. Who the hell do you think you are?' he scoffed.

I took no notice of his tantrum and foolishly continued arguing. I should have walked away from him.

'It's my money, and I'll spend it my way, Adrian,' I said to him firmly. 'Stop behaving like a coolie.'

The words were barely out of my mouth when I knew I shouldn't have said them. He was in the middle of undressing, as he was obviously home to change and go out again.

"So you think I'm your bloody coolie? We'll see who the coolie is around here,' he raved.

He had his belt in his hand, and he swished and swirled it around before speaking again.

'I'll belt you so hard you'll stop speaking to me like that once and for all,' he said, his temper ferocious as he swung out at me, the thick leather belt lashing at my arm, catching me off-guard as I staggered against the door and fell. He hit me again several times as I lay on the floor. The last lash missed my head by inches and caught the door knob as I cowered. I crawled into the bathroom, bolted the door and put the shower on and stood under it fully clothed. My body was stinging with the beating he had given me. I heard the door of the bedroom slam and his car starting up and he was still shouting abuse as I heard the screeching of crashed gears in the driveway as he left.

I took off my clothes and showered gently. I had red welts on my arm and the back of my legs were stinging. Fortunately he had been holding the buckle end of the belt when he had lashed out at me and I had my clothes on. Still, I was badly hurt. It was a broad leather belt bought by me for part of his Christmas. I applied cream on my body, dressed and sat and sobbed uncontrollably on the bed, aching both physically and mentally.

Mrs Fellows came into the Lodge with the children to make their tea before she left. She had heard the shouting.

'My word, Mrs. Greene,' she said. 'My word, are you hurt?'

'Don't worry, I'll be fine,' I said wiping my tears.

I found his belt and cut it into pieces and put it into the bin in the kitchen. Mrs Fellows looked at me and shook her head. She knew exactly what had happened. She was an employee and obviously felt she couldn't take the conversation any further, but she knew. Oh yes, she knew I had an abusive husband.

Adrian didn't come home that night. When he did come home the next day, there was no apology from him.

And so by the late autumn of 1957, my marriage to the man whom I had adored, and for whom I had given up so much, now started to disintegrate, day after day, after miserable day. How could I love a man who had whipped me like some ancient slave?

Mrs Fellows came to see me one evening after visiting Aunt Eileen in the bungalow to say that she had called the doctor much to Aunt Eileen's annoyance.

'She can barely breathe,' she said with sympathy in her voice, shaking her head sadly. 'Why won't she let you see her? She's a stubborn old woman and you have always treated her kindly.'

Aunt Eileen was hospitalised. The nurse at the hospital phoned Adrian to tell him his aunt had pneumonia. Adrian did go to see her, but she was able to speak to him only briefly and asked to see Vali.

Vali had now been moved to a half-way house from the hospital in Edinburgh. She was enjoying the freedom of being able to keep flexible hours but was still under supervision. Her assessment had been good and she was allowed to drive her car, but

always accompanied. I had been to see her and taken her the promised cakes. She told me that her divorce was progressing and she would soon be signing the papers.

'Once I am free of Dean, I'm sure I'll feel like a new woman. I made a terrible mistake,' she repeated to me several times.

I could never speak to her about Dean. He had always been so special for me and despite her accusations I didn't believe he had been unfaithful to her.

I was given permission to take Vali to see Aunt Eileen in hospital. She had not been told the seriousness of Aunt Eileen's condition, but only that she had a little infection in her chest resulting from a very bad cold. She spent almost an hour with her while I sat in the corridor and waited.

'Why is she in hospital if she only has a bad cold. Is there something terribly wrong with her?' she enquired.

I had been told Vali was still fragile emotionally and I replied in a comforting way.

'Vali, she's getting old and they want to keep an eye on her. That's all. She'll be home in a few days.'

'Good,' she said and then paused for quite a while. 'I wouldn't want her to die, she's such a good friend. She has left me all her money after the mistakes Jonathan made. She knows I don't want to be poor and has often given me small amounts of money. You have plenty of money now, so you see, with her money and you looking after me, Jo, I have nothing to fear now, even though I have nothing of my own.'

I didn't answer her and realised how fragile she was. The strange delusion regarding money was still apparent.

She spent a good hour with Aunt Eileen while I sat outside the room.

'It's just a matter of weeks before I'm allowed home. I think I'll live with Aunt Eileen for a while until she's better. She is very poorly.'

'You have nothing to worry about,' I kept repeating almost as if I was trying to convince myself, knowing full well our problems were legion. She was quite cheerful by the time I took her back to the hospital.

Two days later Aunt Eileen died. We never told Vali.

Adrian made all the arrangements for the funeral. She was buried in a small cemetery in Perth, her grave being under some trees. As the priest read the prayers in the gloom of a late October afternoon, a gust of wind blew the bronzed leaves all around us, some dry leaves swirling at my feet; the wind whistling mournfully, a touch of finality as death was now her only companion; the pleasant woman whose attitude to me had soured because of Adrian Greene. He stood silent beside me and I couldn't read his emotions for her, the aunt whom he had loved so well as a small boy.

The sad task of going through her possessions was left to us. Amongst her many papers there was a recent will made soon after she had moved to the bungalow. It left all her money to Vali. The flat in London was left to Frances. There was also an old will amongst her papers which had left everything to Adrian Greene, and it specifically said her beloved nephew in India. Sadly, he was not beloved at the time of her death.

A large photograph of a young woman, obviously taken in a photographer's studio, lay at the bottom of a drawer. He held the photograph to him and the tears welled up in his eyes. From his actions this, I felt, was obviously his mother so I went towards him with arms outstretched wanting to hold him and comfort him in his distress but he pushed me aside and left.

I sat on the couch in the sitting room and put the fire on, immersed in my own thoughts. At least he knew what his mother looked like. All I had was a lock of auburn hair, a few trinkets and dreams.

As he strode out of the bungalow he turned and said, 'That's my money by rights. It's family money. Vali Mitchell has more than

enough to waste. I will speak to Jonathan about this. What on earth was she thinking about? '

I was deeply saddened. How happily Aunt Eileen had welcomed me to her home in London and how pleased she had been to see Adrian. Tragically our association had a bitter ending because of Adrian's poor temperament and Vali's insistence that I had some-how stolen part of her inheritance in collusion with Jonathan, her lawyer.

The room was warmed by the electric fire and I dozed. In my dream Monkey Hill stood out clearly against the horizon but there was no sadhu on the hill. My dream took me into the garden in my father's factory. He was standing in the corner among roses that were large and blooming freely. I heard my father's voice speaking softly to me as he had done when I was a child, 'My Rosamund, my Rosa Mundi is always with me now but our spirits are uneasy for you, our baby.' I woke with a start.

I had phoned to ask him to my wedding but he had rejected me then and when I had written to him when Frances had been born there had been no reply. He had grown Rosa Mundi in a sheltered corner of the garden in Ranchi and now I knew it was in memory of his Rosamund, his flower, his Rosa Mundi. She had lived only a short time but what a perfect love was hers.

I sat and wept for the wrong I had done him. My father had been a faithful man. He had loved my mother and he'd loved me. Had he died too? If so, why had nobody informed me? I had paid too high a price for the false love of Adrian Greene.

thirty | dean's return

Spring and Summer 1958

And so it was spring and we moved into a beautifully furnished new house where I had chosen furnishings and fittings with the help of Alison, and during the many hours spent together we had formed a happy friendship. She was an elegant and quiet young woman with a good sense of humour and I was pleased to see something more than a friendly relationship developing between her and Craig.

She had been on the brink of falling out with Adrian about the décor of the prayer room, as he insisted calling it, much to her annoyance. It had also caused irritation with the builders as Adrian had insisted on small high windows, out of keeping with the rest of the building, giving it a dark and sombre appearance. She had a dislike of the portrait the potter had drawn of me. 'It looks as if you are sad and old, not a young girl. I'll hang it in the prayer room. I'll put all the nasty things in one room, Josephine,' she had laughed.

'That's such a good idea, Alison,' I had said. 'Don't forget to include Adrian.'

I should have felt happy in the house. It was beautiful, new and children played within its walls. Instead I had a feeling of great unease and often went into the Lodge and sat in the sitting room. Mrs Fellows came in one morning while I was sitting having coffee.

'What's the matter Mrs Greene, are you taking badly with the very large lounge in your beautiful new house?'

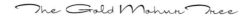
'There's something comforting about this room. Do you sense it? I think people must have been happy here in days past.'

'Yes, I know,' she had said smiling, 'but you should feel comfortable in your new home, as nobody has left a strange imprint here.'

Just as I was coming to terms with the idea of getting Vali home with me soon, we had a letter from Dean saying his mother had had a minor stroke and was no longer able to look after Vali-Jo. He said he had to sign divorce papers and was coming to Scotland bringing Vali-Jo with him. He also had to go through money matters with the lawyers. We had kept him informed about Vali and he had never made any comment about her in his letters other than to thank us for looking after her. He implored me to look after Vali-Jo for a temporary period until matters were sorted out. He would pay for a full-time nanny and asked if he could use the Lodge.

It was late at night before I could speak to Adrian. He agreed grudgingly but insisted that Dean paid rent to him for his stay at the Lodge. He still insisted everything was his. Whose house is it? I thought, but I didn't argue. Communication between us was limited and we spoke as strangers.

Mrs Fellows arranged a girl to help me with the children when Vali-Jo eventually arrived with Dean and I hoped little Vali-Jo and my two would take to the girl whose name was Denise.

We had to handle the delicate situation between Vali and Dean carefully. Dean phoned several times and he didn't think it would be a good idea for Vali to travel to London and neither did the doctors in Edinburgh. He decided ultimately to pay Jonathan's expenses in a hotel in Edinburgh and all meetings with Vali would be held in a room to be booked at the hotel.

I went to see Vali. Jonathan had been in contact with her and she seemed quite calm about seeing Dean. I didn't rush her. She spoke of generalities for a while and then said 'Jo, I don't mind if I see Dean. All I want is to be free of him and his child. I have to get rid of him. I have to get rid of him,' she repeated 'I don't want either of them. I want my old life back. I can't imagine why I married him. I'm not really cut out for married life, children and all that jazz.' She laughed as she spoke and there was a hint of the old Vali about her.

I took her out to lunch and Mr Fellows drove us to a good restaurant he knew. We had grown up together and she seemed to sense my concern.

'Jo, don't worry so much about me,' she said, trying to put me at ease. 'I'll cope with you beside me. Look at how grand we are. Fancy being chauffer-driven to lunch. We're posh.' She giggled and gave my hand a squeeze.

'The doctor has arranged for me to see a Plastic Surgeon next week. I'll be like a film star having plastic surgery to my face. You should have some too, especially to that poky nose of yours,' she laughed. She was starting to be a bit more like her old self, laughing at me and with me.

I was concerned about the meeting with Dean and phoned Jonathan pointing out that Vali was still in recovery and I particularly asked him to stop the meeting if she showed the slightest sign of stress, as I didn't know how she would react at seeing Dean again.

'Stop fussing,' he said. 'I have the matter in hand and everything will be dealt with sensitively. I've spoken to her and she says she can drive to the hotel from the hospital herself. It's only a few miles. The doctors say she's almost ready for discharge and is looking after herself well. She's fine, Josephine. She has obviously regained some of her self-confidence. I'll keep the meeting a short as possible.'

'Play it her way, Jonathan, that's all I ask,' I replied.

I slept fitfully worrying about the proposed meeting between Vali and Dean. There seemed to be a spiritual disturbance in the house, and I felt as if there were movements and strange shadows around

me. I had a repetitive dream of the woman with the light on her face. Each time the shade had come closer and still I couldn't recognise the phantom of my dreams. Fear was my companion, clasping me ever closer each day, and all the silent meditating the sadhu had taught me to calm myself had no effect.

Adrian too was restless and mumbled in his sleep, often wakening, and touching me as if to reassure himself I was still there. So why the aloof attitude during the day which had never changed since he had whipped me, without even an apology for his unacceptable actions?

We were living separate lives under one roof. On a particularly restless night he shouted out in his sleep, 'Missy, come back,' and then sat bolt upright in bed. He had woken me.

We lay side by side, awake and silent, a prey to our separate nightmares.

We lived in a new and beautiful house. We were extremely well off, far removed from the shadow of want and poverty. He had the career he had wanted so much and spoken about so often when we sat together in my small second-hand car beneath the shade of the Gold Mohur tree in India. We had held hands and kissed each other and planned a rosy future for ourselves. And now we lived in a loveless, abusive and violent marriage.

He had stood at the altar and said, 'I will love you forever.' Nobody had told me that 'forever' was but a few short years.

Dean, along with little Vali-Jo, arrived in May on a beautiful sunny day. The Lodge had been aired and cleaned and a cot put in for the child. This was a Dean I scarcely recognised. Troubled, wan and exhausted from his journey, holding a beautiful blonde but bewildered child in his arms.

Mrs Fellows had made an enormous and nourishing casserole for all of us and we had our meal together fairly quietly. The children were not too sure of each other. After our meal we sat in the sitting room for a short while, Frances and Andrew trying to entertain the shy and hesitant little Vali-Jo.

'Well, Jose, where's Adrian?' Dean asked.

'He'll be in later. He's often held up with patients,' I lied.

Later in the week, a worried Denise confided in me that Vali-Jo was often short of breath whenever she tried to keep up with my two.

I reassured her saying 'I'll keep an eye on her. She's had a long journey and will take time to settle to a new environment and adjust to the perpetual noise of Frances and Andrew. Don't over-stretch her in play.'

Dean went to Edinburgh and arranged a hotel for Jonathan's overnight stay and a room where they could meet privately. He had also spoken to the doctors about Vali who had reassured him saying her progress had been good.

As Vali-Jo often tired in the afternoon I made it a habit to let her rest in the Lodge.

Dean had been playing in the garden with Andrew and came in to see Vali-Jo. She was asleep and he decided to make coffee for us. We had not had a chance to speak to each other.

As we sipped our coffee I spoke of Vali, warning him of her mental fragility. There was neither fun nor laughter for us and I told him that Vali, amongst the many strange statements she made, insisted he was having an affair.

'Is it true?' I asked. He sighed deeply before replying.

'Even love affairs need happy times. No, I'm not having an affair, nor have I ever had an affair at any time during my horren-dous marriage.'

'I'm sorry I asked,' I said. 'One other thing, please don't com-ment on her looks. She's not the beautiful girl you married. Her face is scarred and she will need plastic surgery.

'Jose,' he said dully, 'It's terrible to say it, but I couldn't care less what she looks like. She wants a divorce. I am here to give her

one. Her allegations against me are untrue. I won't be contesting anything she says. It's best that we divorce with as little malice as possible. An affair, huh! If only.'

There was nothing more to say about Vali.

'Well, what's with you?' he asked. 'This is your Dean speaking. Plug in to me. I'm sorry, honey. I don't want to pry, but I'm concerned about you. I've been here a week and I hear Adrian's car on the gravel very late each night. In fact it wakens me, that's how I know. Tell me. No doctor is on duty so late *every* night. Honey, look at the state you're in. What's he doing to you?'

'I don't know how to tell you. Just let's say my life has turned into a living nightmare.'

I got up to leave. My emotions were getting the better of me. He came with me to the door. He put his arms around me and put my head on his shoulder to comfort me for a moment before I left the room.

Vali-Jo's state of health started to worry me. I spoke to Adrian about her. She had a very poor appetite and seemed to need to rest often.

'She's possibly just tired and needs time to settle in. She'll soon perk up,' he said. I did then see him pick her up very gently on several occasions. She always put her arms around his neck, smiling at him and kissing him.

This little one needs to be loved, I thought.

thirty-one | a flame extinguished

Summer 1958

Now came the day that would change our lives forever.

Looking back on it now, it seems impossible that there were no clues, no trail of breadcrumbs to lead me to believe it could all go wrong so quickly.

The day had started ordinarily enough, with Adrian at first calm, but when I told him that Jonathan had suggested that it might be a good idea for me to be present at the meeting between Vali and Dean, he flew into a rage.

He ranted on about Vali and Dean, and how we should pray for them, how it was impossible for them to divorce, that divorce was not the way for any couple. I got the uneasy feeling that he was not so much talking about them as about ourselves, but I dared not contradict him when he was in this mood. He held me by the hand and almost dragged me into what he called his prayer room. It was dark and sombre in the room despite the bright day, and I looked up longingly at the small window set high into one of the walls. The dark furnishings seemed oppressive, and as I observed the portrait of myself drawn years before by the potter in India, in the land I still considered home, it was the first time I thought I saw shadows that were not apparent to me before.

'You see it, don't you?' Adrian said suddenly, and I turned to face him. 'You see what you were and what you have become.' The quietness of his voice chilled me as he continued, 'What have you done with your life, and what have you done with mine?'

I was so astounded I couldn't answer and before I had time to register what was happening, Adrian was on his feet and slamming the door shut on me and I heard the grate of the key within the lock.

'What are you doing, Adrian!' I shouted. 'For heaven's sake, what are you doing!'

I could hear him prowling in the hall outside, ranting and raving about the ills of divorce, his voice harsh like the growl of an animal. Silence – and then he was gone. I heard his car speeding away down the driveway, and I began to shout and scream and bang my fists against the door. He couldn't leave me in here! How could he leave me locked away?

He knew the house was empty and I knew the children had gone with Denise to the village on an errand and yet I still hammered at the door and hammered and hammered until the heels of my hands were bleeding, panicking as I tied to hammer out of the room, hammering as if I was trying to batter my way out of my marriage, appalled at what I was doing, and at what Adrian had done and scared at my own terror, wondering what he might do to me next.

Hours later I heard feet on the gravel outside the high window. Had Adrian returned to harm me? Still I called out, my voice all croaked and worn and to my relief it was Mr Fellows who answered.

'Why? whatever are you doing in there, Mrs Greene?' he asked solicitously as he opened the door and let me out, sat me in the kitchen and gave me a drink of water.

I could barely speak, I didn't have to. I could see it in his eyes that he already knew. And there was worse to come, though exactly how much worse, I was yet to find out.

I'd calmed down by nightfall, comforted by the return of Mrs Fellows and the children. Adrian too returned a while later, though he never looked at me and I would not speak to him telling myself

I would never speak to him again, unless it was absolutely necessary.

And then the phone rang.

A call borne of nightmares, but this time I was wide awake. This was the call, the one I would never forget, that said Dean was in hospital and Vali was dead.

'Dead!' I shouted into the phone. 'Dead?' I queried in panic.

It had been a car accident the voice said, though no ordinary one, as I later pieced together the strange and bizarre facts.

Earlier that day, the same time that I was walled up in Adrian's prayer room, Vali had decided to leave the hospital early, in an attempt to meet Jonathan before the scheduled meeting with Dean, to discuss Vali-Jo, the divorce and what was to be done.

She had phoned his room and he had come down into the foyer and taken her to the room that had been booked for the later meeting with Dean, The lawyer, known for his patience with Vali, had tried to calm her by sitting her down and ordering coffee as he had become aware she had had a drink.

Vali had then again spoken about what she considered the flawed wills, her inheritance and the house that should have been hers. He had once again listened to her patiently and tried to calm her fears, and she had then abruptly got up and left saying she would be back in a short while for the meeting with Dean at two. Jonathan had sat and waited.

At this time she had gone to the hotel bar and several waiters and customers attested she was drinking Bloody Marys and tapping her fingers on the bar as if she were counting down the minutes. They had no idea what or whom she was waiting for and were merely observers in the opening stages of a tragedy waiting to happen. She'd gone and stood by the window at ten to two. They were quite precise about the time. Ten to two. Ten to two. They had all repeated when questioned.

Yes, the time was ten to two. Ten minutes before Dean was due, and then quite suddenly, she'd snatched up her bag in a hurry, left without paying her bill and started running out of the hotel and down the steps straight into her car, the waiter running after her to get the money for her unpaid drinks bill. The waiter was but a young man and had been appalled she'd even got into her car and shocked when she'd started it up and got it going in jerks down the street only to turn around suddenly at the corner when she had observed a man crossing the road on his way to the hotel. The waiter had shouted out to her in dismay but she had hurtled the car at the man who was half-way across the zebra crossing.

He had been almost speechless at the ghastly scene he had witnessed but was in no doubt that she had aimed the car at him like a lethal weapon, a stampeding bull, right into her husband, smashing against his legs and then sending him sprawling in the street, rolled up like a hedgehog, blood splattering the tarmac where he landed, rolled and lay, and still she hadn't stopped but had driven away at high speed out of control and straight into one of the plane trees that lined the genteel avenue, slamming the car into the trunk with such force that Vali had been thrown right through the windshield, ending up sprawled against the fence of an adjoining garden like the proverbial rag doll, still and unmoving, her once beautiful face thrown up towards the sky, her blue eyes wide and staring, though unable then, or ever again, to take joy in the clouds or in the sun, or in the deep, deep blue of that after-noon's waning summer sky.

And what of Dean? The waiter, shocked at what he had wit-nessed, still had been able to rush back into the hotel and sum-mon an ambulance.

There had been no mistake, the police had told me later. Vali Mitchell had tried to kill her husband and then had killed herself. Accidentally or deliberately? I would never know.

That Dean was alive at all had been a miracle, but all I could think of first at the news was of my beautiful Vali in her youth, vibrant with a zest for life and the fun of living and laughing. And I had cried all night after the news and all the day after.

The scene as described by the police to me seemed to grow as it repeated itself over and over again in my head.

Should I have seen it coming?

Could I have prevented it?

Was there something I should have done, could have done?

But in the end I knew there was nothing and no answer to the questions that seemed to whirr inside my head.

Only a darkness persisted in my mind and heart.

She had always been a rare thing, a delicate thing, ever since we were children. She had always been the one to break first on a dare, to talk about running away, but never did, had married on a whim and regretted it ever since, had had a child she was not capable of caring for, had spiralled down the tunnel of post-natal depression and never found her way out, had branched off into psychotic episodes fuelled by misery and drink, ignoring every hand that had been held out to help her.

And now she was dead, and Dean in hospital, and Vali-Jo left without a parent to do what parents are supposed to do best: care for her and love her, shield her from all the bad things that the world can do.

Vali-Jo, I thought. Little Vali-Jo, who had never done anything to deserve this.

Vali-Jo, who carried her mother's namesake and my own.

What was to become of that little girl now?

thirty-two | the lord of death

Summer 1958

Craig was stunned into silence and Alison tearful.

Jonathan had agreed to speak at the funeral, silent and stalwart, hiding his innermost feelings. He had been very fond of Vali. And then there was Adrian, standing beside me unfeeling, as stiff as a broomstick, and myself, present in body but where was my spirit?

I had agreed to look after Vali, so fragile and so beautiful. But not this way.

I had arranged for a light oak coffin with pink and white flowers. No darkness of any kind was to touch her, even in death. I had placed a small plaque in her hand, cold but still, whole with nails perfectly manicured. It read. 'I'm with you here darling, Vali, but as I had looked into the open coffin before it was closed, a circular white muslin cloth covering her face, too dreadfully damaged to be seen, a chill ran through me. This then was the omen, the faceless shade that had haunted me and I had been totally unable to recognise what it had meant, nor had the sadhu been able to interpret for me, but then he had no knowledge of Vali.

Dean was there, only out of hospital for a short while to attend the funeral. Crushed and broken, he had insisted he should be present. Luke, his brother, who had arrived from the States, having heard of the accident, stood by his wheelchair and I could hardly bear it, the sadness he was feeling for the woman he had loved, or at least that aspect of her that she had presented for that love. That he would be leaving with Vali-Jo for America shortly seemed to me at that moment more sad still, and I wept long and silently at Vali's graveside, more for our final parting than for her death, for I was only now realising that all this badness, all this tragedy, had swept away the intervening years of misgivings and of doubt, the years of mistaking passion for love and that the one man I had first loved, truly loved had never been Adrian at all.

As I walked away from the graveside a summer storm seemed to be brewing, but it was as nothing compared to the storm within me and for the fear I had for Dean, this once vibrant man, now reduced to a cripple, and yet again I thought of Vali in her halcyon days. What was now to follow?

But had I forgotten Yama, the deity, the Lord of Death, red-eyed, fierce and dark with eyes like heaps of coal, with his green-painted face riding a water buffalo and holding a loop of rope in his hand and a hook with which to pull the souls from the dead and take them to the spirit world for judgement. Yama, too, could judge, but how would he judge the fragile Vali, not harshly I hoped but with some compassion and forgiveness.

And I remembered the Day of Yama. It was during the school holidays when I was about thirteen and a cholera epidemic devoured a local village, near my father's factory, the disease being like a predator in it extreme form. Day after day, hastily shrouded corpses on canvas sheeting with poles at each end and covered with marigolds, were carried swiftly past our factory gates, to funeral pyres along the riverside, the smell of disinfect-ant mingling with burning herbs, rotting corpses and unseasoned wood, the flames reaching out towards the heavens as if pleading for mercy. In all a stench that lingered throughout several days and nights. And then, suddenly it was over and a dreadful silence descended upon us for many days to come, and only then I walked up the hill slowly to ask the sadhu what was the meaning of this.

And so it was with whispered explanations and prayers he told me of Yama, explaining the role of the Lord of Death who could also judge mercifully, and with our palms held together and with the smoke of fragrant dried herbs surrounding us, he explained to me matters concerning Yama; of death, of the soul; the spirit and worlds we knew nothing about.

thirty-three | dead leaves. a dead love

Autumn 1958

Jonathan and Craig had seen to it that I would be financially secure. I was grateful to them. At a meeting in the afternoon before Jonathan returned to London it had been made clear to Adrian, once and for all, that he had no right to any of my assets at which time Adrian had left the room in an ill-tempered and abusive manner. It was when he left that Craig had commented, 'What does he want so much money for, he has a good salary from the Practice and he lives free? Sadly and soon, I was to find out.

Jonathan left for London on the night train and Mr Fellows drove him to the station.

It was well after midnight before I heard Adrian's car in the driveway. He came into the bedroom and started collecting some of his clothes and before he left he spoke with venom in his voice, hissing the words, almost snake-like. 'You're a mean bitch, Jo.' It was the only conversation he had with me, if abuse can be called conversation.

An uneasy quiet descended upon the house. Dean was still in hospital. His progress was slow. Adrian and I scarcely spoke and we barely saw each other. He left for work early each morning and he slept in the downstairs bedroom. On an evening when he was home at a reasonable time I raised the matter of Vali-Jo's health. I was almost afraid to speak to him.

'Adrian, can you please examine Vali-Jo?' I asked. 'There appears to be something far wrong with this little one when I compare her to Frances. Why is she so breathless?'

Scathingly he replied, 'Mind your own business. She's fine.' I repeated my request for him to examine her as I was convinced there was something amiss with this small, quiet and lovable child, who often clung to me and called me Mummy Jo.

He was already agitated. His temper flared.

'Will you stop trying to control me and let me get on with my life, my way?'

I had been traumatised, bullied, beaten and ignored for weeks and months. I could stand his bad temper no longer.

'Control you,' I mocked. 'You have been out of control for some time.'

He grasped my hand and pulled me outside to the Shouting Field which was about to earn its name tragically.

'Yes, I have controlled your life,' I shouted at him as he pulled me roughly, 'otherwise you would still be living in a slum in Calcutta. I should have left you there. That's where you belong. I paid for your ticket to Delhi to sit your exams. Where would you have been without it? I have done everything possible for you. Who paid for you to come to Britain? I did. You have never loved me Adrian. You used me. You are unable to control your money or your temper, let alone take control of my finances and our children. You have tried to destroy me, mind and body. I don't even have permission to go out of the house without your say-so. This nonsense has got to stop.'

I suddenly realised how loud I was shouting.

I calmed down thinking, no, this is not the way and then I spoke to him softly. We were standing apart, facing each other. He had let go of my hand.

'Adrian, look at me. Don't you remember our deep passion for each other? Our love was gentle and so whole. What has happened to us and why? Please give up whatever it is you're doing and return to a family life with me. No decent married man behaves in this appalling way. You don't come home until late at night. You scarcely see the children. Where do you eat? With whom do you sleep? Don't lie and say "no one." I know you are far too highly sexed a man for that. Who has become so important to you that you have lost interest in me, your children, your home and a decent and comfortable way of living? I have given you the things you asked for and craved when we first met. What is it you really want?'

He paced about on the grassy area of the 'Shouting Field' clenching and unclenching his fists. I was shivering with fear and the cold air. Denise had taken the children upstairs having initially heard raised voices. Finally, Adrian calmed down and said, 'I've been offered a short break to do research in London with a woman who has a grant. I will be travelling with Dr Penny Patterson, and living with her in London for three to six months.'

This was the man who couldn't get out of London fast enough to live in Perth. I looked at him in disbelief, and once again my anger rose like bitter bile, choking me, constricting my throat. I should have turned away from him and gone indoors, but still he paced in front of me blocking my path and so I couldn't contain myself and had to speak with harsh disbelief and a great deal of sorrow in my heart.

'Do you really expect me to agree to your going to London with another woman for six months leaving me and the children here? I can't believe this. You're having an affair. How could you, after all we have been through! Who is she, what does she want of you? Does she know you have a wife and small children?' Suddenly I was very tearful, sobs shaking me.

He turned on me, his icy tones betraying the force of his fury. 'Don't be such a stupid bitch, Jo. I have told you repeatedly that I need to involve myself in a research project. Considering you and your cronies, Craig Mackie and that fancy lawyer, Jonathan, have repeatedly refused to release some of your funds to me, and you have considerable wealth, this is now my way of enhancing my career and attaining my goal in life. She has a large apartment and the research papers are all in London. I will work there with her and she will instruct me as to how I can proceed with a research programme.'

'I'm not stupid, Adrian,' I said softly having exhausted myself emotionally and continued speaking to him as normally as possible in the dreadful circumstances I was faced with.

'If this is all above board why didn't you introduce me to her? Why are you out all night? Why can't we sit and discuss this together? What research do people do at midnight? You're a liar. You're sleeping with her. If you leave this house for another woman you'll never set foot in it again. Mark my words.'

He didn't answer and I then asked, again firing questions at him in rapid succession, my tone more strident at each question. 'What about your patients? Have you resigned from your post? Who is replacing you? You can't just walk out of a GP practice. You'll burn your boats behind you if you behave like that. The Medical Profession will be unforgiving. What will you use for money? Have you thought of that? Do you think I am going to keep you and your mistress? Will she keep you?'

I started to laugh and cry hysterically and then stupidly flung one word at him in my rage: 'Gigolo.'

And at that word he took a step towards me and flung his clenched fist into my face, hitting me so hard I fell backwards and passed out for a few moments. The ring on his hand, square cut and large, which I had given him in love for our first Christmas together had formed a weapon against me, tearing and bruising my face, cutting me deep in my cheekbone and just missing my eye.

Crawling on the grass and confused I asked myself, 'When was grass red?' and then I realised the full extent of his violence that day. Blood in my mouth, blood soaking into a patch of earth in the Shouting Field, near the sundial, to be remembered by me forever. And when I came to he was gone.

It was Mr Fellows who discovered me, took me to the hospital where I had sutures put in my face, possibly leaving a scar for the rest of my days. This then was the true mark of my marriage. It was to be the last mark both physically and mentally and now it was Jonathan I needed. I would divorce Adrian Greene.

Mr Fellows, who was a man of few words, was at first silent on our way home but drew into a petrol station to get me a cold drink. He drove slowly and then stopped in a lay-by while I had my drink and then and only then, slowly and succinctly he gave me his advice.

'Look, lassie,' he said, 'I know I am only an employee but I must say this. The wife and I are worried about you. If there's any way you can get out of the situation you're in, try and do it, especially for the bairns.'

thirty-four |
the finlayson curse

End Autumn 1958

The bedroom had been the last call of Adrian's anger.

Two large cases were missing in which he had obviously packed a considerable amount of clothes from his wardrobe, a sign that he had left. Some that he felt he didn't need, and had been bought for him by me, were thrown carelessly on the bed. Was this his final insult?

By the following morning my face was very swollen, and my eye was totally closed. Frances started crying when she saw me, hugging me and refusing to let me go. 'Who was naughty to you, Mummy?' she kept saying.

I went into the study in the afternoon and fell asleep on the couch. The painkillers I had been given made me drowsy. I woke about four o'clock and went into the kitchen. Mr Fellows had come in from the garden and was having a cup of tea. He had a camera with him. When he saw me he said, 'Mrs Greene, I'm going to take a few photographs of you. You might need them.' I agreed.

Mrs Fellows, obviously wishing to comfort me, said she would stay on a little while after the children were in bed and have a cup of coffee with me. 'It'll be good to unburden yourself a little,' she had said.

We had coffee together and I took a couple of painkillers. She then spoke of matters I had vaguely suspected. At first she was embarrassed at the state I was in but loosened up and told me what I had long suspected, but now putting into words my worst fears.

Adrian had, indeed, been involved with a woman, a Dr Patterson, she said. He had rented an apartment for her and this is where he spent a great deal of his time. Unable to suppress my curiosity I asked, 'What is she like?'

'I don't rightly know,' she replied, 'but I have a friend, a nurse, who lives in the same block of flats. She described her as sturdy of build, plain, possibly older than him, but very self-assured. She has often been seen in the small shop nearby always buying cigarettes. She's a heavy smoker apparently.'

The sorrow I felt had left me as had the rage. I was unwanted and unloved and yet a strange sense of relief started to take over my feelings. He had gone, taking his violence out of my life and surely the path of fear that I had trod for so long would now end.

Mrs Fellows had become increasingly embarrassed as she told me the story of Adrian's deception and then with a worried look said, 'I'm so sorry, what will become of you and the bairns when he stops giving you money and wants you to leave the house. I'm so sorry,' she repeated several times and then paused and looked at me strangely. 'If I'm mistaken and this is only idle gossip, please forgive me.'

I started to laugh almost hysterically and put my hand over hers for a moment saying, 'Mrs Fellows, don't worry about me. The money is a legacy from my mother's side of the family, the Finlaysons, and the house is mine, it cannot ever be sold and will pass to my heirs.

At this she seemed to pale visibly, rose, went through to the kitchen and made fresh coffee. When she returned she put down the tray and sat down almost hesitatingly, saying, 'So you're a Finlayson and then continued in a strange whisper. 'Have you heard of the Finlayson curse?' I shook my head.

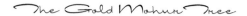

'Sadly, I'm afraid the Finlayson curse has been a story around these parts for many long years. A young village girl kept secret company with one of the young Finlayson men. Very rich they were. He got her pregnant and then abandoned her. She lived in poverty and the little girl she had out of the liaison died as a child and so she cursed the Finlaysons, saying her curse was powerful and would touch the young Finlayson women and they too would die young.'

'There are many stories like that in large wealthy families,' I said 'and not really for believing.' I then tried to make light of the situation saying, 'She should have cursed the men and not the poor women who had done nothing to warrant such a curse.'

She smiled at me in a strange way and we finished our coffee. I was tired and aching in body and mind. I thanked her for her sympathy and concern and went to bed.

I was alone now and made doubly sure the house was properly locked up at night. I also asked Mr Fellows to change the locks on the doors. The children played happily together and the days were busy for me but the nights were troubled and my concern for little Vali-Jo increased.

I thought of the story Mrs Fellows had told of the Finlayson curse. Could such a thing be possible? I questioned her further one day while I was helping her in the kitchen and she told me that several female members of the family had died young starting with the grandmother for whom this land had been bought and for whom the original house had been built. I thought of my mother Rosamund, my real mother, in her twenties dying of malaria in India, and Vali. Was this just coincidence? All young lives cut short.

Not now, my subconscious screamed out to me. No, I mustn't let myself believe this and I looked at my children playing in the grass in the Shouting Field. Who would look after them if I was gone? And then a dreadful sweat, born of fear, broke out all over me as I thought, what of frail little Vali-Jo, carrying my name and much loved by me.

And now the nights were restless for me, strange dreams and thoughts crowding into my mind, often of my time in India. And on a night of great unease I dreamed I was back in my father's factory. I was climbing Monkey Hill and could see the sadhu standing still at the top with his arms outstretched in supplication and as though he was warding off something.

I was a small child in my dream and as I climbed and then stood with my back against him he was protecting me from a strange unknown force and I was no longer afraid. He kept pushing his hands forward, warding off an unseen enemy with the palms upturned saying, 'Bus, bus, (enough, enough).

I woke, covered in perspiration, but a strange calm was within me. It was indeed enough. The desire I once had for Adrian Greene was long gone.

thirty-five | a slow recovery

Winter 1958

Dean was like a sturdy tree, knocked to the ground in one fell swoop in the storm of Vali Finlayson's insane rage. Why had it happened?

After many weeks and several heart-wrenching visits to the hospital, he was showing some improvement, and in a phone call, during which he seemed to be regaining some of his old exuberance, he told me he had decided he would be going home for Christmas as he needed the comfort of his family. His brother Luke had made the arrangements.

So it was, that with heavy heart and with little Vali-Jo in my arms I visited Dean in hospital for the last time on the day he was scheduled to leave for America. Had fate decreed this was our final parting?

I walked slowly with Vali-Jo, down characterless white corridors until I came to his room. The door was ajar and his face lit up as he saw Vali Jo, who ran towards him. I stood back apace and when he had cuddled his little daughter he turned to me.

'And how's my Jose' he said, but as yet he had never commented upon my scarred face. Luke came into the room and took Vali-Jo away with him to buy her a drink. I sat beside him and took his hand in mine. My emotions were getting the better of me to see this fine young man reduced to a possible invalid for life. It was Dean who broke the silence, and at last commented on my appearance saying softly. 'Oh, my Jose, why do you let Adrian treat you so badly? Are you to live the rest of your life as a battered wife?' And at last I was able to tell him with as little emotion as possible, I had decided to divorce Adrian.

Luke came back into the room and we left Vali-Jo with Dean for them to have some private time together and Luke accompanied me to a small waiting room where I expressed my real worries to him about Vali-Jo. Understanding my fears were genuine, and not borne of eccentricity, he said, 'Jose, I hear what you're saying. You've been like a mother to Vali-Jo. I give you my word she'll be seen by specialists when we arrive in Boston, as will Dean. They will both be well looked after. I promise you that.'

As we walked back down the corridor to Dean's room he turned to me and said sadly, 'How is my brother going to cope with his injuries and a sick child. God help us all. Dean won't be able to accept being an invalid.'

We returned to the small clinical room where Dean sat cuddling his daughter. Dean now had a false joyfulness about him. I went up to the chair to kiss him goodbye and tell him to take care of himself and Vali-Jo. He encircled me with his uninjured arm and kissed me full on the lips.

'Come on, Jose. Don't you remember what I used to say? Jose Willis will always kiss her Dean. Kiss me properly, Jose,' he laughed.

It was a false laugh. It was a false time, but the emotions we had obviously felt for each from our early days of love were now slowly rising again to the fore, especially for me and I had hope in my heart that when the grieving was over for Dean, one day we might have a new beginning.

I accompanied them to the station. They were to go by train from Edinburgh to London and then take a flight the next day back to America. The train was at the platform and not much time was left for us to speak. I kissed Vali-Jo with tears in my eyes and turned to Dean. He was trying to stand up from the confines of his wheelchair.

He put his arms around me. He had always been a strong, well-built young man. I couldn't believe how light he seemed in my arms. I wept as he tried to embrace me. He didn't want to let me go. Vali-Jo seemed bewildered.

'You will come to the States and I will walk when I meet you at the airport. I swear it,' he commented with determination in his voice. He was still holding me when a guard who was passing said, 'You will have to let him board now, Miss.'

Luke helped Dean onto the train. I stood and waved them goodbye. I walked down the platform slowly and alone, with my back to the man I loved, while the train pulled away, just as my father had done all those years ago.

A part of my life was ending. Would there be a new beginning?

I had made an early start to arrive in Edinburgh on time and now needed some breakfast. I asked Mr Fellows to stop at a small café. I persuaded him to join me. He noticed I was tearful and tried to comfort me.

'He's a good man, Mrs Greene. Men sometimes marry the wrong woman.'

I smiled at him saying, 'Well, you've done all right for yourself, Mr Fellows.'

'Aye, the wife's a good lass,' he admitted. 'She's a bit out of sorts the last few days. I hate to say this but we won't be working for you much longer.'

'Huh! Am I that much of a nuisance, or is she unwell?' I asked.

'No, even with all the problems it's been good working for you. You have been very considerate, but it's like this. The landlord of the flats we live in wants his property for redevelopment. He's offered us a small sum to vacate quickly. We can't afford to rent in Perth. Rents are going sky high.'

'Well, you can stay in the bungalow,' I offered on the spur of the moment. 'Mrs Fellows has the keys anyway and cleans it out occasionally. Move in when you like. The only problem is the piano.

Can you arrange to shift it into the sitting room? Aunt Eileen was a fairly well-accomplished player and maybe the children could learn.'

'Good Lord! We couldn't afford the rent on such a place,' he exclaimed.

'There's no rent, Mr Fellows,' I assured him. 'It will be comforting to know there's someone living near at hand in case of emergencies. I don't expect any extra work from you.

You have done more than enough to help me.' Mr and Mrs Fellows moved happily into the bungalow at the end of the week.

The children whinged after Vali-Jo had gone. It was nearing Christmas and I took them shopping and bought them the best television set I could find. This would entertain all of us during the long winter nights.

A certain lightness of atmosphere pervaded the house. The fear I had left me. Alison and Craig visited often and just before Christmas Alison told me excitedly that they were to tour Europe on an extended holiday. She had never been out of Britain.

The days were full but the evenings spent alone brought with them memories, and the snowman the children had built with the help of Mr Fellows was so close to the window that at night I pulled the curtains to hide from his almost leering stare, the coals for eyes and the carrot for a nose together with one of Adrian's old scarves draped around his neck formed something of a menacing sight when the skies darkened.

I decided to clean out my bedroom, make it my own, my very own without the feel or the smell or the presence of Adrian. I threw out the clothes he had left behind and decided to freshen all the drawers and cupboards he had used. The drawer where he kept his smalls and socks seemed to be most distasteful to me and as I removed the lining paper from the drawer, his passport and a few letters lay secreted under the paper.

I removed them and sat on the bed to read why he had kept them in such a place, but then paperwork of any sort was no friend of Adrian Greene.

I picked up Adrian's passport first and flicked through the pages aimlessly remembering how he had such difficulty in getting this passport and the difficulties he had caused Craig about the paperwork involved. Huh! I said out loud and thought back to this particular time in our lives. So this was the man who wanted to conduct complicated scientific research. Not much of a chance of success there, I thought bitterly.

I stopped suddenly. There was an Australian visa for six months in the passport.

'Oh my God. Oh, my God, what did I marry?' I murmured.

I couldn't believe what I was reading. The visa had been granted to him when I was pregnant with Andrew. Also enclosed in the passport was a letter offering him a post as a research assistant in Australia, with a possible extension. The letter was from a Professor Brownlee. It was what he always wanted. Why didn't he go and what on earth was he going to say to me?

The next two letters revealed more, sadly much more.

The first letter from a Lynn Brownlee thanked Adrian for the wonderful graduation present and for the magic sexy weekend spent with her. She said in the letter she was looking forward to their life together in Australia and was pleased that Daddy had appointed him on her recommendation. The next paragraph brought back to life the strange telephone call I had in the London flat. It said. 'I will look after your beautiful little girl as if she were my own. Ad, I'm so sorry your wife died in childbirth. Sweetheart, I'm a little over two months pregnant. Daddy was a bit cross at first but said he would be pleased if we married quickly. I'll be back from London soon.' It was signed 'from your darling Lynn.'

The second letter shocked me to the core, full of bitterness and ending, 'I aborted your child, you lying bastard.'

Disbelief and horror seized me in its grasp. I could now explain why he had held the sleeping Andrew in his arms and whispered, 'Forgive me Lord.' His was the sin.

He had stood at the altar of God and said to me with such passion in his voice, 'I will love you forever.' Nobody had told me how short was his forever.

I had thought of divorce, talked of divorce but now I had to do something concrete about it.

I phoned Jonathan, who initially tried to persuade me to think again, saying it was a blip in my marriage as we had gone through so much, so soon together. And then I told him the whole truth and sent him the photographs Mr Fellows had taken of me and the papers I had found. Jonathan was shocked that Adrian had even contemplated bigamy. And so my marriage was over and Jonathan agreed to start divorce proceedings.

Penny Patterson would now only be a ripple in the rough seas of our divorce.

thirty-six | a new era

1959

Letters from Dean gave me cause for concern.

Doctors had confirmed that Vali-Jo had a heart condition and the medication they had put her on had shown some improvement. I had a letter from Luke thanking me for my concern. A certain amount of optimism ran through his letter but I couldn't share his hopes. Was Vali-Jo's condition congenital, or was it something hidden in the darker side of life; perhaps the result of Vali's excesses and heavy drinking or even was it the Finlayson curse that Mrs Fellows believed in?

In the main I had remained whole though sometimes in the darkness of the night in my dreams I heard a soft voice saying, 'You're home, Missy.' It woke me. What had happened to the man whom I had loved? The hurt was still palpable. But in the main life had dealt me a reasonable hand. I had a good home, two beautiful children and enough money for a comfortable living. Was it enough for me if a solitary life was to be the price?

The children seemed content and I kept Denise on to help with their ever- growing activities. I taught them and Denise to swim. I threw away my old clothes and visited the boutique that Alison frequented. I selected smart outfits and got rid of my dowdy image, had my hair styled in the fashion of the day, had facials and bought special creams to hide the scar on my face. Styles had changed dramatically as had the very demeanour of young women. They were vibrant and self-assured. It was 1959 and I was only twenty-nine. Why shouldn't I be fashionable?

I couldn't expect Mr Fellows to transport me indefinitely. I asked him to select a small car for my personal use. The larger car would be kept. I paid for lessons every other day and soon got used to the roads. The car Mr Fellows chose for me was a Triumph Herald, a car of the times, colourful and smart, in two-tone blue and white.

I passed my test but was a bit apprehensive of driving on my own. It was the hilly terrain I found difficult at first as I was accustomed to the flat roads of Calcutta.

Mr Fellows accompanied me for the first few days. I was busy with the children and my self-confidence was starting to return.

Despite my loneliness, the time seemed to pass quickly. The children had become used to not having a father in the house. Nobody mentioned Adrian Greene.

It was mid May when I had two very worrying phone calls from Dean. He asked if we could go to America as soon as possible. Despite specialist care Vali-Jo was not showing any further improvement. There seemed to be a problem with the way her heart was functioning. After the second call I applied for a visa to the States. Dean had said 'Jose, please come. I need you here beside me at this time and through the dark days that are approaching.'

I phoned Jonathan and told him of my plans and arrangements were put into place for Mr and Mrs Fellows to look after the house in my absence and Craig, ever reliable, was asked to look after my financial affairs.

It was the end of June before we were able to leave for Boston. Frances and Andrew were excited for the sake of being excited. I was leaving with a heavy heart. Although looking forward to seeing Dean I knew I would be faced with a very sick little girl and a damaged man whose love of life had been dimmed by misfortune.

We took an early morning PANAM flight from London and the children were still sleepy when we boarded. Luke was to meet us in New York and we were to have a couple of days in a hotel before going on to Boston. He thought the journey all in one day would be too much for the children.

It was a Monday morning when we arrived in Boston. Dean's father had taken the day off from work as the construction site for the houses they were building was quite some distance from where they lived. I was expecting an ordinary comfortable house. I was surprised by the sheer beauty of the place. Dean had said, 'It's a nice patch, Jose, you'll like it.' It was more than a nice patch. It was sheer luxury.

As I looked around me at the beautiful setting I thought how could Vali have given up Dean and a comfortable home and trashed her future for the sake of drink.

The children were quiet at first in a strange environment. Dean and Vali-Jo were not at home when we had arrived. He had taken her to the hospital for a check-up as they had put her on yet a further new medication.

Dean brought Vali-Jo home late in the day. I went forward to the car and took her in my arms. 'You've come to see me, Mummy-Jo' she said smiling. She had recognised me.

Dean put his arms around us. I was pleased to see he was able to walk, albeit with a heavy limp. He seemed pale and drawn. As we went inside the house he took Vali-Jo gently from me and put her on the couch in the sitting room and propped her up with pillows. I had to go to the cloakroom and wipe away my tears. I could scarcely believe Vali-Jo's health had deteriorated so quickly. Frances was very gentle with her as was Andrew, who was all for giving her his little car which he rolled on the floor continuously. While Vali-Jo was pleased to see them she became breathless with the excitement. We had to calm the children down, and Val-Jo was fed by a nanny and put to bed early.

Dean and I took Frances and Andrew to the garden to let them run about. They had felt cooped up in the hotel in New York. Dean's mother had prepared a room for each of them which she had decorated beautifully. I thanked her for her thoughtfulness and kindness. She had made a good recovery after her slight stroke but said she tired easily as she was still on a lot of medication. The arrangements she had made for us seemed to be long-term ones and I now feared the worst for Vali-Jo.

After our evening meal, Dean suggested we go for a walk in the grounds of their home. I noticed he sometimes used a stick while walking. We sat quietly on a bench together, not far from the house. This was no time for small talk and frivolity between us. We were both damaged in our own way. He put his hand over mine and said softly, The doctors say Vali-Jo's time is limited and they are doing all they can for her. Jose, you will be here with me until the end? I can't stand it alone. I know how she clings to you.'

'I promise I'll stay with you and Vali-Jo as long as you wish,' I said. He sighed before he replied, 'I feel ill and tired, Jose. How much more of this can I take?'

We stood up to go indoors. Dean pulled me to him and kissed me. I was surprised at him, but even more amazed at myself as I responded to him. I stood facing him holding his hands and he was apologetic saying, 'I'm sorry, I shouldn't have done that. You're still married to Adrian but I need you so badly at this time of my life.' I too needed him but for very different reasons. I knew I loved him but was my love returned or did he have a need only for my strength and sympathy at this vulnerable time? We walked back slowly to the house and he then said, 'Well, how is your divorce progressing?' 'Horrendous,' I replied. So many dreadful things have happened in my marriage. I don't want to burden you with them. I married a violent and manipulative man. How stupid I was not to listen to the advice of friends and family. I hope the divorce is granted soon.'

For me the days seemed to merge one into the other. Vali-Jo continued to look frail. Andrew and Frances tried to entertain her. What did life hold for her? I was uneasy but didn't speak about her medical condition. We were living in a dreadful cocoon of sorrow whilst a way of life carried on outside.

Dean had not been able to help his father with the paperwork of the family run business as he had been giving his undivided attention to Vali-Jo. Luke had been busy on site. Dean's father Matt was worried that the paperwork was piling up and asked if I could help saying, 'Dean says you're pretty good at accounts and have been trained in accounting while in India. Can you help out, Jose?'

Time had been hanging heavy on my hands and I was glad to be working with Matt. I was amazed at the large amounts of money being handled. It took my mind off my problems and the imminent death of Vali-Jo.

Matt and I stopped one afternoon for a tea break. We sat and chatted for a while. I told him a little about my background. He was quite distressed when I told him the story of my real mother and how I had never had a proper family.

'Jose, would you consider marrying Dean?'

I was taken aback.

'I'm already married. I'm waiting for a divorce, as you know. Besides, it's manners to wait until you're asked,' I said smiling at him. We returned to our work and nothing more was said. Deep down, however, I feared that Dean, after Vali-Jo, might want to wipe the slate of his past clean and start again. I, unfortunately, was a reminder of his past. Would he really want me?

I was able to help considerably both with Vali-Jo and in the office thus relieving some of the pressure off Dean and Matt. Dean came into the office and helped with the paperwork for three days running, giving Matt a break. I was amazed to see how quickly and accurately Dean handled paperwork, unlike Adrian.

'You're not so stupid, Jose,' he teased after the second evening, revealing a small glimmer of his former self.

I was working with my head down. I knew he had stopped and was looking at me. There was something different in the way Dean looked at me recently. This was a more mature man, a man of want and needs and I somehow felt shy and blushed.

'Oh! *Jo-see.*' That's how he said the word. He was smiling broadly. 'You blushed. You must be thinking naughty thoughts about me.'

'No, Dean, it's the other way around. Let's pack up for today,' I replied.

I was pleased to see a spark of fun still existed within him. We cleared the desk and as we were going out of the room he held my hand and drew me to him gently, kissing me, holding me close and whispering, 'I'll never do anything to hurt you. You know that.'

Each day I noticed that the nanny put Vali-Jo on the couch and carried her back and forward to the table for her meals. I thought this little child's life has no fun in it at all. No matter how long she had, we should give her some joy in living.

I went to the hospital with Dean and Vali-Jo for the next hospital appointment. The weather was warm and I asked if we could put her in the swimming pool. We could carry her in the pool while the children swam. We could also carry her in our arms and dance to music. We could put her on the swing very gently. The doctors agreed with these suggestions. Little Vali-Jo seemed so much happier as she felt she was taking part in all the activities that were going on around her. Matt cooked endless barbecues. We tried to let Vali-Jo take part in some way in the everyday lives of Frances and Andrew.

Dean and I often sat in the garden together long after everyone else had gone inside. The smell of the barbeques seemed to linger in the warmth of the evening. I never spoke of Vali to Dean, but these were the times when there was anger within me against

Vali and the mean and selfish things she had done. Day after day, month after month, we were to watch a child die, all because of her thoughtlessness and I had to break my heart watching Dean limp – possibly for the rest of his life.

By the fall of 1959, when the leaves were starting to show their glorious colours, Vali-Jo worsened. My visa was running out and Luke had the task of helping me obtain an extension on compassionate grounds. I hoped that Vali-Jo would be with us for Christmas. Yes, she was, but at what cost to us, each and every one of us trying to pretend everything was as it should be. We all knew we were trying to entertain a dying child, helping her enjoy the last days of her life but breaking our own hearts in trying to do so. Fortunately the children seemed unaware of our torment, and gave the proceedings an air of normality, even if Dean dressed up as Santa for the children with a heavy heart.

We took Vali-Jo back to the hospital the next day. They could no longer let her out of hospital and no amount of love or medication could save her now. All that was left to us was a heartbreaking vigil at the bedside of this beautiful, innocent child.

The hospital had a small chapel and each day I prayed within its walls trying to calm my spirit. I knew now Vali-Jo would never recover.

During the last two days of her life Dean and I never slept. We dozed through exhaustion at her bedside. Dean had Vali-Jo, half-cradled in his arms. She tried to put her little hands around his neck but her strength was seeping away and on the thirtieth of December she died. Dean put his head down and wept silently with the dead child in his arms. So many times she had said softly in the last month of her life, 'Mummy-Jo, you are here' and smiled at me.

I touched Dean on the shoulder. He pulled me down beside him.

'Dean, we will have to let go now,' I said to him softly.

A nurse came into the room and persuaded him to leave. Luke came to collect us. Dean was given a sedative and I went into my room and slept through exhaustion. It was Luke who made all the arrangements for the funeral.

The following week I lived in a sad and shadowy haze. My children were, however, my priority and I had to hold my emotions in check for their well-being. Frances asked for her young companion several times and we told her Vali-Jo was to be in hospital for some time. Vali-Jo's nanny looked after the children while we all attended the funeral.

We were a family, a family drained of emotion, shadowy and purposeless, without Vali-Jo as the pivot of our activities, and I knew it was time for me to return to Scotland.

Dean came to see us off at the airport. The children were in tears as they didn't want to leave their now familiar surroundings nor the man they had come to love. Andrew in particular had become very attached to Dean. I, in turn, was now parting from the man I had giggled with as a teenager and danced with often. We had been torn apart by the jealousy of my half-sister Rose and I had wept with him at the death of his child. I had always loved him in so many ways. My greatest regret was that I had introduced him to Vali Finlayson. If there was such a thing as the Finlayson curse, then it had touched us all.

He held me close for a short while and thanked me.

'Look at me, Jose. Am I to die a childless cripple?'

'You're not a cripple, Dean and as for childless, that's up to you,' I replied.

He said he would be in touch.

thirty-seven | home to perth

1960

It was all different when I came home, snowing and cold.

Somewhere across the sea Vali-Jo was deprived forever of laughter, growing into womanhood and the very joy of living, and Dean too, so far away. It felt as if a vast hole had been ripped through the curtain of my life.

But amongst all this sadness and deep sorrow, a glimpse of joy and light shone for me. Alison and Craig had decided to get married and arrangements were well in hand at the time of my arrival. And it was an excited Alison who came to see me, telling me of her experiences on the Continent and how much she had loved her trip. It was to be a small wedding but a spark of her joy lifted my spirits and I was pleased, once again; to have the friendship of Alison at my door, but I had to cast a shadow on her joy as I gave her the news of little Vali-Jo's death.

Mrs Fellows would also have to be told out of earshot of the children who were busy rediscovering their surroundings after their time in America.

I missed Dean. I expected to hear his voice at every turn. Mentally, my feet hadn't really touched Scottish soil. Part of me still seemed to be in America and I missed the bustle of the Mitchell household.

Large bundles of mail in date order awaited my attention and as I sat in the kitchen drinking a cup of tea and reading my mail while Mrs Fellows cooked, I asked, 'Any news?'

She didn't speak for a minute or two and seemed upset as she stirred the contents of the pot rapidly.

'Well, it's like this,' she said eventually. 'Dr Greene, your husband, came in one morning. He collected the rest of his belongings. He didn't look too well.'

'Without your excellent cooking who can look well?' I teased.

She turned round and looked at me without smiling and then spoke awkwardly. 'He stood in the study, or as he always insisted calling it, the prayer room and looked at the picture of you that the potter drew. He was in there quite a long time. The door was open and I followed him. Your lawyer had phoned to inform me that while you were away he was not to remove anything from the house other than his own possessions. I could have sworn he had a tear in his eye. There was such regret on his face.'

She sighed and shook her head. 'When he saw me he merely said goodbye, Mrs Fellows, and left. It was if he was never to come back.'

'He's never to enter this house again, Mrs Fellows,' I replied briskly.

'Mrs Greene, I think you should phone your lawyer,' she said in worried tones. 'He has phoned several times during the last two weeks asking when you were to be back. Ever since your husband returned from London, he too has phoned constantly wishing to speak to you and each time he seemed increasingly agitated by your absence.'

'I'll think about it in a few days,' I replied without really taking her remarks seriously.

Mrs Fellows looked at me almost in horror.

'Are you *no awfie* worried?' she said slipping into dialect.

I sighed as I spoke, 'When I compare it with death, no, Mrs Fellows. Dean, his family and I have had a harrowing time. Little Vali-Jo died soon after Christmas. There was nothing more the

doctors could do for her. We kept her as happy as possible. I'm still too upset to put up with nonsense from anyone let alone my husband who should have signed the divorce papers by now. It's over a year this farce has been going on.'

'Well and how have you been?' I asked, changing the subject.

'Getting weary without enough to do,' she smiled. "It's been a long times for me without any *bairns in the hoose*,' she laughed.

Mail from Jonathan advised me that Adrian was now seeking custody of the children and wanted a private meeting with me as soon as possible. He asked me to phone him. I took no notice of the letter. I was rather tired of being badgered by one problem or another. The children needed attention and my love as Vali-Jo had taken up a great deal of my time. I had to see to their welfare. Frances was school age and Andrew would have to go to a pre-school group. I needed to keep them happy and well-adjusted. I knew I might have difficulties in the future without a father figure.

Mr Fellows came in to see me about the cars and several household matters. He was pleased I was back. 'Excuse me,' he said. 'I hope you won't take it amiss, but you look well since you've come back from America, even though you must have been saddened after the death of little Vali-Jo. Poor *wee mite*. Mrs Fellows and I are very upset. God rest her soul.'

A fortnight after my return to Perth, Adrian phoned early in the morning irate that I had changed the locks as he was unable to gain access to what he had persistently called his house. The ensuing conversation was anything but polite.

A phone call the following day from Jonathan was frantic. 'Josephine, stop telling your husband to go to hell when he phones you. I strongly suggest you have a meeting with him as he is refusing to sign the divorce papers and says he will seek custody of the children. He wants a meeting with you and has spoken of reconciliation despite the fact you have refused all along. This divorce must be finalised soon or you might run into problems with him. He maintains that in his religion there's no such thing as divorce and you'll always be married to him, despite the ruling of the courts.'

A week later Adrian phoned again and I agreed to meet him for lunch in a restaurant in town. He said his car had broken down and was being repaired so I was to collect him from a flat he had rented. I chose a Monday to meet him knowing the restaurant would be quiet.

The nights were dark and lonely for me. The children were company but didn't make up for adult conversation. The weekend before I was to meet Adrian I was particularly troubled, and slept little.

The sadhu came to me in spirit. For the short time I did sleep I had a strange dream of him. It was a mysterious dream giving me a sense of foreboding. I previously had a repetitive dream of him pushing something unseen and unsavoury away from me. This night I dreamed he was sitting down in a small clearance in a forest. He was in a safe place but I was entangled in the tentacles of bushes and trees. With great difficulty I managed to set myself free. The thorns had ripped my clothes to shreds and my arms were bleeding. The scar on my wrist had become a gaping hole and blood was spurting from it.

The dream then became much more peaceful. He beckoned to me. I found myself sitting opposite him in the lotus position, just as I had done when I was a child, and wearing the blue dress I had worn on my last visit to my father in Ranchi. He put his hand out and touched my wrist. The blood stopped flowing. Instead of the bare earth of Monkey Hill around him, a swathe of green grass surrounded him. Small multi-coloured, flat daisy-like flowers were growing through the grass. They disappeared as I tried to touch them. The beads around my neck were of the type sadhus wore, seeds of fruits strung together. A garland of small marigolds nestled amongst them.

Once again, the sadhu was chanting in my dream. Only the chant was strange. .He was saying, 'Khuthum hua, khuthum hua, (It's finished, it's finished). He stopped for a while. He spoke softly saying 'Jo ba ba, the spark of my spirit I gave to you won't hold much longer. You must now rely on your own strength. The time has passed. Be at peace now and walk cautiously. The old path has ended. Tread this new path with joy and don't go back and never look round with regret in your heart. Don't return to the old path even if you find it welcoming. I have prayed hard and long for the ring of sorrow around your life to be removed. Hold fast now, don't give way to fear.'

I woke with a start on Monday morning, not knowing if the dream was for good or evil or was it born of fear of Adrian Greene whom I was to meet in a few hours time. Was this the end of the terrible path the Sadhu had predicted and which I had trod or was I the last member of the Finlayson Clan to be touched by the curse? Was I going to die? Yellow marigolds were often put on dead bodies being taken to the burning ghats, and these had been wound round my neck as a garland in my dream. I took a cool shower to get the uneasiness out of my mind. I had to be strong against Adrian when I came face to face with him. His personality had been forceful and he had been able to manipulate me in the past. I dressed in a dark green suit with a matching blouse that I had bought in America with the help of Dean's mother. I wore high-heeled brown boots that looked good with the outfit. I did my make-up carefully and sprayed myself with a light morning fragrance. I looked in the mirror and thought. Well, I have only myself to please now. I would not go back to the dreary, down-at-heel image of myself. I used the Herald to drive round to where Adrian had rented a flat. He was standing outside looking thin and shabby in a suit that I recognised as the one he had worn at Vali's funeral. He didn't have on an overcoat even though it was a chilly morning.

He put his hand out for the car key as I stopped beside him saying, 'I'll drive.' He immediately wanted to take control, and as I hesitated, he tried to make the most of my one unguarded moment by saying gently and with a smile, 'You know I always drive you, Jo,' but it was too late. I gained my composure.

'I'm sorry, it's only insured for me to drive,' I lied. It was the first time I had driven him and he was uneasy, but I had put down my marker that I was now in control. From the outset of this meeting I wasn't going to let him browbeat me.

He got into the passenger seat reluctantly. I drove to the restaurant without us exchanging a word. We were ushered to a table in a bay window. The midday sun caught his face as he sat down opposite me. He had started to grey at the temples but was still the handsome man I had fallen in love with although not well groomed. I felt a great pity for him and for his foolishness. For a moment a strange softening towards him seemed to encompass me and I almost put my hand out to touch his, to reassure him, to comfort him, as I had done in the early days of our love, but all at once I noticed the ring he was wearing that had damaged my face and as a snapshot of that dreadful day flashed before me, I returned to the reality of our position and the dream of the night before was still fresh in my mind. Had it been a warning? The appearance of the waiter brought me back fully to reality and Adrian's voice ordering the table d'hote. I asked for some grilled chicken and a salad.

This meeting was unnecessary but I was now at the point of doing almost anything to finalise my divorce. Jonathan had repeatedly been instructed by me to tell Adrian that I wouldn't consider reconciliation. For a brief moment I wondered if I had acted correctly. Was I depriving my children of a father? Could he change?

He finished his soup before he decided to speak at all. The first thing he asked for was his aunt's money. He didn't seem to understand that his aunt's will left the money to Vali.

Vali had left her money to me. I had agreed to let him have the equivalent amount that his aunt had left Vali. This was a good-will gesture on my part. The money had never been willed to him. There was, however, a proviso. He had to sign the divorce papers and return them to Jonathan first. Once this was done the money would be released to him.

I now spoke as softly and gently as was possible in the circum-stances. I didn't want a hideous argument in a restaurant.

'I'll give you all your money. When have I ever taken anything from you? You have always taken from me. The only thing I want from you is a divorce. I can't live with you, Adrian, so please stop asking for reconciliation. You are as a stranger to me now. You attempted to commit bigamy and abduct Frances when I was pregnant. You got a young girl pregnant and she aborted your child when she found out you were already married. How stupid do you think I am? Oh, yes, I know about that too, Adrian. You see, I found the letters you so carelessly left in your drawer. How could you have done that to me at such a vulnerable time?'

He shook his head. He didn't deny anything.

'I'll get counselling. I won't hurt you again, I swear. I've fool-ishly hurt myself too, you know,' he said dramatically. 'Please come back to me, Jo, I do love you.'

I knew it was a lie, but he was very persuasive.

We ate together in silence and by the time I had finished the physical and mental agony he had caused me seemed to rise between us like a spectre of great evil. 'Counselling? Adrian, what counselling is there for someone as manipulative as you?' I asked.

'I'll never divorce you, you're my wife,' he said belligerently.

I spoke without raising my voice. 'I don't care if you sign the papers or not. Sign or starve, take you pick.' I said cruelly. From his demeanour I knew he had no money. But still he persisted in threatening me, trying to force me to return to him.

'I'll take the children away from you,' he said like a sulky child, knowing what he proposed was impossible for him.

I still managed to keep cool and replied softly but with an undertone of anger in my voice. 'Don't raise your voice here, Adrian, and stop being idiotic. No court will give you custody. You have made no attempt to see the children. You have no job, little money and no home. You may be daft but the judges in the courts are not. You see, I'm not as illiterate and stupid as you think. I've increased the money left to me by my natural mother several times over. So who's a stupid bitch now? You have given up a good way of life for strange and unrealistic dreams, well beyond your capabilities, to say nothing of your violence towards me.

Research, huh! I have given my children a secure and loving home. What have you ever given them? All you have ever said to me is I want, I want, I want. You have had no thought for anyone else, let alone the children you've fathered.'

I was pleased there were only a few people in the restaurant and our table was well away from them as we were now struggling to try and be civil to one another. and I was losing my temper with him. I wouldn't have liked them to hear our conversation.

He continued eating and dropped his belligerent tone.

'Our children,' he said almost in a whisper. He continued in his old dictatorial fashion. 'Marriage is for life. It's a wife's duty to obey her husband and carry out his wishes. You did agree to love, honour and obey at God's altar. I only disciplined you. I want us to reconcile. I do love you, Jo,' he repeated. 'I have never stopped loving you. You are out of control. You never do anything I say, you please yourself. You're like a whited sepulchre; you're going rotten inside. Look at the way you're dressed.'

I had no answer for him, and now knew he could never control himself or his vile temper as his voice was rising as he spoke. If we had been alone he surely would have struck me.

We finished our meal in silence. I got up from the table and paid the bill.

We got into the car and I drove him to his flat. I thought of his attitude regarding discipline. It frightened me. Would he have hit the children in a fit temper as they grew and called it discipline? How far would he have gone? If he had whipped me like some ancient galley slave with his leather belt what would he have done to Andrew as he grew up? It put a chill through me. I stopped the car at his flat and turned off the engine and looked at him.

'What happened to you?' I asked. 'What I felt for you was almost like worship. You must have known that. Why then did you try to destroy me? Why do you have no answer for me? You wanted my money, my house and the children I have borne. You got none of these and now you want me back. Not in love, but because your ill thought out plans have not worked out in your favour.'

He was losing his temper. I recognised the set of his jaw.

I asked him to get out of the car. He had to have the last say.

'You went all the way across an ocean to sleep with your boy-friend, Dean Mitchell. He must be bloody good in bed. You're just an upmarket whore, Jo. Aren't you?'

I replied to him speaking slowly and deliberately, keeping my temper in check. 'If that's what you think, then why don't you give me a divorce? Why are you asking to come back to me? Your idea of discipline is not the law of this land. Here it's called assault and battery. Leaving your wife and small children is desertion. Sleeping with women other than your wife is adultery. That's what such sins are called on this planet, if not in your prayer room.

As for bigamy; if you had succeeded in your crazy plot you would surely have been found out. A prison sentence is what most people get for bigamy. Didn't you know that? Oh, yes, and finally, this is what I really think. You are irresponsible and a disgrace to the medical profession.'

I paused. I knew what I had to say next was difficult for me.

'Vali-Jo is dead.'

He seemed shocked but didn't say anything.

He got out of the car and banged the door as hard as he could. It almost felt as if he had hit me once again.

Two weeks later I heard from Jonathan that he had signed the divorce papers and taken the money.

Craig heard he had managed to obtain a temporary post in Edinburgh and was living in a small flat near the practice. He never made any attempt to get in touch with the children despite the fact that he was given supervised access. There was no further talk of custody and I agreed that Jonathan send him a further ten thousand pounds being what I thought Aunt Eileen may have given Vali.

thirty-eight | lighter hearts

Spring 1960

A very excited Craig and a pregnant Alison came to see me. Craig had many strange worries about parenthood. Today his concern was nappies, much to my amusement. Craig and changing nappies certainly didn't go together.

They were very sorry to hear about Vali-Jo. After much baby talk the conversation turned towards the inevitable business.

"Josephine, you will realise when you go through the paper waiting for your attention that I am now your tenant and I have paid you rent. Good heavens, what a noose,' he laughed.

I thanked Craig and told him that I hoped my divorce would be coming through soon as Adrian had accepted the money I had offered him.

Craig reassured me that I had made him a fair and generous offer but murmured, 'I don't suppose he appreciated it but sincerely hope it won't be wasted.' For once we spent a stress free-and pleasant evening together, and offered to help Alison in every way possible during her pregnancy.

Spring, fresh and green, heralded in brighter days and the shoots of recovery from sorrow lifted my spirits and renewed my zest for life. The children were my joy and each night I slept without fear. A small cloud did sometimes dampen my spirits and it was the lack of communication from Dean. His mother wrote to me regularly often sending small interesting presents for the children. I wrote and told her about my divorce and a part of her reply disturbed me.

Dean is grieving more than I could ever have imagined, she wrote. He goes for long walks on his own and refuses to socialise. He works hard with his father. Matt has been offered a good price for the business. He's getting on in years now and will probably take the opportunity to sell. Luke is to stay on as a director of the company but Dean wants to take his money out of the business. He's very fragile.

For three months I heard nothing from Dean. I had returned from the hairdressers when Mrs Fellows told me she had signed for a cable. It was from Dean and read 'Arriving fifteenth June. Can I have the Lodge? Will explain everything.

I sent him back a one word reply: Welcome.

He was obviously coming to bury Vali-Jo's ashes.

Mrs Fellows and I cleaned the Lodge and awaited his arrival. I thought he would phone from Edinburgh and ask me to collect him. No such call came.

The excitement turned to disappointment for the children. Frances was the optimist. Before she went to bed she put her arms around my neck and kissed me.

'He'll come, mummy,' she said trying to comfort me.

I woke late the next morning to the noise of the children squealing and running around.

'Will you two stop that racket,' I shouted. 'It's too early for nonsense.'

I heard a deep laugh and thought. Mr Fellows has taken leave of his senses. For one dreadful moment I thought it might be Adrian but he never laughed like that with the children.

I showered and dressed quickly. I went into the kitchen to find Dean and the children having breakfast. I think I must have stood with my mouth open for quite a few seconds. Dean got up from

his chair and came over to me and gave me a hug. I was so pleased to see him.

'Forgive me. There's a valid reason why I'm late. From the time I got out of the train in Edinburgh it was like a black comedy. Some of my luggage went missing. I had ordered a new car to meet me at Edinburgh. This part of the confusion was my fault. My instructions said Edinburgh. They thought the airport not the station. The paperwork for the car was also incomplete. I eventually stayed overnight in Edinburgh as it got very late. I drove through very early this morning and slept an hour or two in the Lodge. Did you not hear the car?'

'Where did you get the keys to the Lodge?' I asked.

'Jose, don't you remember giving me the duplicates when I was last here. Thank you for arranging everything in the lodge for me down to the coffee.'

'Well, let's see this confused car' I laughed.

Dean had ordered himself a beautiful Mercedes. I was amazed. Why had he bought a car when he was only here to bury Vali-Jo's ashes?

'It's big enough for all of us to scramble into,' he commented looking particularly at Andrew, whose very demeanour yelled out joy at seeing Dean. The children went outside to play after their initial excitement. He took me by the hand and we followed them and sat on a bench to watch them at play. He was tired after his journey. He put his hand over mine as we sat together. The sun was gaining in warmth and as the children played we never spoke. I felt such a comfort in his presence. One child is missing, I thought sadly. Poor little Vali-Jo, she should be running around with them. Maybe Dean had the same thought in his mind. I got up and went into the kitchen and got lemonade for the children.

He rested after lunch and stayed in the Lodge until he joined us for our evening meal. He was unusually quiet and I wondered if he wanted to be on his own. After the children were in bed he came into the sitting room with me.

'Dean, would you prefer to be in the Lodge on your own and eat on your own and have some quiet time? Is the perpetual noise of the children annoying you?' I asked.

'I didn't come all this way to be on my own. I'm here for a while to see if this Scotland of yours likes me and if I like it. I have one more sad duty. I cannot mourn forever. Help me over this last hurdle.'

Dean had difficulty in discussing the interment of Vali-Jo's ashes. I didn't raise the matter. It took him a week to speak about it.

'Jose, I have arranged a minister on Friday,' was all he said, and all he seemed able to say, as emotion seemed to choke him and tears were not far away, so I made all the final arrangements for him.

The little plot was close to Vali's grave and a headstone had been arranged some time ago. Denise took the children to Alison for the morning and I decided to drive Dean to the cemetery. I had waited in the driveway for some time and had eventually gone back into the Lodge to find him standing in the bedroom with the small urn held fast in his arms.

'Dean, its time,' I said to him as gently as I could.

His eyes were red with shed and unshed tears. 'How can this be fair and right? This is my child I'm holding.'

'No, Dean. Your child is in the spirit world. You are holding her mortal remains. You have to do the right thing now and then keep her memory in your heart and mind.'

I took the urn from him and he followed me to the car.

The minister was waiting for us at the cemetery. A few prayers were said and Dean put the urn gently in the grave. I put a small teddy bear in with the urn. Vali-Jo had always loved soft toys. The tiny grave was closed and he walked to the car without looking back, walking so slowly as if he never wanted to leave.

I had a small posy of flowers for Vali-Jo and a single white rose for Vali. I put the rose down on Vali's grave and intended to say a prayer for her but what do you say over the grave of a woman who had tried to kill her husband?

I walked back slowly to the car. Dean was sitting in the car almost motionless waiting for me. I drove him back home and we had a sandwich lunch before taking a walk together in the 'Shouting Field,' while we waited for the children to be brought home by Denise. We walked the length of the field and as we turned he put his arms around me and kissed me. I pulled back quickly.

'Why does Jose always kiss Dean if she doesn't mean it?' he said.

This time he didn't say it in fun as he usually did. There was such a sadness about him.

'I can't mourn any more,' he said. 'God forgive me. I have walked alone and questioned and mourned and wept until I felt I was the only person why had known sorrow. Yes, that's how I felt. I saw girls and boys and children laughing and playing thinking Vali-Jo should be doing this. Why was I the only one?' I held his hand in sympathy and before I knew what we were doing we were kissing again. I had my arms around his neck and his body was warm and comforting against mine. How gentle and relaxed he was with me but would I ever wholly forget the passion of my first love, and would I love that way again? I pulled away from him.

'I'm so sorry. It was an impulse. No, to hell Jose,' he said, 'I'm not going to apologise. I wanted to do that, I meant to do that. It was no accident. I'm not going to stand back again and see somebody else take over your life and then hurt you. We have met and parted in three countries. The time never seemed right for us. Is it now? Vali-Jo loved you and I know you loved her to the bitter end like a mother. I feel no guilt at kissing you on this dreadful day. I think her little face would have lit up if she had seen us.'

I was amazed at his outburst. I smiled at him and we went inside. He seemed to be waiting for me to say something.

'Dean, I know what you're thinking. Yes, couples do get back together again. Yes, it was a very passionate relationship in the early days of my marriage, and I won't deny it. However, what Adrian did to me was unforgivable. I will never go back to him.'

We heard the children come in. They seemed to have an abundance of balloons with them and the noise was deafening. I hoped they hadn't proved too much for Alison.

Just before we turned in for the night I gave Dean the front door key to the house.

'This is just to make sure I don't have to jump up every two minutes to open the door for you.'

"Oh, Jose, as if. It's every five minutes that I would expect you to open the door for me,' he was able to tease.

thirty-nine / and for all the days of my life

And so it was.

Craig and Alison had a baby girl.

Dean and I got married soon after my divorce and we had a boy named after his father Matt, but he was sturdy and called Butch. A girl three years later when I was thirty-four, named Emma, red-haired like her mother and grandmother before her. She changed the tempo of our lives with her pranks, and often frantic activity.

I had borne four children God and been good and gracious to me. They were healthy and would be cherished and loved. I had an easy-going loving husband, fun to be with, who was always there for me and the children. He loved all four children as his own, but sometimes in rare and silent moments we remembered the missing child. Vali-Jo.

There was no grand passion, but a deep and understanding love, concern and reliability, and Craig's famous word that I had mocked at in my youth: compatibility.

What of the children that had been deserted by their biological father and what of their father?

Frances became quite an accomplished pianist. The Shouting Field outside was never developed as a garden. Dean made the mistake of buying her a pony, other animals followed and she eventually qualified as a vet.

She started practising in the London area and I was distressed when she left home. Dean repeatedly said, 'Stop worrying, Jose.

You've warned her to be careful of animals from aardvarks to zebras and have told her the dangers of men from eighteen to eighty.'

I found it very hard to let go. Frances had the income from the flat that Aunt Eileen had left her and which had been let. I never returned to London. The memories would have been too painful. Each time I thought of the flat where Adrian and I had spent the early years of our married life, the silly giggling voice that had ruined my marriage seemed to ring in my ears.

Andrew studied law in Edinburgh. He changed his name to Andrew Mitchell by deed poll. Dean was very touched by this gesture. I sat at Andrew's graduation and cried, much to Dean's embarrassment. Andrew spent some time in India trekking in the foothills of the Himalayas. He had always been interested in the stories I had told him of the country I had loved so well and he had to see it for himself. I tried to persuade him to go to Calcutta and visit the grave of his grandmother Frances, but he refused. He said he knew no father but Dean and no grandparents other than his American grandparents. He came back elated but also saddened at the poverty he had seen in India. He did, however, manage to contact a genuine charity dealing with abandoned children for me to donate to them regularly as the memory of the little beggar boy who had virtually died in my arms was ever with me. He obtained a post as a lawyer in Dundee.

In 1982 when I was fifty, I had a phone call one morning from a lawyer in Edinburgh asking to speak to Mrs Greene.

'There is no such person here.' I replied. The lawyer persisted saying he was phoning me on instruction from a Dr Greene. Eventually we agreed to an appointment in Edinburgh, on a Monday morning.

The receptionist ushered us into a bright and attractive office. A young lawyer in his early thirties rose from his desk to greet us.

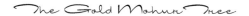

He addressed me as Mrs Greene, an error which got the meeting off to a bad start. I could see Dean getting annoyed and he quickly took over the conversation.

'I'm Mr Mitchell and this is my wife, Josephine Mitchell. I would ask you to be brief and to refrain from calling my wife Mrs Greene. Please address all your remarks to me and I will handle them. I suggest you be brief as I consider this meeting totally unnecessary.'

The lawyer introduced himself as Mr Simpson and said he was under instruction from Dr Greene. He had a file in front of him and a brown paper package.

Dean and I had been married happily for over twenty years and he didn't like the idea of the past raising its ugly head.

The lawyer spoke hesitatingly, unsure of himself. 'First, Mr Mitchell, I should point out Dr Green's contention is that he is still married to your wife and she is Mrs Greene. According to him, his religion does not recognise divorce. Dr Greene is terminally ill with cancer of the lungs. He has been a very heavy smoker.'

I was really shocked at this statement as Adrian had been against smoking, in fact the *biris* smoked in India used to be a source of great irritation to him.

'Surely not,' I remarked.

The lawyer continued. 'Secondly he has asked for his body to be cremated and his ashes buried beside his Aunt Eileen. When he made this request he knew he was to go to a hospice and asked if you, Mrs Mitchell, could visit him as he had only a short time left according to the doctors at the hospital. It need be only for a few minutes if you can cope with it. There's also this parcel. It's to be given to you and you only, under instruction from Dr Greene. That is all.'

Dean looked at me, nodded and said, 'You reply Jose, honey.' He knew it was very personal.

I chose my words carefully and without emotion.

'I don't know about his religion but the law granted me a divorce on the grounds of adultery, desertion and assault a long time ago and I haven't seen Dr Greene since the divorce. I suggest you contact my solicitors for confirmation.'

I gave him Jonathan's name and address. Jonathan was due to retire and I was sure he didn't need a resurrection of our past troubles. I continued speaking.

'I agree to have his ashes interred and I will do the needful if they're sent to me by courier. I will not be coming back to Edinburgh to collect them. I will accept the parcel. As far as the visit to the hospice is concerned, I will discuss it with my husband after this meeting.'

We were about to leave and Dean was already standing, when the lawyer raised his hand.

'Just a moment, please,' he said, 'there's another rather strange and painful point, not raised by Dr Greene. A woman came to see me last week, by the name of Dr Patterson. She said she had been looking after Dr Greene for some time. I think she is some sort of elderly relative who lives with him. Do you know her at all? She came in here to see me and asked for funds. She's an old woman – very large. She seemed to have some sort of problem with her legs as she was using a stick. Late sixties, I would say. She asked, as you were still married to Dr. Greene – by his way of thinking – if you could pay some of his bills as he was heavily in debt and an eviction order was imminent from the rented flat they live in. She explained that Dr Greene had not worked for many years. Her story was that he never had a permanent post after his divorce and apparently returned to India for quite a few years returning to Edinburgh and the flat he had shared with Dr Patterson for many years.'

He stopped and looked at me for an answer.

Dean interrupted at this point saying curtly, 'Certainly not.'

I couldn't believe what I was hearing and explained the situation to the lawyer saying. 'Mr Simpson, the Dr Patterson you speak of is not an old relative. She's his mistress. He left me and the children for her. There's no way I will pay any of her debts, because that's what this request is about. If Dr Green is terminally ill he will obviously not be going back to his house or flat or wherever they may be living. I gave Dr Greene a considerable amount of money at the time of the divorce. What has he done with it, I wonder? Dr Greene never knew how to control his finances.'

He looked at me in disbelief.

'Are you sure there's no mistake? She must be years older than him.'

'Oh yes, Mr Simpson. He made a terrible mistake don't you think?' I replied sarcastically.

I picked up the parcel and the address of the hospice and left the room with Dean. We lunched together and discussed what I should do. After lunch Dean drove to a quiet spot and we sat silently together, each of us immersed in our own thoughts. Dean put his hand over mine to comfort me as he had always done.

'Jose, honey, that woman is a liar to the end. What bloody nerve asking you of all people for money. She can go to hell. What I can't understand is why he never married her and why he persists with this nonsense that he's still married to you. I am proud of you in regard to the burial of the ashes. It's a dying man's wish. I'm glad you granted it. My advice regarding the hospice is don't let the ghosts of the past haunt you. See him for five minutes and put an end to it. It's pointless anyway.'

I thought for a while and agreed with him. I had the address on the top of the parcel I was holding. I knew it was Adrian's prayer book without even opening it. I couldn't understand what he had done with the thirty-five thousand pounds I had given him. It was a lot of money all those years ago. He should have at least bought a flat for himself.

We found the hospice quite easily. Dean decided he would sit in the car while I went in. I was becoming increasingly nervous, remembering how I had feared Adrian. My hand automatically touched the scar on my face and a strange dread seemed to well up within me. .Dean, sensing my unease, spoke softly.

'It's just five minutes, Jose. It will do no harm. Just take it as a visit to an impoverished dying man.'

The hospice was clean and sterile looking. I found a doctor and asked if I could visit Dr Greene. He took me into a side room and indicated I should sit on the small chair near the bed. An emaciated man, whom I would never have recognised as Adrian was lying on the bed with an oxygen mask on his face. Was this the man I had loved so passionately? He had been vibrant and athletic. Sadly, as I looked at him the only emotion I felt was a deep pity. He seemed to be dozing. I waited but he didn't speak. I said quite loudly.

'I'm Josephine Mitchell.'

He stirred and looked at me with sunken grey eyes. A nurse came into the room to help him into a semi-sitting position and straightened his pillows, moving his mask just a little to enable him to say a few words to me.

'Josephine Greene, you'll always be Josephine Greene,' he said in a whisper. He raised his hand and tried to smile.

'I've been to see your lawyer,' I said.

He nodded his head ever so slightly. I sat there silently. There was really nothing to say. The love had gone and so had the bitterness – a long time ago. He seemed to doze again. He knew who I was, obviously. After a while he said in a hoarse whisper. 'Missy, you're my wife. My Missy.'

I nodded my head. What was the point of trying to argue with a dying man who was now really a total stranger to me? He closed his eyes and a tear ran down the side of his face. Was this supposed to be some sort of death-bed apology for what he had done to me? His breathing was laboured. I sat a few minutes longer. He opened his eyes and with great difficulty said, 'Gold Mohur. I always loved you.'

Neither of us spoke again. I sat quietly beside him and thought of the early passion of our lives, the quarrels and the eventual rage between us. We had now reached the end of a storm. Just a few quiet moments were left to us. Was he too thinking of the past?

The nurse who had left the room to give us some privacy came back after a short time, put the small oxygen mask back on his face and said, 'He is getting very distressed. I think you should leave now.'

She took me to a side room at the far end of the wards. She very kindly made me a cup of tea.

'He has only a short time left; he seems to think he's your husband,' she said. 'He was once, for a short painful time, many years ago.' I replied.

'I'm sorry,' she said and left the room.

I sipped the hot tea slowly. A wave of pity engulfed me. Why had he deliberately, after so many years, made me remember India? What had he done when he returned and why had he never wanted to see the children?

We had sat in the old Morris 8, as young lovers and looked at the Gold Mohur trees on Red Road in Calcutta. We had only known each other for a short time. He was tanned and handsome and I had fallen passionately in love with him. Strangely enough I couldn't remember what he had really looked like. I only seemed to recall the bad times, the temper tantrums and the violence. I dug deep for happy memories of him.

The late evening sun shining on the Gold Mohur trees had given them a special glow for us. There was a heat haze on that day. Masses of brilliant red flowers, nodded in the slight breeze of the evening. I remembered what a wonderful sight it was against the stark white marble of the Victoria Memorial and the swathes of green grass of the maidan.

'Missy,' he had said. 'This is how you are for me. Bright, flamboyant, and glowing like the flowers of the Gold Mohur and I love you for it.'

What he didn't say was the ferocity of his jealousy and violence and his strange obsession with an older woman would blow away the blossoms of our love and passion, just as the monsoon in its ferocity would blow away the blossom of the Gold Mohur tree and dash the glorious red umbrella-shaped flowers to pieces.

I finished my tea and joined Dean in the car.

'Well, Jose,' he asked.

'It was as you said, a poor sick man dying of cancer. The man I knew had long gone. I am only sorry to see that his life is ending so tragically by his own stupidity.'

We drove home silently. Adrian Greene had lied to the bitter end. .He was still living with Penny Patterson. What had prompted him to do it? What had driven him? He died a fortnight later.

I phoned Craig and told him I was burying Adrian's ashes. Dean didn't come to the cemetery. I think it would have been too painful for him. Craig came. It was more appropriate. I had asked a priest to say a prayer over his grave. I had arranged a small plot near Aunt Eileen's grave, and had ordered a headstone simply stating his name, date of birth and death.

I wanted to bury his prayer book with him and had it in my hand. I opened the brown paper that the book, well thumbed and worn, was wrapped in. Two photographs and the ring that I had thrown back at him fell out. They were the photographs that Juliana's husband Richard had taken at our wedding. Craig looked at the photographs for a few minutes.

'He adored you then, Josephine. The lure of the West was too much for him. The night you got engaged and you wore that attractive green dress I remember him saying, "Look at my Missy, isn't she fabulous."'

I shook my head.

'Did he say in later years, 'Look at my Missy, how successfully I have broken her spirit and destroyed her love for me?'

'Josephine don't' was all Craig said.

He handed the photographs back to me. 'My Missy' was written in Adrian's writing at the back of the photograph of me standing on my own. It put a strange chill through me to read his writing.

I put the book, the photographs and the ring in the grave along with the urn and then had the grave closed. It was my final act for his unforgivable wrong. I had erased his memory from my life forever.

Craig stood and said a prayer for him.

I turned and walked away. I had no prayer to offer.

We sat in Craig's car, for a short time in the evening sun before he drove me home. We had known each other for what seemed to be an eternity. He was greying at the temples and was heavier than when we first met. An ageing Viking. I smiled inwardly. Only he was unscathed.

Five of us had met in India. Our lives had been intertwined. Our ambitions had given us great joy, great wealth, and sadly death. Two of us lay buried in a strange cemetery far from what had been considered home. Was this the hand of kismet? The strangest thought came into my mind. In my rage and hurt when he had left me for another woman, I had sworn that I would destroy him. I had no need.

Adrian Greene destroyed himself.

Those who come into this world cannot stop in it forever.
So do not hope to do so, and do not remain in grief for
those who have gone.

END

Printed in Great Britain
by Amazon

20431852R00151